THE
PENTHOUSE

Catherine Cooper is a journalist specialising in luxury travel, hotels and skiing who writes regularly for national newspapers and magazines. She lives near the Pyrenees in the South of France with her family, cats and chickens. Her debut, *The Chalet*, was a top 5 *Sunday Times* bestseller. *The Penthouse* is her fifth novel.

 @catherinecooper
@catherinecooperjournalist

Books by Catherine Cooper

The Chalet
The Chateau
The Cruise
The Island

THE
PENTHOUSE

CATHERINE COOPER

HarperCollins*Publishers*

HarperCollins*Publishers* Ltd
1 London Bridge Street,
London SE1 9GF
www.harpercollins.co.uk

HarperCollins*Publishers*
Macken House, 39/40 Mayor Street Upper
Dublin 1, D01 C9W8, Ireland

First published by HarperCollins*Publishers* 2025
1

A catalogue record for this book is available from the British Library

ISBN: 978-0-00-867255-3 (PB)

This novel is entirely a work of fiction. The names, characters and incidents portrayed in it are the work of the author's imagination. Any resemblance to actual persons, living or dead, events or localities is entirely coincidental.

Set in Sabon LT Std by HarperCollins*Publishers* India

Printed and bound in the UK using 100% Renewable
Electricity at CPI Group (UK) Ltd

MIX
Paper | Supporting
responsible forestry
FSC™ C007454

This book contains FSC™ certified paper and other controlled sources to ensure responsible forest management.

For more information visit: www.harpercollins.co.uk/green

For Toby and Livi, who make me proud every day.

He is happiest, be he king or peasant, who finds peace in his home.

JOHANN WOLFGANG VON GOETHE

Set on the twenty-fifth floor of the brand-new Golden Peaks building, this exceptional split-level riverside penthouse close to London's South Bank has to be seen to be believed. Benefiting from its own private roof terrace as well as two bedrooms, three balconies and views of St Paul's Cathedral and the City, this penthouse offers city-centre living with every modern convenience, plus the highest quality fixtures and fittings. Access is via a private lift from the ground floor, with a 24-hour gym and indoor swimming pool also available to residents, assuring them the highest level of security and privacy. Available for occupation in September 2008. Price on application.

1

December 2008

Newspaper report:

Fears are growing for lead singer of girl band Breathe, Enola Mazzeri, 23, who has been missing for at least 48 hours.

The pop star attended the Ultimate Starz Awards ceremony on Saturday December 6, at which Breathe won the People's Choice Award 2010, along with prizes for best album and best single.

The Breathe lead singer was last seen at an after-party the same night at Enola's luxury penthouse apartment, also attended by fellow Breathe members and boy band This Way Up.

According to reports, Miss Mazzeri was asleep when the last guests left.

The alarm was raised by Enola's manager Emery Askew when the pop icon failed to appear at a rehearsal on Tuesday. No sign of Miss Mazzeri was found when a security guard unlocked her penthouse at the exclusive Golden Peaks Thames riverside development at the request of the police.

A police spokesman said: 'There did not appear to be any signs of disturbance or break-in at the flat, although it remained in some disarray from the party held three days earlier.

'Miss Mazzeri's bank cards have not been used since and her phone was found in the apartment, along with her two Maine Coon cats which are being cared for by relatives. However, her passport appears to be missing, along with her house keys.

'Though there is currently no evidence that Miss Mazzeri has come to any harm, her friends, family and fellow band members state that Enola going missing in this way is entirely out of character and that they are extremely concerned for her safety. All avenues of enquiry currently remain open.

'We appeal for anyone who has seen Miss Mazzeri or has any information about her where-abouts to get in touch, or for Miss Mazzeri herself to contact us in confidence to let us know that she is safe and well.'

Enola's mother Kimberley Mazzeri added: 'Please come home, my baby. All we want is to know that you're OK.'

2

May 2004
London
Enola

The queue isn't only out of the door, but also around the block.

Thankfully, I managed to persuade Mum not to come with us while we wait to audition for TV talent show *The Chosen*, even though she wanted to. I made it a condition of me coming here, that she'd leave me and Becki to it.

Becki is having the time of her life. She's always been more into this kind of thing than me, and I wouldn't be that surprised if she had conspired with Mum to get us here. I've had about enough of auditions, Mum's had me going to them pretty much since I was born. 'Let's practise again,' Becki says. 'By the look of the queue we've still got at least another hour.'

I sigh. 'I think we're as good as we're going to get,' I

say. 'You wouldn't want to make your voice tired, would you?' In reality I'm not worried about her voice; I just don't want to practise any more. Mum had us singing together for hours last night and I've totally had enough of it.

But Becki starts up anyway, warbling about how there is only me in her life and when she gets to my part about me meaning the world to her I somehow can't help but join in. And then I see a cameraman heading towards us and realise why Becki chose that particular moment to start singing.

We sing the song all the way through. The camera is still on us and I'm already mortified – it is surely going to be even worse doing all this in front of three judges. I've done masses of performances and competitions throughout my life, but none so far where there was the potential for me to end up on TV embarrassing myself. My friends might see it. What if I do something wrong and humiliate myself? I wonder briefly if we can bail and go home. But Mum would never forgive me and there'll be no way I'd be able to drag Becki away I'm sure.

As we finish Becki beams at the cameraman and the boy wearing a black T-shirt labelled 'Crew' next to him.

'What's your name?' he asks, brandishing a black and red notebook.

'I'm Becki and this is Enola,' she says, inclining her head towards me. 'And together, we're Fizz!'

He nods and scribbles something in his notebook. 'Nice one. Well, best of luck to you both!' He taps the cameraman on the shoulder and indicates three identically dressed boys further back in the line who are doing some kind of synchronised breakdance, saying, 'Let's go and take a look at them.'

'Name?' Emery, the notoriously 'difficult' and unofficial chief judge barks.

'Becki!' she squeals.

'Enola,' I mumble.

'And together we're Fizz!' she squeaks.

He nods. 'Right. And what are you doing for us today?'

'"Endless Love",' Becki says.

He rolls his eyes. 'Seriously? Give me strength. You're the fifth act today to do that.'

Fuck. Maybe we should have got here earlier. The judges must have already seen dozens of acts – they've probably had enough, want to go home and have already decided who they want to put through.

I glance at Becki, and see her face fall momentarily, though she quickly recovers. 'I'm convinced we'll offer the best rendition you've heard today,' she says smoothly. 'But we're here to please. If you'd rather hear something else, we can do something else for you, of course.'

'Oh you meanie,' says Susie, the 'nice' judge. 'Ignore Mr Grumpy-pants,' she adds, addressing us. 'He clearly got out of bed the wrong side this morning or perhaps his mummy didn't cook his eggs quite the way he likes. You perform exactly what you want, my darlings.'

Becki gives me a meaningful look. I can almost see

her thought process, stick with 'Endless Love', which we've practised over and over, or try something else? And if so, what?

I stare back at her.

'How about "Respect"?' she says to me, and then looks at Emery.

He nods approvingly. 'That's more like it, let's hear what you've got then, Fuzz.'

'It's Fizz,' I correct, and Becki gives me a dirty look.

He holds up his hand. 'My apologies. Fizz. Off you go.'

We sing 'Respect', a cappella, as is required by *The Chosen*. It's a really hard song, much harder than you might think with long, high sustained notes, a lot of very fast sections which are easy to trip up over, it's tricky to keep the rhythm and tempo right without any backing track or even a metronome and apart from anything else, we simply haven't sung it anywhere near as often as 'Endless Love', which has always been one of our favourites.

Emery regards us, totally expressionless, through the entire performance. Susie nods in time to the beat and gently taps her hand on the table, smiling. The third judge, Paulo, seems to find it hard to tear his eyes away from Becki's ample cleavage.

When we get to the end of the song, for a few seconds the room is entirely silent. I feel myself blush and wonder if we can go yet. How will we know when to leave? Becki glances at me and then looks expectantly at Emery, who is staring down thoughtfully at his note-book, chewing the end of his pen.

'You,' he says, pointing his pen at me. 'What was your name?'

'Enola,' I say, trying to sound confident, but my voice cracks and it comes out weirdly.

'Emma?'

'Enola,' I say, louder and more clearly.

He nods. 'Enola. You've got a great voice and, while your look,' he moves his biro slowly up and down to indicate my carefully chosen outfit of low-rise jeans, a handkerchief top and favourite Converse, 'currently isn't quite right, you're a beautiful girl and with a styling you could be quite something.'

Even though I hadn't particularly wanted to come to this audition, I'd been talked into it by Mum, and in spite of his compliment being extremely backhanded, I feel a little stab of excitement.

'You though . . .' he continues, turning to face my friend.

'Becki,' she offers, but there is a wobble in her voice and I think we already both know what's coming. We watch the programme avidly, and I've seen him do this many times before.

'You are not at the same level. Nowhere close, I'm afraid. You're a pretty girl, with a nice enough voice, but if you two stay together, performing as a pair, you will hold your friend back.'

I glance over at her and see tears forming in Becki's eyes.

'What I would like,' he continues, still looking at Becki rather than at me, 'is to hear Enola singing by herself. I'm sorry, my dear, I know that's harsh, and isn't the outcome you were hoping for, but it's how it is. You aren't the first people I've said that to, and I'm sure you won't be the last.'

The cameraman behind the judges moves and does something with his lens – I assume he's zooming in on Becki's face.

'Obviously you should do it, Enola,' she forces out, hoarsely, tears streaming down her face. She takes my hand.

I shake my head and the cameraman moves again. 'I don't want to, not without you,' I say, but I can already feel myself weakening, and a part of me knows that I am simply going through the motions. Playing the role that is expected when Emery does this. The favoured one is meant to buckle and agree to go on alone, and they always do.

Plus, I am very aware that we are being recorded and, at some point, what is being filmed might be shown on TV – we've already had to sign a release form while we were in the queue. Mum would never forgive me if I refused to sing alone simply out of loyalty to my friend. And if I'm being honest, I am not Mother Teresa, I am not sufficiently altruistic to give up the potential fame and fortune which could be on offer here, much as I love Becki.

Emery likes me. He thinks I have something. I hadn't wanted to come initially, because I thought it would simply be yet another boring audition that wouldn't change anything much. I had thought we'd get a quick 'thanks but no thanks' and that would be it. But this is suddenly very different. It is a potentially life-changing opportunity. I hate to admit it, but perhaps Mum had been right about all those classes being worth it.

I get that I've got a nice voice, and I can dance quite well, but being a singer was always Mum's dream, not so much mine. When she has a few too many glasses of wine, she'll tell me that she's convinced she could have made it big if she hadn't accidentally got pregnant with me and Roxie, then pats me on the arm as she says: 'Of course it was all worth it though,' somewhat insincerely as she helps herself to another glass and wipes away a tear.

I've finally managed to persuade Mum to let me give up most of the dance and singing classes I've been attending since I was a child, citing A-level stress, but really I just want more time to hang out with my friends. I've never aspired to sing in crap pubs or on cruise ships. It's the kind of thing that Mum thinks would be a brilliant way of life, but which I've never been remotely interested in. Roxie has never had Mum on her back in the same way that I have – so I've always seen my 'talent' as a bit of a poisoned chalice.

But this is different. Everyone knows what happens if Emery gets behind you. Your life is not going to be one of singing in pubs and on cruise ships. It will become a whirlwind of red carpets, film premieres, fame and fortune, almost overnight. Number one records. Appearing in all the magazines. Maybe a celebrity boyfriend. Smart hotels. Perhaps even a world tour.

But I've watched *The Chosen* many times and I know very well how this scenario is meant to play out. I know they want the storyline and the drama. I imagine the swelling music they'll lay over the pictures as the audience hold their breath and wait for my decision. No one ever says 'yes' to this kind of request straight away, that isn't what the producers of the show want, and it isn't what the audience wants.

I shake my head again. I look at Becki and touch her wet cheek. 'But you . . .' I say, my voice hoarse.

Emery sighs loudly. 'Look, love, we haven't got all day. There's a queue of people behind you. You're good, granted, but some of those waiting behind might be even better. My world is certainly not going to turn around you. Are you going to sing or not? I don't mean to be crude, and I'm going to keep my language PG as this is a family show, but you need to defecate or get off the pot.'

Becki squeezes my hand as the cameraman moves towards her again. 'You need to do it. I insist,' she says, her voice little more than a whisper. She hugs me and then leaves the room sobbing.

I swallow hard. 'OK,' I say, with way more confidence than I feel. 'I'm going to sing.'

3

July 2004
A Secret Location in Spain
Enola

'Enola, meet your new bandmates, Angel and Sophie. Together, you are Breathe, and you can take on the world,' says Emery, who, just like that, has morphed from head judge into our producer.

We are in an enormous glitzy villa in the south of Spain somewhere, they did tell us but I forget the name, well away from the cameras.

To cut a long story short, after that awful audition, the one that made Becki cry and the one that meant that she hasn't spoken to me since, I sang 'Wonderwall', and that, followed by a series of other songs on several shows, got me through to the final.

I didn't win. I came second. Angel and Sophie got knocked out in earlier rounds – they didn't even make the

14

final show. But Emery's people contacted us individually afterwards and said he had plans for us all.

I've never been anywhere like this before in my life, and if I hadn't gone to that audition and been picked up by Emery, it's likely I would never have done so in the future either. I dread to think what a villa like this costs to rent per week.

It's not that I haven't been abroad before, I have, but only once, when me, Mum and Roxie got a coach through the night down to the south of France and spent two weeks in a tent on a huge campsite with massive pools and a naff disco for us to go to in the evening. We had a great time, living on baguettes, runny cheese and peaches, drinking Orangina and spending all day at the beach.

Even that felt pretty exotic, but I've never been anywhere remotely like this. My room is enormous, with its own bathroom, there's a massive terrace overlooking the sea with a gigantic pool and a hot tub. There's even a chef to make our carefully calorie-controlled meals every night.

I didn't meet Angel and Sophie during the filming of *The Chosen* because we were in different heats, but I can see instantly that as well as them both being a few years older, they are nothing like me. I try not to judge people on appearances, but it's hard to imagine that we will have anything in common. Except music, I guess. Focus on the positive, I tell myself.

'Hi!' they chime in unison, looking my outfit of

knock-off 501s and my favourite River Island T-shirt up and down. I feel suddenly dowdy compared to them in their seemingly carefully curated outfits, full faces of make-up, fake tan and perfectly coiffed hair.

'It's so lovely to meet you!' Sophie squeaks.

'And you,' I say, uncertainly. I wish it was just me here in this lovely villa. Or that I could be here with Becki. We'd have such a laugh, taking the piss out of the stupid clothes that Sophie and Angel are wearing and the frankly ridiculous voice exercises vocal coach Kendra makes us do.

I wonder if Becki will ever speak to me again? Tears spring to my eyes. It's not fair. It wasn't my fault that Emery liked me and not her. She told me she wanted me to go ahead and sing alone on *The Chosen*. If she didn't mean it, she shouldn't have said it.

'I love your look,' Angel says with a sneer, making it entirely clear that she means the exact opposite. 'So . . . natural.' She is obviously a gym bunny, perfectly toned with delicately sculpted biceps and a washboard stomach peeking out from under her crop top. Of the two of them, Angel is definitely the scarier.

I try to smile graciously but I can tell it looks more like a grimace. 'And I love your . . . shoes,' I say, picking something entirely at random to compliment, even though they look hideously uncomfortable and not the kind of thing I would ever want to wear in a million years. But it seems like I picked the right thing to say as she preens. 'Thank you. They're Louboutins. A birthday present from my daddy.'

'And speaking of look,' Emery says, 'it's time to meet your stylist. And then we'll get on with rehearsals. Plenty to get on with and no time to waste.'

I expected the stylist to be some kind of fear-inducing, matronly woman, but actually it turns out to be Dan, camp as Christmas and the first friendly face I've seen since I got here. I'm relieved to find that he doesn't try to force me into skimpy little clothes like the other two are wearing, but instead, says that we will simply 'refine and enhance' my look together, which seems to basically mean wearing more expensive and nicer versions of the kind of thing I'd usually wear anyway, so I'm OK with that. I try on Seven for All Mankind and Acne jeans, which make my bum look more pert and my legs slimmer, True Religion and Dior T-shirts, and Converse almost like my usual ones, but newer, cleaner and some designer label versions. There is also a high-heeled version that I'm less keen on, but I can just about live with. He does the same with the other two, Sophie is all Ralph Lauren slick, while Angel is Juicy Couture sportily sexy.

In spite of the luxurious surroundings, the next few weeks are punishing. We are up early to a breakfast of fruit and a small bowl of porridge and nuts, before vocal exercises with Kendra, a quick lunch of salad and grilled fish or meat, an afternoon of dance training, before a healthy dinner (no alcohol or even fizzy drinks in case they cause bloating) and early to bed. Our mobile phones have been confiscated, no one is allowed to call us, and we're only allowed to call home every other day, on the landline, and someone sits in with us. We're told this is for reasons of confidentiality and security, but I hate it. I feel like our every move is being watched and monitored, and that they don't fully trust us. We are Emery's new supergroup, and we apparently have to be kept top secret until he is ready to reveal us to the world. It should be exciting, but it only serves to make me feel lonely.

And then, a few weeks later, they launch us.

4

August 2004
London
Enola

Emery has yet another similar yet different talent show to *The Chosen* coming to TV for the autumn. The launch is live from Hyde Park, the idea being that the concert will have a festival ambiance, and Breathe, as I have to remind myself Angel, Sophie and I are now called, are opening the show with our first single. It's called 'Loud and Proud', and I had a large hand in writing it. As well as the audience of 60,000 in the park, they're expecting a UK TV audience of 10 million.

It's hard to process that – the idea of 10 million people watching us! Performing a song that I wrote. Absolute madness.

When we were in Spain, which already feels like it was months ago even though we only got back last week, and the team were banging on about security, privacy and secrecy while we were rehearsing, they were also at the same time drip-feeding pictures of us to the showbiz pages of the newspapers and some of the pop mags on the rare occasions we were allowed out of the villa.

There were shots of us lying by the pool in bikinis chosen by Dan in *Heat* magazine, taken by the in-house photographer, but which look as if they have been taken on the sly through the hedge. There are ones of us out together as a threesome in the local town in a couple of the Red Tops, as our publicist Trixie calls *The Sun* and *The Mirror*, all in long dresses, cork wedges and sun hats, and again, seemingly candid. As if someone spotted us while we were out and about wandering the streets like any three girls enjoying a sunny holiday. I remember spending the whole sweltering afternoon trying not to trip over my dress, which was too long, or fall off my wedges, which were too high, fretting about sweat stains and wondering when I could go back to the villa and dive into the pool or lie in my lovely air-conditioned room. I never wear stuff like that out of choice. And as well as all that, Trixie was there the whole time just out of shot, telling us to act natural and talk to each other, to make each other laugh. I felt like a total spare part, as even in this fake kind of set-up Angel and Sophie aren't interested in even pretending to talk to me. I had to nod and smile at no one like the chorus member in an am-dram production you can tell no one likes even from your seat in the audience.

The photographer Tom seems like a nice guy, just

doing what he is told I'm sure. And Trixie explained that Emery had a 'relationship' with certain journalists and newspapers, and would give them 'exclusive' pictures and stories when he chose to, but they were set up to look as if they'd been 'snatched' to make them seem more interesting to the readers.

Mum was utterly beside herself about me being in the papers, and would give me a rundown of what had appeared each week on my calls home.

'I loved that dress you were wearing in the picture in *The Sun*!' she gushed last time. 'The one when you were out in the local town with the other girls. Was it Temperley?'

'I'm not sure,' I say. 'I just wear what I'm told to. Dan wanted me to wear a dress that day to match the others.'

She sighs. 'You're so lucky. I'd have given anything for the kind of opportunity you have now. That villa! And those beautiful clothes! One of the best voice trainers in the business! If only I—'

'I know, Mum,' I interrupt. I already know she wishes she hadn't been so young when she got pregnant. I don't need to hear about it yet again.

'I'm keeping a scrapbook so that you can see all your cuttings as soon as you get back,' she says. 'I can't wait for the concert! I'm going to see if I can get Roxie to come along too – I'm hoping a VIP ticket to your Hyde Park event will be enough to persuade her away from her computer screen. She sends her love.'

I feel a pang. I miss my sister Roxie, and I worry about her. She's becoming more and more introverted, to the point where she pretty much refuses to leave her room. She dropped out of school before she'd even done her exams – said it was all a waste of time and she couldn't bear to be around the other kids any more. I did what I could to change her mind, but she was having none of it.

I hope she will come to the concert – I'm sure getting out more would do her the world of good. And even though I'm nervous about it, I'm also really excited. Not just about performing, but also because I'll get to meet Max from This Way Up again.

There's a section in *The Chosen* where the contestants like me sing with already-established stars. I sang with Liam from boy band This Way Up, a song he and I wrote and put together in just a couple of days called 'All The Way'. Everyone knows you get more votes on the show in that section if you write something new – and it was quite a good song, even if I say so myself, and for the show it was staged with a full band and dancers. That was exciting, but Max is the one that I've always had a massive crush on, along with just about the rest of the world. Max was paired with someone else that show, and I only got to say a quick hello before I had to go off with Liam to rehearse some more. But there was a spark between us, I'm sure of it.

'Enola? I'd like to introduce you to Max. Lead singer of This Way Up.'

It's kind of ridiculous Trixie introducing me to Max in that way because surely everyone in the world knows who he is, most of all me. This Way Up were the first band that Emery propelled to stardom almost overnight and I've been a huge fan since their first single came out five years ago. With his dark hair, dark eyes, and smooth Irish accent, he's just gorgeous. Breathe opened the Hyde Park show, This Way Up closed it, and I still can't believe that we are here in the same room, let alone sharing the same stage. And obviously there's an after-party.

Max shakes my hand in a surprisingly formal way and I feel like I might fall through the floor or die. 'Good to see you again, Enola,' he says. 'Great show tonight. That's quite the voice you've got.'

'Oh! Thank you,' I say, blushing scarlet.

'Here, you've got something . . .' he leans forward and touches my hair. I'm vaguely aware of a photographer behind him who is circulating the party, taking pictures, and am momentarily blinded by a couple of rapid flashes as his camera whirrs. 'There. That was in your hair,' Max says, handing me a large piece of gold foil, one of the many thousands that rained down from above the stage as our set finished.

I smile back. Behave like a star, I tell myself. You have every right to be here. As much as Max. As much as any of them. 'Thank you. Your set was great too. I really like your new single,' I say.

For fuck's sake! Is that the best I can come up with? Don't sound like a star-struck fan, I tell myself. Think of something intelligent to say. Memorable. Interesting. 'I loved the key change,' I add.

Oh God. Really? But amazingly, it seems like that

was the right thing to say after all. His face breaks into a grin. 'You did? That was my idea! Liam said it was cliched and naff.'

'Liam's wrong,' I say, confidently.

He clinks his glass against mine. 'You're a girl with good taste,' he says. 'I can tell.'

The next day, the picture of Max picking the gold piece of foil out of my hair runs huge in several of the papers, with headlines such as 'Remember to Breathe, Enola!' and 'MAX-imum romance?' The angle of the camera makes it look like his face is much closer to mine than it actually was.

It gives me a warm and fuzzy glow all day. I'm sure nothing will come of it. But a girl can dream.

5

January 2024

Newspaper report:

Vintage girl band Breathe will join former rival band This Way Up this summer for two legacy concerts in Las Vegas on June 30 and July 4.

This Way Up shot to fame in the late 1990s under management of pop supremo Emery Askew, followed by Breathe in the early 2000s after the three girls were discovered on Emery's talent show *The Chosen*. Both bands had a string of number one hits around the world, including Breathe's high-energy debut 'Loud and Proud' and This Way Up's slow-dance classic 'U and Me'.

But the dream came to an abrupt end for

Breathe when lead singer, Enola Mazzeri went missing in December 2008 after a star-studded awards ceremony in London.

In spite of a wide-scale investigation, and many rumoured sightings all over the world almost to this day, no confirmed trace of Enola has ever been found.

Many were questioned by police over her disappearance at the time, including members of both bands, but no arrests were ever made or charges brought.

The remaining two members of Breathe, Angel Williams and Sophie Moffat have opted not to draft in a third singer for the reunion performance.

Angel said: 'We pray every day that Enola is still out there somewhere, living her best life. We hope she is happy, wherever she is and whatever she is doing.

'As Breathe we are extremely excited about our first performances for more than fifteen years, though, of course, deeply saddened that they will also be the band's first performances without Enola. Our hearts remain torn in two by her disappearance, and these concerts will be a tribute to her – we hope she would, or even better, hope she will, be proud. We will be leaving a microphone for her on the stage and if she were to rejoin us between then and now, it would be everything we hope for, a true miracle.'

Angel, now aged 44, continued to enjoy a moderately successful solo career in the few years following Enola's disappearance, as well as a short-lived marriage to Italian football star Gianni Caperelli, while Sophie, also 44, quickly left the music industry to set up and run a wellness retreat in Ibiza. Angel continues to perform occasional concerts at small venues and at private events.

Pop duo This Way Up broke up around a year after Enola's disappearance, citing musical differences. Lead singer and songwriter Max Heaton now lives in LA, having had a brief spell as an actor and then forging a new and very successful career as a property developer. Liam, after struggling for many years with alcohol and gambling addictions, now runs a construction company in Manchester.

It has been rumoured that the two bands will be performing some of their respective songs together at the Las Vegas legacy concerts for the first time ever.

The hotly-anticipated concerts sold out within minutes, with tickets selling for up to $700, and resale prices believed to be well into four figures.

6

24 June 2024
Las Vegas
Angel

Wow Sophie has changed. I almost didn't recognize her at first.

Back in the day, though the vast majority of the fans fancied Enola the most, we all had our place and people who liked each one of us best. Me, the haughty, fit one, with the incredible body and designer clothes. Enola, the girl next door, the one you'd like to go for a night out with, your female best friend who you secretly fancied. And Sophie, the beautiful, mysterious one. With a kind of Mona Lisa vibe. Feline.

After Breathe split, we didn't keep in touch. But I know she ballooned in weight because of those bitchy 'look at them now!' articles in the following years when she'd occasionally be spotted out and about in Ibiza and someone would send a picture in to *Heat* or one of the papers. And then she got a gastric band fairly recently, she's now stick thin (to the point of being gaunt and unhealthy looking if you ask me) and puts her name to just about every dodgy 'natural' supplement going. Guess she needs the money to keep that hippy wellness retreat of hers going.

'Sophie! There you are!' I gush, kissing her on both cheeks as she opens the door to her suite. 'How lovely to see you!'

'And you,' she says, stepping back to let me in. I'm pleased to see that her suite, while it has the same enormous windows overlooking the Strip, isn't as big as mine and doesn't have such a good view. In the distance I can see the Sphere, today lit up like a smiley emoji. When we flew in yesterday evening, over the desert and mountains into the surprisingly large airport seemingly in the middle of nowhere, the same ball-shaped building looked like a somewhat creepy all-seeing eye. I definitely prefer the emoji.

Rather cutely they have had these ragdoll things made to look like us, which sit on the beds in among a mountain of cushions. Mine has curly blonde hair and the thigh-high boots I often wore back then, while Sophie's has a pixie cut and baby-doll dress. Admittedly they are the heyday versions of us: I have pretty much left the boots behind, though other than that, I like to think I haven't changed that much. Sophie, however, is showing her age and has grown her pixie cut out into a somewhat lacklustre bob.

Today she smells of patchouli and is wearing what

looks like a white sack, which I recognize is by a 'hot new designer' she's been promoting on her Insta page, no doubt a sponsored arrangement. Her face is much more lined than it needs to be – she lives somewhere sunny now and should probably invest in some better sunscreen. She's clearly never had Botox or filler, but maybe she can't afford it or has some ethical objection to it, I don't know. I guess some people like that 'natural' (aka old) look these days, but you wouldn't catch me going without my tweakments.

I sit down on the deep blue sofa which is about the size of a double bed, pushing myself to the back. Sophie perches on the edge of an almost as enormous matching armchair opposite me.

'Well, this is weird, isn't it?' I say.

She smiles wanly. 'Yeah. Very. To be honest, when Emery rang me, I assumed it was some kind of wind-up to start with. One of those prank shows or something.'

'Did you? Why?'

She shrugs. 'I dunno. I've been out of the music game for so long, the idea of performing now just seems . . . well.'

Sophie sighs deeply. Fuck's sake. No one *made* her do this.

'These days I'm just a clean-living, middle-aged hippie who lives on a hill in the middle of nowhere,' she continues. 'I'm hardly the hot young hard-drinking party animal that the papers loved to write about all those years ago.' She pauses. 'And even if I *was*, even if . . . well, the band was always about Enola, really, wasn't it? We all knew that, even back then. Even if we didn't want to admit it.'

Speak for yourself, I think. The papers are still interested in me, though admittedly less because of the performing, but more because of my much publicized and *Hello*-sponsored wedding to much-younger-than-me footballer Gianni Caperelli, followed by our almost as equally publicized and extremely acrimonious divorce.

'I don't think that was the case at all,' I say lightly, though a large part of me knows she is right. 'We each had our own loyal fan base.'

'If you like,' Sophie concedes, in a way that clearly indicates she doesn't agree in the slightest. 'Anyway, initially I said "no" to Emery. I wasn't interested in any of this any more. But then, well, it's a ridiculous amount of money they're paying us for a couple of nights' work, isn't it? The retreat I set up in Ibiza . . . it does OK, but performing in these two concerts means that I could offer some free spaces to women who would really benefit from a visit to my place but can't afford it. It would be nice to have more of a cushion behind me to know that I can continue to help the women who come to the retreats, and I figured that if I did these concerts, I wouldn't have to worry for several years.' She pauses. 'Or at least, I wouldn't have to worry about finances.'

Instantly I wonder if we are both being paid the same. We'd better not be. I mean, I get that I'm not as young as I once was, and it's several years since I've released

31

a new song, but I'm surely a much bigger draw than Sophie is.

Once Enola was gone from Breathe, I finally got my moment in the sun, in fact, more like a few years in the sun. I did OK for a while, picked up some new fans, snagged the rich celebrity husband. I still get the odd booking, but as they dwindled, so did Gianni's interest in me, and I was traded in for a younger, more successful version. The bitch.

But as for the concerts that are coming up, I am more current, and more of the fans will be coming to see me rather than Sophie, I'm sure of it.

We've got a few days of rehearsals together, us and the boys, though they are hardly boys any more – they must be pushing fifty. And then the real thing. Two concerts. The last one on Independence Day. Then, hopefully back into the limelight for me. Sophie can fuck off back to Ibiza, I don't care. There's been a pleasing amount of press around us since the concerts were announced back in the summer – a lot of it annoyingly about Enola, speculating about what might have happened to her, of course, but it is what it is. Our back catalogue has already seen an uptick in sales and downloads. I'm hoping to relaunch a solo career off the back of this. I don't need the money – I got a good settlement from Gianni because my lawyer was better than his – but I miss being properly famous like we were. And I've still got it, I know I have.

The concerts need to be good. I'm not the big name I once was, admittedly, but I've kept up with my music, writing, singing, and still do the occasional (usually private but big bucks) performance at a rich bitch's fortieth birthday, or the odd nostalgia tour with some others from our era. I like doing those – I get to see somewhere new, a bit of adulation, and I'm often the biggest name on the set list.

I'm pretty sure Sophie doesn't perform any more, and I'd be surprised if she's bothered to try to keep up whatever voice skills she might have had, but whatever, she's basically just backing vocals for these concerts. It was agreed in advance that there were to be no complicated dance routines, partly because we are no longer in our twenties (though I am still very capable of some excellent moves, as I pointed out), but mainly because there isn't a huge amount of rehearsal time and so a team of dancers is being brought in to do all that side of things. There's also a full band, light displays and indoor pyrotechnics, the works. A lot of money has been thrown at it, rightly. We remain the big names behind it all, and people are coming from all over the world to see us perform.

Us, and the boys.

Max and Liam.

A lot of history there, much of it, not good. Much of it, still secret.

And each of us, for our own reasons, will be sincerely hoping it stays that way.

7

August 2004
London
Enola

I can't believe it when Max calls me the day after the launch concert. At first I think it's one of my old mates winding me up. But then I remember that I don't really *have* any old mates any more, most of them gradually fell away after *The Chosen*, with not inconsiderable encouragement from Becki, who took the line that I had stitched her up in the audition room and that it had probably been my plan to use her as a prop to propel myself to stardom all along.

I feel a pang. I miss her. I hope, in time, she'll come around and we can be friends again. I called and texted to invite her to the concert, but she never replied.

But, but, Max is calling me, and he's asking if I want to go to a party with him this evening.

'Liam's throwing a birthday party for his brother,'

he says, 'at The Ivy. So it's a proper, small event, just friends, not a huge party with journalists, musos and all the other various hangers-on who are usually there, so it'll give us a proper chance to chat. Hang out together away from the madness.'

'Great,' I say, blushing. 'That sounds lovely.' I feel weird about seeing Liam again after what happened between us, when we were on *The Chosen*. I managed to avoid him at the concert and the after-party yesterday. But I'm not going to pass up the chance of a date with Max because of that. And besides, I doubt Liam gave what happened a second thought, I realize that now. Probably barely remembers. I still sometimes wonder if I should have told someone about it at the time.

'Pick you up at seven?' Max asks.

'Yep. Sounds great.'

'Nice. See you later.'

It's only when I replace the phone that I realize I didn't give him my address. Or, for that matter, my phone number.

The doorbell rings bang on seven. I've been ready for ages, but I let Mum answer even so as I figure it'll both give her a thrill to answer the door to Max from This Way Up, and not rushing to the door might make me look maybe at least a tiny bit cooler than I feel. She shouts up the stairs for me, 'Enola! Max is here for you!' and even Roxie ventures out to peer over the banister before retreating back into her room.

I amble down slowly, uncertain in my much-higher-than-I-am-used-to shoes, taking care not to trip on my dress. It's not my usual look, but I'm going out this evening with Max from This Way Up, it's The Ivy, and I want to make an effort.

It's not Max at the door though, it's a man in a uniform. Behind him is an enormous black limo, one of those long ones like some girls go to hen parties in.

For a second I wonder if I've made a mistake or if this is some kind of elaborate wind-up, but then the man says, 'Miss Mazzeri? Mr Heaton is here for you.'

Mum kisses me on the cheek and squeezes me hard. ''Bye love! Have an amazing night! Don't do anything I wouldn't do,' she snickers.

I feel myself go red. God, she's so embarrassing. The chauffeur, as I guess he must be, opens the shiny limo door and I slide in.

Max is there, right on the other side of the enormous car, and I dither momentarily about where to sit until I notice that someone else is there too, a woman, older than Max.

I feel a lurch of disappointment. I had thought this was some kind of date, but it looks like I got it all wrong. Maybe he's invited lots of people along and it's just a night out like any other. Maybe that's why he's in such an enormous car.

'Enola!' he says. 'Come and sit here with me and have some champagne.' I cross the car – how weird is that? – and Max hands me a glass. 'This is Danute, This Way Up's publicist,' he adds.

The woman smiles at me, a lizardy smile that looks

entirely false. Breathe's publicist Trixie terrifies me, but this woman seems even worse.

'Enola. We're so pleased you were able to come along this evening,' she purrs. 'We thought that, after the papers were so delighted by the pictures of you and Max together at the Hyde Park after-party, it might be nice to continue the storyline.'

Storyline?

'It's such a nice, positive one,' she continues, 'good for both bands, we feel. The right photographers have been briefed to be there this evening, so when you get out of the car, can I suggest that you're careful about what happens with your skirt, as they'll be waiting – I'm glad you're in a long dress, that makes it easier. Let Max get out first, perhaps he could even take your hand as you do so? Yes, that will be good, makes him look chivalrous. People like that kind of thing, don't they? Big smiles, don't say anything to any fans or the paps, and then straight into the restaurant, maybe leaning in to Max a little to whisper something in his ear as you go. That sound OK?'

But I am barely listening to her instructions – I'm only thinking about what she means by 'storyline' and by 'we'. Who is the *we* who thought this date would be such a good idea? I feel tears come to my eyes and fight them back. Is this all this is? A PR exercise? A set-up for the photographers? A *story*? I thought Max had asked me out because he liked me, because he wanted to get to know me, like he said. But it seems like that isn't the case at all. Does he even want to be here? Would he rather be with his mates, or even, much worse, with some other girl?

I give myself a mental shake. I need to play the game, I can't show how disappointed I am. 'Yes, that's fine,' I say to the PR woman, even thinking of a follow-up question to her spiel which I barely registered. 'Will there be photographers inside at the event too?'

She frowns. 'We don't think so. There shouldn't be. But you never know exactly who you can trust, so it's best to be on your best behaviour just in case, and,' she rubs the bottom of her nose, 'definitely none of that, OK? This Way Up and Breathe: it's important that both groups are seen as wholesome because of the fan demographic. Mainly kids.'

'Um, right, yeah.' I've never done drugs, never plan to, and am quite shocked that she thinks it's something that I need to be told, but this is a different world I'm in now and I need to get used to it.

The car slows and I can see cameras start to flash behind the blacked-out windows even before we get out.

'Ready?' Max asks. 'I'll go first like Danute says. We'll go inside quickly, it's not like we're on the red carpet and need to hang around and wave or anything.'

'Not too quickly,' Danute warns. 'You need to make sure the guys have time to get some nice shots of you, otherwise this whole thing is a waste of time.'

I don't feel that spending an evening with Max Heaton would ever be a waste of time, but it seems that her agenda is very different to mine. I only hope Max doesn't feel the same way.

'And then later, get reception to call the driver when you're ready to be picked up,' Danute continues. 'They've got his number. Have a nice night,' she adds, without feeling.

The door is opened by a doorman, Max gets out to shouts of, 'Max! Max! Over 'ere!' from a couple of large men with huge cameras. He offers his hand to me as Danute suggested and I step carefully out, forgetting to smile and looking down at the ground as they shout, 'Enola! Enola! Are you and Max an item?' We scurry quickly towards the door, which is swiftly opened by a man in a suit – I've no idea where he came from – and we launch ourselves into the hallway. There was no time to do the leaning and whispering or whatever it was that Danute suggested. I don't care if I haven't given her what she wants, but whether it turns out to be a proper date or simply a publicity stunt, I don't want to let Max down or make myself look stupid.

'Sorry about all that,' Max says. 'This evening isn't how Danute made it sound, I promise. I probably should have warned you about her before I picked you up, she's always like that, doesn't care how she makes people feel at all.'

I feel a jolt of optimism. Perhaps Max does actually like me?

'I wanted to invite you, honest I did,' he continues. 'It was only when Danute suggested that I take Angel along as my "date" to the party – apparently her agent had been in touch and suggested it – and I said I'd already asked you that she decided she needed to get in on the action and micromanage. But she's gone now, so we can get on with our evening and enjoy ourselves. I'm looking forward to getting to know you better.'

I smile. 'And I you,' I reply, which is the understatement of the year. This is everything I've ever dreamed of.

8

24 June 2024
Las Vegas
Liam

It's a long time since I've been anywhere like this. The hotel we're staying in is mental. It's got something like 5,000 rooms and, here in the enormous atrium, the solar system is represented by spheres made of what look like fresh flowers that hang from the ceiling, which is, in turn, some kind of infinity screen covered in twinkling constellations. Now and again the space-themed roller coaster roars through above the check-in desk, accompanied by the screams of the people riding it, before disappearing out of the other side. I didn't have to queue to check in, or even check in at all, Emery has people who do all that for us. It's like the good old days of This Way Up – not having to lift a finger. Which is a relief in this heat. It's something like 40 degrees outside, but luckily so far I have been whisked from one hyper air-conditioned place to another, so I've barely broken a sweat.

My suitcase goes straight from the limo that picked us up from the airport to my suite without me even laying eyes on it. The suite on the fiftieth floor is bigger than my flat, and certainly much cleaner. The bed is round – round! – and so high it has three steps to get up to it. The person showing me around presses a button and it starts to revolve. Bizarre. Why would anyone want a bed which revolves? A 70s-style mirror on the ceiling I could understand, but sadly no such luck.

On a coffee table there's an enormous platter of fruit and chocolate with my name written in red sauce at the front of the white ceramic plate, and in front is a classy-looking notebook with the cover of the first This Way Up album on. Max and me, posing moodily in black and white, look impossibly young and fit.

'I hope you are pleased with your room, Mr Hardy?' asks the uniformed bellhop, who is hovering in the door-way. I realize he is probably waiting for a tip and thrust my hand into my pocket. Have I got any cash?

'Uh, yes, it's great,' I mumble. I pull out my hand – a £20 note and a couple of pound coins. I didn't think to get any dollars. I figured it was better not to have too much cash on me – me and gambling don't exactly have the best record, though horses were always my thing rather than casinos. Even so I was hoping to stay away from the tables, but the way the hotel is arranged, it's almost impossible to come in or out without going past them.

I look at the useless cash and push it back into my pocket.

The bellhop nods politely. 'I am pleased. If we can help with anything at all, don't hesitate to call reception or room service. So unless you need anything else . . .'

'No, that's all good, thank you.' He nods again and retreats from the room. As soon as the door closes behind him, the phone rings. In fact, three phones. One on the bedside table, one in what is notionally the living room, and one somewhere else – I guess the bathroom. Always wondered why anyone would want a phone in the bathroom.

'Hello?' I say, warily. Who uses a landline these days? And how do they know I'm here?

'Liam! It's Max. I'm in the bar – we've got a VIP bar all to ourselves so we don't need to mix with the normals. Come and find me. It's been a while hasn't it? Lots to catch up on. Sorry about calling your room – I didn't have your mobile number. Isn't this great? It'll be like old times.'

I swallow hard. 'Yeah. Great.' Old times. Do we really want it to be like old times? A lot has happened. A lot that can't be undone or forgotten about. 'Give me a few minutes and I'll be there.'

9

25 June 2024
Las Vegas
Angel

We will be performing in Las Vegas' newest venue, The Cube, and as well as this being our reunion concert, it's also the venue's inauguration. It holds 20,000 people and is made up of giant LED screens both internally and externally, covering something mad like 15,000 square metres and capable of displaying literally millions of colours. BREATHE is currently spelt out in giant letters on the outside, and 'with This Way Up' is scrolling around – though the typeface for that is much smaller, I am pleased to see.

For our big entrance, Sophie and I are being lowered from the ceiling in baskets with the graphics of hot-air balloons behind us, the way they've set the lights and projection up makes it look like we are out in the desert outside – it's incredible. I used to think our sets when we toured before were impressive because we had a lot of trucks following us around and fireworks at the outdoor venues, but things have come a very long way since then, especially out here in Vegas.

Once our baskets land on little podiums just above the stage, gates at the front of them open automatically and two hot male dancers take our hands to lead us down a couple of steps (they will be bare chested and in tight silver trousers which leave nothing to the imagination for the actual performance) and this is when we will actually start singing.

By now Sophie is to my left on the stage, and to my right is the pointless microphone that has been placed in order to 'honour' Enola. I'm not entirely sure whose sappy idea that was, and we're not even the first band to do this. But it's hardly as if she's suddenly going to turn up mid-performance and start singing, is it? I saw the idea was attributed to me in the media, but I certainly never suggested it – I guess Trixie put it out in a press release. I imagine it will have been her who came up with the idea too. I hope they've thought it all through and set the mic up so that it isn't live and can't cause feedback. Either way, the set designers have made sure that no one can miss it, it is covered in lights that seem to race up and down, and there's something that looks like a lit yellow ribbon which flashes 'tied' to the top of it for fuck's sake. Even when Enola's not here, somehow everything still has to be all about her. I believe the idea of an onstage ABBA-style hologram of her was even discussed at one point, but that was discounted, thank fuck.

45

'OK, girls, you ready?' Emery asks. Girls. Ugh. We are in our forties now, we are not 'girls'. Emery was creepy at the best of times and he has not aged well. He's now balding and paunchy and his jeans are too tight, a kind of horrific and unpleasant echo of what the dancers will be wearing. Arguably we all owe our success to him, but I've never liked him at all: I don't think any of us did. Not even Enola. She was his pet, but mainly because she sucked up to him to make sure she always kept her place centre-stage. He never had any qualms about pushing us too hard – the image of the band always came first – and he has a heart of stone. Doesn't care about anything except making money and looking important.

'Soundcheck please,' he calls. A backing guitarist and bassist strum a few notes each in turn. The drummer does a lacklustre kind of *badoom-tish*. Sophie sings an arpeggio, and I'm relieved to hear that her voice still sounds in pretty good nick – it was much more than I was expecting.

I lean into my microphone to do the same. There is a sudden shout, a creak and a whoosh of air, and something large, heavy and black falls to the stage in front of me, missing me by mere inches.

10

'What's this?' Max asks, thrusting a newspaper in my face, so close that I don't stand a chance of actually seeing whatever it is I'm meant to be looking at. Not that I need to. I don't know exactly what it is this time, but I can guess the gist. It's always the same.

We've been together almost two years now. Everything was brilliant to start with, but now, not so much. It took a little while for his jealousy to show its true colours, and as Breathe's success has grown and This Way Up's has waned, it's got worse and worse. I should have become used to it now. Or at least unsurprised by it, and on the whole, usually I am. But that doesn't make it any more fun.

I gently take the paper from his hand to look at. 'It's a picture of me at the *Enola Beautiful* launch party, you can see that,' I say, handing it back to him. 'I invited you. It would have been lovely if you'd come. But you said you didn't want to.'

He sniffs. 'Yeah. Didn't want to spend the evening with a load of cooing women having to play *Mr Enola* again. At least one of the papers has taken to calling me that in headlines now. In headlines!' He moves his face closer to mine and hisses, 'Do you understand how humiliating that is for me?'

I flinch. 'I'm sorry you feel that way,' I say, trying to keep my voice even. 'You know how the papers like to give people labels. No one takes any notice. I don't think they mean anything bad by it.'

He moves back, thrusts the paper towards my face and I recoil as he shouts, 'Oh, you don't, do you? Well as long as that's how *you* feel about it, that's fine. Obviously what *I* feel doesn't matter.'

I can't bear it when he gets like this. The easiest thing to do is try to shut it down. I hate being shouted at, it scares me.

'Of course what you feel matters,' I say in my best soothing voice, trying to avoid the newspaper, which he is still flapping far too close to my face. 'It matters a lot. I'll have a word with Emery. See if he can do something. Maybe he can ask the journalists . . . not to write that. Perhaps Trixie can tell the key people . . .'

He pulls the paper away and moves closer to me, not just his face this time, but his whole body. I resist the urge to step backwards because when I do that it always winds him up further. 'More to the point though,' he continues, 'it looks like you took full advantage of me not being there.' His voice is low and menacing. 'Looks like you had a brilliant time,' he spits. 'It looks like I missed out on a *really good evening*. Unlike some,' he spits.

'Yes, it was a fun night,' I agree blandly, not knowing exactly where this is going. It was a good night, the beauty people were happy with it and the press were kind, on the whole. We got some positive coverage, but nothing particularly out of the ordinary or noteworthy happened, as far as I'm concerned at least.

'But obviously, for me, it was work,' I continue. 'It was the launch of my make-up brand, as you know. They thought it would be good press to have a launch party, and as it turned out, it was. Most of the papers and the women's mags came along, probably thanks to the open bar and the excellent goodie bags. But I'd much rather have been home with you, watching a film or something,' I add, gently touching his arm. This isn't true – I enjoyed my night out and I can stay at home and watch a film with Max any time. But I've learnt from experience that that's usually the right thing to say.

Not today though it seems. He snatches his arm away and thrusts the paper in my face again. 'Oh really?' he sneers. 'So if that's the case, why are you standing so close to Finty?'

I take the paper gently from him, taking care not to rile Max further by snatching, and look at it. In spite of myself, I actually laugh. Finty is an actor, new on the scene, admittedly quite good-looking but at least twice my age, probably more, and not someone I would be interested in in a million years.

'Seriously? That's what you're upset about? You think . . . I was flirting with him? That we're having an affair? Or what?' I giggle. 'Don't be so ridiculous.'

'Don't laugh at me!' he screams, and I feel flecks of spit hitting my face. 'I don't know. I've no idea what's going on. It seems like I'm always the last to know everything. You tell me.'

I look at the pictures again. For fuck's sake. 'Look,' I say, pointing at a petite blonde, heavily pregnant woman chatting to Emery in one of the other pictures of the party. 'You see this woman? Her name is Clara. We had a long chat, she's lovely. Her baby is due in three weeks and she's really excited about it – he or she will be her first child. Their first child. Clara is Finty's *wife*.' I pause to study the pictures a little more.

'If you look closely,' I continue, 'you can see that in the picture taken of me and him, she is actually standing right next to him. See?' I ask. This time I push the paper into Max's face. 'See the pattern on her dress? See this picture of me and Finty? See the same pattern on what looks like an arm, in the edge of the picture? Her dress. Her arm. Pregnant wife, right next to her husband. She was there the entire time I was talking to Finty. But even if she hadn't been, I wouldn't have been flirting.'

I shouldn't have to explain myself like this. I shouldn't have to go forensically over who I spoke to and when and why, every time I go out without Max. Apart from anything else, even if I *did* ever want to do anything I

50

wouldn't – the paps with their cameras are always there. It would be impossible to keep anything secret from anyone, least of all Max.

Max, when he's in a good mood, is perfect. The dream boyfriend. Good-looking, attentive, will do anything to make me happy, always surprising me with little gifts and outings, what more could a girl want? And that's even before you get to the fact that he is Max from This Way Up, the boy most girls would give their right arm to be with. But this kind of thing is happening more and more, sometimes I'm not sure how much longer I can deal with it.

He looks at the paper, back at me, and throws it on the floor like a toddler having a tantrum. 'If you'd only stayed at home with me . . .' he whines.

'Max! It was the launch party. You know that. I'm the face of the brand. I couldn't *not* go. You are being ridiculous.'

He starts to cry. Oh God. Not this again. 'I'm sorry Enola,' he sobs. 'It's only because I love you so much. I can't bear the thought of anyone else touching you, trying to take you away from me.'

I take him in my arms and let him sob into my chest. He's making my T-shirt wet and snotty, and the gulping sounds he's making are grossing me out.

'It's OK, Max, I know,' I soothe, because I don't want to start a row about this now. 'You don't have to worry. No one is going to take me away. Please don't cry. Everything is OK.'

11

25 June 2024
Las Vegas
Angel

'I'm fine!' I insist, knocking back yet another large vodka and tonic. 'Honestly, this is all a huge fuss about nothing. The gantry fell, it no doubt wasn't secured properly, it didn't hit me or anyone else. Nothing happened apart from a light smashed. I just hope they can replace it in time for the actual show.'

Sophie is drinking a chamomile tea, wrapped in a foil blanket like you see people wearing after car crashes or marathons, still snivelling as some first-aid people fuss around her. So pathetic. What a drama queen. 'We could have been killed!' she wails. 'Either of us! What if . . .'

'If its and buts were blood and guts,' I say, 'actually no, that can't be the phrase, but there's one . . . anyway, there's no point fretting about what might have been. No one was hurt, everyone is fine. Seriously, Sophie, you need to pull yourself together and we need to get on with it. We're wasting time, it's not as if we've got all the time in the world to rehearse, is it?'

Various young men dressed in black are roaming about the stage with walkie talkies, climbing ladders, shouting stuff to each other and there's even one hanging from the lighting grid, holding a giant torch and peering and fiddling. The toppled gantry is still lying heavy on the stage while people bring in trolleys to load it onto. A couple of other stagehands are sweeping up the broken glass. I'm surprised to feel a slight shiver as I look at the now-dented light at the top of the huge fallen tower. In spite of what I said to Sophie, I feel a modicum of unease. If that light – one of the old-fashioned enormous types brought in as a nod to our past, more of a prop than anything else and much heavier than the modern stuff – had hit either of us, we'd have no doubt been very seriously injured. Or even killed.

12

Letter delivered to Brilliant Records:

Enola I love you I would do anything for you anything at all and one day I will prove it watch out for something right when you least expect it. I love your new hair cut I don't think Max is good enough for you you should find someone better. But dont worry because I am always here for you Enola love you love you love you

Letter delivered to Enola's home:

You're a stupid bitch Enola I hope you die. One day I will make it happen. You should watch yourself

13

October 2008
London
Enola

My new penthouse by the river, just off the South Bank, not far from Tate Modern, The Globe, Tower Bridge and plenty of other fabulous places, is amazing. I love it so much. The building isn't actually finished – I am the only person living here at the moment, which is admittedly a bit strange, but as soon as I saw it, I knew I had to have it. It is perfect, way nicer than anything else the property finding people suggested for me.

During the day there are builders coming and going as they finish off fitting out the other apartments, which look like they are pretty much done from the outside at least, and they've still got the whizzy gym and riverside garden to finish off, but at night, it's as quiet as the grave. Kind of spooky if you think about it too much, so I don't. And anyway, after the hurly-burly and full-on nature of my days, I like the peace and quiet. You'd think that it would be noisy living on what amounts to a building site, but the spec is so high in these flats that the insulation is amazing – I don't hear a thing. Not that I'm around much during the day though, and by the evening and at weekends, all the builders have gone.

As my penthouse is the biggest and the most expensive apartment in the building there is a lift just for me and my own private entrance so I don't have to go through the lobby. I can go straight from the car park or my very own ground-level door up to here on the twenty-fifth floor without seeing anyone, and at level minus 1, the lift also opens on the other side so that I can go out directly into what will eventually become an underground gym and pool. Right above the gym, there will be a communal garden overlooking the river which I probably won't realistically be able to use as I'd attract too much attention, even among the no doubt well-heeled residents who will eventually occupy the rest of the flats. But that doesn't matter because I have my very own roof terrace, and it is fantastic. Part of the reason I chose this building is because of the private high-spec gym, so I'm looking forward to that being finished, hopefully in the next few months.

These days, I can barely go anywhere without people noticing me. A lot of the time, it's nice, people want an autograph or to say hi. But sometimes it's weird, people (guys) are leery and letchy. So to be able to do something simple like go in or out of my place to the gym without any make-up on and not have to talk to random fans when I'm not in the mood means a lot – that's why I love the private entrance. And as for the gym, not needing to worry about anyone snapping a picture of me looking sweaty in my workout gear or using that machine where you open and close your knees which always feels a bit obscene will be big plus. I know that almost everyone in the public eye says this, and most of them don't mean it, but I genuinely am a very private person.

And as well as all that, there are three massive balconies and my view of the river . . . wow. I can see across to St Paul's, over to the Canary Wharf, and well beyond.

It was a relief to move out of Mum's. Since I became famous, she's been more embarrassing than ever. She hangs on my coat tails as much as she possibly can. I get that she gave up a lot for me, and that I'm basically now living her dream, but . . . it's awful trying to deal with her sometimes. She dresses too young, turns up at parties and events using my name (and they always let her in), some of the paps even take pictures of her now, and she absolutely loves it.

Roxie had already left home by the time I gathered up enough strength to tell Mum it was time for me to move on. Roxie's in a crappy bedsit in a not very nice area, but seems happy as a clam – says it's much easier not having Mum bothering her about why she isn't going out and having a social life when she just wants to be left alone. Neither she nor I go home to Mum now all that much, but Roxie and I meet up fairly often in places that aren't too crowded as she can't bear noise and I'm more likely to be left alone if the place is reasonably quiet.

When I moved out of home, it wasn't only about wanting a bit of distance between me and Mum, I was also looking for more space and freedom. But mainly, I wanted more privacy, and a place to call my own. Just for me and my darling Maine Coon cats Apple and Bella, who I adopted shortly after I moved in. They have their own luxurious, purpose-built, enclosed 'catio' on one of the balconies.

I rented for a while in a gated development while I looked around, but it made sense to get on the property ladder, everyone said so. And I wanted something that was all mine, which no one could take away from me, and that I didn't have to share with anyone.

Max wanted me to move in with him, but I told him I didn't want to do that. I'm not ready to live with him all the time, at least not until he gets over his jealousy, though I didn't put it quite like that. But we are still very much an item. And I do love him. I really do.

I think about how he was when we first got together, how attentive he was, how much fun we had. When we went to that theme park and pulled faces for the roller-coaster cameras. When we dressed up in 1920s clothes and went punting in Oxford with a champagne picnic. When he surprised me with a visit to Paris in a private plane, where we ate oysters in an art deco restaurant and had dinner at the top of the Eiffel Tower.

But that was back when he was already the big pop star and I was still the wide-eyed newbie, thrilled to be going to expensive restaurants, being flown in private jets and meeting people I'd only seen in the papers or on TV before.

We celebrated at The Ivy when Breathe had their first number one, the same place we had our first date, the first time we had kissed. When our next single got to number one, we had champagne at home together because Max said he wanted to spend the evening just with me, not share me with anyone else. And I was flattered, I loved that.

Even now, he loves to organize surprises for me, sometimes to celebrate a special event, but sometimes just because. Private after-hours shopping in my favourite designer shops. A beach picnic on a private island in the Maldives. A trip in a speedboat along the Thames because I'd said it looked fun when I'd seen it in a film. He's really thoughtful about things like that, which goes a long way to making up for his failings. Mum absolutely adores him and he's adorable with her too, even pops around to see her sometimes when I'm not there, which she's always thrilled by. Not everyone has a boyfriend who will do that kind of thing.

As time went on, Breathe went from strength to strength, while This Way Up was on the decline. They still do OK, their singles make the top 10 usually, but not always number one. They had to cancel a couple of dates on their last tour because ticket sales were slow. Meantime, there's a Breathe feature film coming out next year and we're about to set off on our sell-out Out There European tour, which, to add insult to injury, This

Way Up are making 'guest appearances' at in a few key cities. Next year, a full world tour is planned.

Maybe the tour will kickstart This Way Up's career again. I think if that happened, things would be better between us. I don't want to give up on Max. If he could get over the jealousy, he would be perfect. I could see myself spending my whole life with him. No one is ever the full package are they? I think that, for me, Max is as close as it's going to get.

Another reason to move was to escape the weird letters. I get that it's normal that people in my position have fans and that some people get a bit obsessed. Most of the letters aren't threatening, but a few are, and that can be a little unsettling.

Mum's address was well known, thanks to her, she's made no effort to keep it a secret because she loves me being in the papers and she loves it even more if she manages to get a comment in too. She'd even make tea for the journalists when I was being doorstepped.

But as far as I know, this address is still not widely known by the general public, though I imagine it won't be that long till Trixie decides to leak it to her favourite snappers – it didn't take long at my rented place anyway. People seem to think it's hard to find out where famous people live, but it isn't. Once one journalist or photographer knows, they all know – same with the fans.

I am still receiving some letters, but fewer than I was. The police are aware, but they say that letter writers are usually all talk and no action, and obviously they can't do anything about it unless they know who is sending them. They don't believe I am at risk, and have told me not to worry beyond taking the usual sensible safety precautions.

So for all these reasons, right now, it's much better I have my very own place. And I love it.

'Here's to privacy,' I say, clinking my brand-new Waterford glasses with Roxie. I'm not having a proper housewarming – I go to enough parties as it is, and I'm keen to keep my penthouse as my own private sanctuary as far as possible. I might have a party eventually, maybe after the Ultimate Starz Awards, but I don't want to have any of the rest of the band here yet. Instead I've invited Roxie up for the night and have ordered a takeaway to be delivered from a Michelin-starred restaurant. I don't care about that kind of food much, but I know Roxie doesn't have any money and probably doesn't eat anything much other than beans on toast, so I wanted to show her a bit of the high life for a change.

In spite of us being twins, we don't have much in common. But we are very close, in a way which only twins can be, and when I don't see her much, I miss her terribly. She's the absolute opposite of Mum in the way she views celebrity. Roxie won't come to parties and isn't interested in that side of my life at all, so these days I only usually get to see her if I invite her to something just for us. Like tonight. It's been getting harder and harder to get her to meet up lately, but she seemed happy to come here as long as I sent her a taxi so that she didn't have to go on public transport. 'All those people,' she'd said. 'All those germs. It's too unhygienic.'

I think back to when we were children and used to mess around in the way I'm sure all identical twins do – swapping places at school so that the teachers didn't know who was who. Mum was furious one time when I sent Roxie along to one of the millions of dance competitions she made me do and she only noticed when Roxie got out of the car – Roxie can't dance at all so there was no way she could take my place there. In the early days of Breathe, Roxie even stood in for me during a couple of photo shoots to see if we could get away with it – and I'm pretty sure we did.

There was one Breathe party she came to with me when it was all very new – I persuaded her to get her hair and make-up done and come along; we wore matching outfits and the press had a field day. But she found it overwhelming, left early and never wanted to come again. She'll still do the occasional interview for me if she can do it over the phone, sometimes even for radio, and we both find that quite fun. She'll usually slip something in that she knows I'd never say, a little private joke between us. I like the fact of getting one over on the journalists – I tend to do it to ones who I don't like much. I might try to persuade Roxie to stand in for me in public some time at something small again – she might even enjoy it if she didn't have to interact too much once she'd got over her initial reservations. It could even help bring her out of herself. But I don't want to push her – don't want to freak her out.

'Cool place,' Roxie says, approvingly, snapping me out of my reverie. 'Max seen it yet?'

I shake my head. 'Not yet. He will do. But I need something . . . just for me for a little while.'

'How are things going with him?' she asks, taking a sip of her champagne. 'Ugh,' she says. 'This is vile – I don't see what all the fuss is about around champagne. It's just fizzy wine with an inflated price tag. You got any beer?'

I get up, go to my enormous fridge, which is one of the best things I've bought since I moved in, and hand her a Sapporo beer. She eyes it suspiciously before cracking it open and taking a large gulp. She looks at the large can approvingly and gives a nod.

'Nice. Anyway, you were saying . . . Max? Things OK there?'

I sigh. 'Yeah. Mainly. When things are good, they're really good. He can still be quite . . . jealous though. And sometimes that's hard.'

Roxie is peering at the beer can and I'm not entirely sure if she's listening. Never mind, I don't really want to talk about Max anyway. It's hard to make people understand how his and my relationship works, even someone who knows me as well as Roxie. I tell her just about everything – we don't have any secrets from each other – and while I *have* told her about my issues with Max, I've tended to play down his jealousy. Though I suspect, given how well she knows me, she'll be surmising more than I actually say.

If I'm honest with myself, I'm embarrassed by it. Part

of me knows I shouldn't stand for it, but a larger part loves him and doesn't want to give him up. Also I know he loves me, and I can never know for sure if someone else will love me in the same way. Especially now that I'm rich and famous, there are plenty of men who will be much more interested in that than in the real me.

But I don't want to talk about this now, so I change the subject, like I usually do when this comes up. 'And what about you?' I ask. 'You seeing anyone?'

I know she'll say no. Roxie barely steps away from her computer and her internet forums these days. She doesn't seem to interact with anyone in real life more than she can possibly help, and it's hard to imagine her actually ever having a relationship. If she did, I'd no idea if it would be with a man or a woman, she's never really expressed any interest either way, and even though she's my twin, asking would feel like a breach of privacy.

'I'm not seeing anyone,' she says. 'Can't be bothered with all that.' She pauses. 'But you know you said that thing about Max and his jealousy?' she continues, leaping back to where I left off almost as if I'd never asked the question. 'You'd better hope he never finds out about what happened with you and Liam, hadn't you? Then the shit would really hit the fan. For both of you.'

14

'Did you hear what happened at the girls' rehearsal?' I say. 'Sounds like it could have been really nasty.'

'Some issue with one of the stage lights,' Max says. 'It fell. Nearly hit them. Everything's been stopped and they're checking the whole rig now before anyone can do anything else.'

'But they're OK?' I ask, not that I give a shit. Conniving little bitches, both of them. Nearly as bad as Enola. Shame, really, she seemed all right when she first came on the scene. Until it turned out that she wasn't.

Max takes a final drag of his cigarette and stubs it out. 'Yeah. Apparently Sophie's a bit shaken up and has gone off to meditate or something and Angel's making a fuss about it eating into their rehearsal time. You know what she's like. And she has a point, our first rehearsal is due in an hour, and at this rate, it's going to be set back. We need to rehearse too, we don't want them outdoing us, do we?'

I try to laugh, but it comes out as a somewhat bitter bark. 'We've always been better than them,' I say. 'They've just had the lucky breaks. The press. The tits. Enola going missing didn't exactly do Angel any harm either.'

Max gives me a look as if I've said something shocking and I'm about to apologize, he and Enola did have that thing going on after all, even if it was a long time ago, but then he simply lights another cigarette and stares out across the hotel courtyard thoughtfully.

'That was all a very long time ago,' he says. 'We were children. Barely formed. Knew nothing about anything. We're all different people now.'

15

September 2008
London
Enola

'You just don't love me as much as I love you,' Max is snivelling. 'If you did, you wouldn't do things like that.'

Oh God. Somehow I find sad Max even harder to deal with than angry Max.

But I've had enough. I'm going to be strong.

He is sitting on my Gamma and Dandy sofa, head in his hands, sobbing. I can see the lights of the London Eye through my window and I think about how much I'd love to be in one of those pods, on my own, slowly going on a journey to nowhere and seeing a view not that different from the one I can see from my balcony, but without having to deal with this.

In public, he is great. We're the perfect couple. He's attentive, he brings me drinks, he holds an umbrella over my head when it rains, he gently puts his hand on the small of my back as we leave a room together as he guides me out. I love it when he does that, it makes me feel treasured. Protected.

But then, when we get back to the privacy of wherever we're going, my place, his, a hotel room if we're away, wherever and whenever, the accusations start. Why did I spend so long talking to so and so? Didn't I notice that he was staring at my boobs? Why was I wearing such a low-cut dress anyway? I never used to dress like that! What did I say to whoever, was I talking about him? I'd better not have been slagging him off. And so on.

Sometimes I argue. Defend myself. Say that I wasn't flirting, because I never do. That I was just out having a good time, socializing, like anyone. But mostly I don't bother because it gets me nowhere. He's never got physical with me, but sometimes I feel like it wouldn't take much to push him to that.

And this is what set this off. As usual. A conversation with some boring bloke twice my age who I didn't especially want to speak to, but Emery had made me sit next to at a charity dinner because apparently he's a fan of mine and Emery wants some favour from him, I forget what. It's well worth my while staying in Emery's good books though to make sure I keep my place at the front of the stage, so when it comes to that kind of thing, I generally do what I'm told.

Emery's mate was dull and old, but a perfect gentleman, even kept his eyes on my face which plenty don't manage to do, and there was no gratuitous touching or anything like that.

I steel myself, try to keep my voice steady. I don't want to rile Max. But enough is enough.

'You spent the whole night talking to him!' he wails. 'Why would you do that if you didn't fancy him?'

I take a deep breath. 'Because Emery told me to, like I said. You wouldn't want Emery giving the Breathe lead to Angel, would you? He needs to like me the best.'

He reaches out for my hand. 'And I need you to like *me* the best,' he whines.

Oh God. 'Max. I *do* like you the best. I love you.' I feel tears pricking behind my eyes. 'But I can't cope with this any more. You don't trust me. It's exhausting.'

He peers at me, silent for a second or two, but at least he stops that awful crying. 'What are you saying?' he asks, hoarsely.

I sit down next to him without dropping his hand. 'Max. I'm sorry,' I say gently, a sob forming in my throat, 'but I don't think I can carry on with this. I love you. I don't want to end it. I really don't. But I have to. We have to.'

He looks at me in horror and then starts shaking his head as fresh tears come. 'No, Enola, no, no, no, you can't . . .'

He is bawling now, pawing at me. I start crying too. I love him. I don't want to do this. But . . .

'Please!' he shouts, launching himself off the sofa onto the floor, taking both my hands. 'I'll do anything. I'll be less jealous, I promise. I do trust you. I do. It's just that you're so beautiful and I'm nothing without you, nothing . . . please Enola, please!'

I turn my face away from him and shake my head. This is awful. Awful.

'Max,' I say. 'Don't do this. It will be hard, for a while, but it'll be OK, in time we can probably be friends, and . . .'

'It won't be OK!' he shrieks. '*I* won't be OK. Ever.' He puts his face in my lap and continues to cry these horrible huge, heaving sobs. I stroke his head. I am hating this. I don't want to hurt him. And yet.

We sit there for a few minutes, both crying. And after a while, he lifts his head and looks me directly in the eye.

'If you leave, Enola,' he says, his voice steadier now, 'I will kill myself. I mean it. I wouldn't be able to go on without you. There would be nothing left for me.'

16

September 2008
London
Charlie

I've got a ticket to the London concert of the Out There tour! It's mainly Breathe, but This Way Up are also joining them for some of the dates.

If money was no object, I would go to every single Breathe concert in every single city on the tour, which is twenty-five dates around Europe. I've seen them in concert before, as many times as I've been able to afford, and they were always amazing! But obviously I can't go to every one, even though I've already given up my job to have more time to devote to Enola. I get nearly as much on benefits as I did from my awful job and this is so much more worthwhile than washing test tubes in some crappy lab.

No one else seems to notice, but Enola needs a friend. She looks sad in the pictures, even when she is smiling.

And the other day when I was waiting for her outside a party, I watched her leave with Max and I don't know what he said, but her face changed in an instant. And he was holding her arm too tightly as they walked. I bet his fingers will have left bruises. They're not as happy as they make out, I'm sure.

I've been re-reading through some old interviews – I read or I listen to every single one she does – and she's always dropping hints that things aren't that good if you take the trouble to read between the lines like I do. It's just that most other people aren't paying attention and don't bother to think about what she might really mean. I mean, 'Max is my soulmate,' who says that unless they're being coached to do so by their partner? No one. Or, 'I can't imagine a life without Max now,' – surely that means that's *exactly* what she's thinking about? Otherwise why imagine it at all, let alone mention it in an interview?

I'm sure we could be friends. If only we moved in the same circles, I'm certain I could be the confidante I'm positive she needs. It makes me sad to see her so lonely, not knowing that I am here for her. I would do anything for her, but most of all I would like to be close to her and know that she is OK.

I have never felt like this before. I got a bit obsessed with someone a few years back, when all that stuff happened and I got the restraining order, but now I can see that I was wrong and it was little more than a silly kid's crush. Those feelings were nothing compared to what I feel now. I am sure I am meant to be there for Enola, to help her. And we could have such fun together too! It's so frustrating, not being able to get close to her. It would be the best thing for both of us, I know it would. We have so much to offer each other.

I know where Enola lives, the building is right by the river, and her new penthouse looks amazing. Obviously I have never been in the penthouse itself – that would be the absolute dream! But one day I put on the one suit I own which I bought from the charity shop for my court appearances, and went to the sales office pretending I was interested in buying a flat so I could look at the brochures and know that I was close to Enola. Sometimes I hang around outside to watch her come and go, but I am careful to keep my distance because I don't want a rerun of what happened before: she is far too important to risk anything like that. I don't send letters to her apartment because doing that kind of thing played a part in what got me in trouble last time. When I have something to say to her, which is often, I send it to the record company. I hope she gets the letters. I'm sure someone like Enola would take the time to read letters from her fans.

The tour will finish in London so I have that to look forward to. I can't wait. But first they will be doing their concerts in mainland Europe, so waiting is what I will have to do. I am going to the airport tomorrow to try to see them as they leave. Their publicity people have 'leaked' where they will be departing from, and I will be watching. But I've learnt from experience that you have to go softly softly with this kind of thing and I'm not even going to speak to Enola until I know the time is right. I am careful with the letters, I don't put my name on them and I only ever say nice things. Though admittedly I do send quite a lot. No more than one per day is OK though, isn't it?

17

26 June 2024
Las Vegas
Angel

Sophie and I have most of the day off today while the boys rehearse, and then tomorrow they will put us together onstage. I spend most of the day at Caesar's Palace, shopping. They have all the designer shops here, it's amazing, and you barely even have to go outside to get to them, which is a relief because it's simply too hot to do so. The ceiling of the shopping mall is painted so that it looks like real sky, but it's neither too hot or too cold, and when you're in the really smart bits, there are no crowds either, which can't be said for most of the city. A couple of the shop assistants recognize me, which is always a thrill, and even the ones who don't are scrupulously polite and never snooty like they are in some places. Got to love USA-style service.

After I've been shopping I pop back to the hotel spa

for a quick massage and then we all have a photo shoot together at the most giant pool complex I've ever seen. After we've posed on the real sand beach and in the various cabanas and Balinese beds, danced to the DJ set, floated on pool rafts, frolicked in the water misters and whizzed through the shark tank on a slide, we watch the sun go down over the mountains with a few cocktails. The section we're in is closed to the public while we do our shoot, so it's just us, plus all the hair and make-up people, the photographers, lighting technicians, set runners and a few journalists, of course. For the first time since the two bands have arrived in Vegas me and the boys have quite a laugh together, and even Sophie seems to have less of a stick up her arse than usual, so afterwards, once we've had time to dry off, get dressed and freshen up, we head out for dinner together, just the four of us.

We shake off the various managers and other people in our entourage and while there is one security guy stationed outside the restaurant, his presence is pretty pointless. It's true that the concerts sold out quickly, but sadly we are very much not the big deal we used to be. I can't see that anyone will be trying to get in and mob us.

Part of that is obviously because we are not the big stars we once were, we are older, in Liam's case, fatter, and in Sophie's case, uglier and more boring. But it's also because, whether we like to admit or not, and I more than anyone do *not*, Enola was always the biggest deal out of all of us. With her gone, we are somehow less than the sum of our remaining parts.

And now, more than fifteen years on, it feels weirdly awkward us being together without her. In the same way that we're doing that pointless thing of leaving a microphone out for her on the stage, though we barely mention her, we might as well have set a place for her at the table and added an empty chair.

Trixie booked Tapa Tapa for us as apparently it's the new place to be seen in the city. Fortunately, the venue is hip and buzzing, so somehow Enola's absence isn't quite as jarring as it might be in the kind of white tableclothed places that management sometimes want to send us to.

Here, we are sitting at a high table on leather cushioned chrome bar stools and ordering our own food and drinks from the bar, though Brilliant Records will be picking up the no doubt extortionate tab, as Liam was careful to ascertain. Feels refreshingly normal.

'To absent friends,' says Max, raising a glass. We raise our glasses too and murmur, 'To absent friends.' Christ. Is it going to be like this all night? I certainly don't want to be reminded of Enola – I doubt the others do either.

There is an awkward silence.

Max clears his throat. 'So,' he continues, 'as we've all been apart for a while, and haven't really had time for all four of us to have a proper chat yet, why don't we start by updating everyone on what we've been up to?'

Liam rolls his eyes and laughs. 'What is this? Some kind of corporate ice breaker?'

Max looks momentarily hurt and then composes himself. 'Fuck off, Liam,' he says, good-naturedly. 'You got a better idea?'

'I do, actually,' Liam says. 'Two truths and a lie. More interesting than just wanging on about ourselves. No one wants to listen to that. Or at least I certainly don't.'

I'm already quite drunk because those cocktails we had at the pool were delicious and very strong and, looking around the table, I don't think I am the only one. No one looks entirely sober, except Sophie who is now teetotal, of course. Is Liam meant to be drinking? I thought once you'd been through rehab you were meant to be on the wagon for good. Maybe there are different ways of doing it, I don't know.

'What are we, fifteen years old?' Max grumbles, but Liam has always loved games like this and ignores him. He and I used to spend hours playing 'Who Would You Rather?' on tour buses – he never seemed to tire of it.

'OK, I'll start,' I offer, thinking about what I can say that is going to paint me in the best possible light and remind them all that of those of us who are left, I am by far the most successful, at least musically. 'Number one, my first solo single, "Big You Up", was the biggest seller in the UK of 2009; number two, I won *Heat* magazine's "most fanciable female" for three years in a row; and number three, I have two million followers on TikTok.'

'I think it's the fanciable female one which is the lie,' Liam says. 'Enola won that all the time, didn't she?'

He gives me a smug look. He knows exactly what he's doing. He never had much time for any of us, but he's never really forgiven me for telling a journalist about him not being able to get it up a few times when

78

he was wankered. It's hard to believe we did that 'friends with benefits' thing for a while, looking at him now, but he was fit in his day. 'No,' I say, airily. 'She only won it twice.' Basically I only won once Enola was off the scene, but, whatever, I won each time for the next three years. I might have won even if she hadn't gone – who knows? 'The TikTok one is a lie,' I add. 'I'm not even *on* TikTok. Don't need to be when I have so many Insta followers.'

'Ah well,' Liam says. 'I lose that one then. So I guess that makes it my go. Number one, I've got a couple of rich female clients who tell their husbands I'm doing some menial job which takes five minutes and I spend the rest of the time shagging them senseless, *and* they also pay me and give me lunch; number two, I have five cats; and number three, once a year me and my ex-girlfriend from ten years ago meet and have no-strings-attached sex, just because we can.'

'You dirty dog,' Max says, 'I hope three is the lie. But I think it's two. You're not responsible enough to look after all those cats.'

Liam smirks. 'Yeah. You're right. I hate cats. But Tara's still fit as, and as long as her new husband doesn't find out, it's just a bit of fun. She decided she couldn't put up with all the drinking and gambling in the end, but when it comes to that,' he makes an unnecessarily obscene gesture with his hands because we all know exactly what he's talking about, 'we're perfectly matched. Honestly, the things she'll let me do . . .'

'Right, moving swiftly on before we all hear far more

detail than we want to,' Max interrupts, 'Sophie. Your turn.'

'Um . . .' she takes a large swig of her pointless non-alcoholic drink. I'm guessing she's so boring these days she can't think of anything interesting enough to say about herself for the truth bits. 'Number one, I now run a retreat for women in Ibiza. Number two, I have severe allergies to seafood and nuts. And number three, I can do the Rubik's cube.'

Yawn. Is that as interesting as she can get even when she's lying? 'Number two?' I guess. I don't remember her being allergic to seafood back in the day. We used to love going out for oysters at J Sheekey and bitching about Enola. We also made sure we looked our best when we went there as the paps knew we loved it too, along with plenty of other celebs, and there would almost always be at least one photographer there. Sophie has never been able to hold her drink, and I once convinced her she'd given one of the waiters a blowjob in the loos. Another time I told her she'd spilt a drink on Victoria Beckham and then told her how much she fancied David. As far as I know, she probably still believes both to this day. It's perhaps a good thing she's teetotal now.

She shakes her head. 'No. Number three is the lie. The seafood allergy is weirdly new and annoying as they do great prawns where I live. I spent ages trying to complete the Rubik's cube when we were on tour, but never mastered it.'

An anticlimactic quiet falls around the table until Max interrupts with, 'I guess it's just me left then.' He leaves a dramatic pause and then gives himself a little drum roll by tapping his hands rapidly on the table.

'Number one, I have a collection of classic cars at home but have never learnt to drive, because there was never any need when we were taken everywhere in limos; number two, I've got a cameo role in the next Bond film; and number three, I know what happened to Enola the night she disappeared.'

18

October 2008
London
Kimberley

I lie back in the bath, enjoying the scent and feel of Enola's Rituals bubble bath I've helped myself to. At home I wouldn't normally bother having a bath of an evening – a quick in and out of the shower is fine, but my daughter's bathtub is about the size of a small boat and has a huge porthole-style window next to it so I can look out over the Thames and the lights of night-time London twinkling. Honestly, that girl doesn't know she's born.

I've dimmed the lights and lit a couple of her Diptyque candles – she's got so many I'm sure she won't mind. And even if she does, well, what of it? I'm doing her a favour, here babysitting her cats while she's away for a few nights at whatever event it is this time. They're the most spoilt cats in the world and she doesn't like to leave them alone for too long. The size of the stupid 'catio' thing she has for them on one of the balconies! Their own little jungle gym with lounging platforms, all fully enclosed so that there's no chance of anything bad befalling them. Designed by some big-name architect, apparently. Nothing but the best for Apple and Bella.

It's not exactly a hardship, being here in Enola's penthouse, obviously, I don't mind doing it now and again at all. In fact, I'd do it more often if I was asked, but I think Enola feels like I'm somehow muscling in on her space when I'm here. Normally she has some fancy-schmancy cat sitter who looks after the little critters when she can't, but this time she wasn't available, apparently. It's not the first time I've done this and I'm sure it won't be the last. My place is quite a trek from here so when she wants me to do it, I stay over. I'm doing my daughter a favour and it's only fair that I make the most of it when I'm here.

I get out of the bath and put on a robe – it's so thick and soft it feels like a hug. Enola's name is embroidered on the breast in red stitching above a logo which I think belongs to some posh hotel – I forget which. Enola gets gifts like this all the time. She doesn't know how lucky she is.

Back in her living room I help myself to a bottle of champagne from the fridge, along with a chilled glass and some snacks which are made of seaweed or some such, and take them over to the glass coffee table in front of the enormous sofa. I flick the huge TV on – I mean really, who needs a TV that massive? – and start watching the latest episode of *The Apprentice*. Fucking hell. What a load of knobs.

I'm about halfway through the bottle when the buzzer rings. Enola didn't say she was expecting anyone, but maybe it's a delivery of another of the thousands of gifts she gets. I haul myself up, swaying a little. I'm already a bit drunk, I should probably eat a proper meal. Maybe get a takeaway. I know Enola has an account at a place round the corner – I'll charge it to that.

I answer the buzzer. 'Hello?'

'Kim? It's me. Can you let me up?'

My heart gives a little leap. It's Max! He's such a good boy. We've become quite good friends since he's been seeing Enola, and he'll often pop round to my house for a chat. He loves hearing stories about Enola, what she was like when she was little, and what she's been up to lately that he might not have heard about. I've no idea why he thinks I'd know – she hardly tells me anything – but he's always asking. Especially about other men. I tell him she's only got eyes for him, but, well, in spite of his good looks, money and fame, he seems pretty insecure. Bless him.

'Enola's not here, luvvie, it's just me. I'm babysitting the cats.'

He sniffs. 'Yeah, I know. It's you I wanted to talk to. I'm worried. I need to talk. It's urgent. Can you let me in? It's pouring with rain and I'm desperate for a pee.'

I look around the penthouse, I'm not sure why, it's not like Enola's here, is it? What is Max worried about? Is it something to do with Enola?

I'm sure she'd want me to let him come up. She wouldn't want me to leave him outside in the rain! And she knows Max pops in on me sometimes, and she doesn't mind at all. Says it's cute.

'OK. Come up,' I say, pushing the buzzer. I dash into the bathroom to give my hair a quick brush, find another champagne glass in the kitchen, and wait for the private lift door to open.

19

November 2008
Paris
Enola

We are travelling by private jet today. Before Breathe, obviously I'd never been in a private jet, and each time I get to go in one now, I feel like Chardonnay Lane-Pascoe in that old TV series *Footballers' Wives*. The seats are wide, beige and leather, and we are being served champagne in real glasses, with little canapés like you'd get at a party. Even though the plane is small, I'm relieved to see we have two pilots because really, what if something goes wrong? Luckily for this tour we have been travelling most of the time by bus, but now and again, for logistical reasons apparently, we go by jet.

I still don't like flying much. I'd never been on a plane before I joined Breathe. Even though it's always ultra luxurious – we either fly on private jets or in first class – I don't enjoy it. It doesn't seem natural, being so high up in the air in something so big and heavy. I was never very good at physics at school – how on earth do these things stay up? And it's claustrophobic, breathing the same air as everyone else. Made even more so by having all the rest of the band in such close proximity.

The relationship between me and the two other girls is becoming increasingly toxic. Even the press has noticed and snarky articles are appearing about how Sophie and Angel are forever out on the town without me. Not that I particularly *want* to go out with them, but, well, it would be nice to be invited once in a while. I don't get the impression they even like each other that much, or that they are close in any way, but rather that they like the attention they get from the photographers when they go out as a pair.

I've also started to suspect that at least one of them is selling stories to the papers about me. Nothing major, because it's not like I ever do anything I shouldn't, but little bits and pieces have been coming out that they've been privy to which most people haven't – me being late for rehearsals a couple of times, or me coming out of the loo with paper stuck to my shoe, that kind of thing. No more than a small paragraph in a showbiz column about something inconsequential usually, but it's annoying and, if I'm honest, also quite upsetting. I'm not sure which one is doing it and I don't have proof yet, but I am working on it.

But I haven't had a lot of time to think about that right now – I want to make the most of our tour. It's our first one outside of the UK, and apart from having to spend so much time with Angel and Sophie, I've been really enjoying it, even if it has been exhausting.

We've already done Holland, Germany and some Scandinavian countries, which was brilliant – I loved being in the snow and I even got to see the Northern Lights.

Max and Liam have just joined us as our support act for the next concerts – first Paris, and I'm told that after that, we will be back on the bus for most of the home stretch – Toulouse, Barcelona and then just one flight to London – so that's a relief.

Max is sitting next to me, holding my hand. We're in a 'good' phase at the moment, not too many rows. After his big outburst in my penthouse, things have settled down.

We talked literally all night that night, and of course, by the end, I'd agreed that we would give things another go. I don't know if he'd really go through with killing himself, but I can't take the risk. No way I could have that on my conscience. And since then, he has made a lot more of an effort with the jealousy stuff anyway. Perhaps it was just one of those things he somehow needed to get off his chest.

The tour, even though it's been full on, has given both groups a lift, because there's been quite a lot of extra publicity for both bands, not just Breathe, so Max is in a better mood. This Way Up have only just joined us for their guest appearances, and I think the time apart did Max and I some good.

I think I've managed to make him understand why

I don't want to live with him full time in a way he can accept and which doesn't make him feel too undermined and jealous. That I need some time for me. That we can enjoy our time together more if we don't have to think about domestic tasks and argue about whose turn it is to take the bins out.

And since Max arrived on the tour, it's been brilliant between us. During the first part of the tour, with Angel and Sophie having nothing to do with me, I actually felt pretty lonely.

I do love Max. I do. I am hoping that the tour will give us time to reconnect. To have all of the good bits and none of the bad bits which were happening before we left. All the day-to-day drudgery taken away. I hope it can help us remember how things were when we first got together.

Because they were really good then. I'm sure they were. It's sometimes hard to remember now. But there's barely been time to think about any of that at all so far. Though the schedule for the rest of the tour looks a little more relaxed, so I'm hopeful there'll be a little bit more downtime. That we might actually get the chance to go out and do something. We can spend some proper time together then, doing something nice. I hope.

I look at Angel, who is pretending to perform a lap dance for Liam. Rumour has it that they're shagging in an unofficial, non-relationship way. It's kind of an open secret, which, so far, Trixie has managed to keep out of the papers because it doesn't tally neatly with our wholesome image.

Liam is allowed his reputation as a bit of a tart obviously because he's a boy – just not with Emery's precious popstrels unless they are in a relationship, or at least potentially heading that way. And I happen to know that Liam and Sophie have spent at least one night together so I'm not sure what's going on there. Angel puts her arms on the seat either side of Liam, leans in and whispers something in his ear, he looks at her lasciviously and whispers something back. I glance at Sophie, who is looking daggers at them both from the other side of the plane.

None of my business. I don't care what's going on between them all. Although I have subtly made sure Emery knows about it. It's no secret that I'm his favourite, and it's very much in my interest to keep things that way. I like being lead singer, I wouldn't want him to take that away from me. And me and Max being in a relationship works well for him, for our brand.

All of these things make me appreciate Max more. I don't miss being single at all. I really don't.

Once we have arrived in our suite, I fill the huge clawfoot bath and tip in some of the Hermès bath oil from one of the pretty little deep-green bottles, pour two glasses of champagne, and slide in beside Max. I have left the curtains open and we can see the Eiffel Tower in the distance, all lit up. This is what it's all about, I say to myself. This is what it's all for. This is what makes the bad moments worth it.

'God that journey seemed long. Glad we're finally

here,' he says, downing his champagne and pouring another, topping up my glass too. 'Did you see the way Sophie was looking at Angel earlier on the plane? Wasn't happy about Liam having his face halfway into her tits at all.'

I laugh. 'Yeah. Not sure what's going on there. Has he been with both of them recently do you think? I know he and Sophie had a night a while back.'

He puts his arm around my shoulders. It's awkward sitting in that position in the curved bath and I'm already too hot – I should have run the water cooler – but I don't say anything or move away because Max is trying to be nice and I don't want to ruin the moment.

'Not sure,' he says. 'Don't care. We're lucky though, you and I. We've got each other. We don't need anyone else.'

20

November 2008
Paris

Online news report:

A petrol tanker has crashed into high-end shopping centre Galeries Monique in Paris, causing a large explosion. Surrounding streets have been cordoned off and the public is being warned to avoid the area.

The crash happened just after 11 a.m. when there were many staff and shoppers on site. Several people are believed to have been taken to hospital, though their condition is currently unknown.

Firefighters wearing breathing apparatus are in attendance and it is believed that further casualties continue to be evacuated from the site.

It is so far unclear what caused the crash, and terrorism has not yet been ruled out.

'It was absolute carnage in there,' said Skye Miller, a high school student from America currently on holiday in Paris. 'There was a loud bang and people started screaming and running for the exits. I didn't know what had happened until we got outside. I feel lucky to be alive. I only hope everyone else made it out.'

Another eyewitness claimed he had seen Breathe's Enola Mazzeri and This Way Up's Max Heaton browsing engagement rings in a jewellery shop shortly before the incident, but this report is, as yet, unconfirmed.

21

November 2008
London
Charlie

Oh my God. Oh my God. Oh my God.

What is going on? Was Enola really in the shopping centre? Who was driving the tanker?

Did someone arrange this? Someone who wants to hurt her? Someone who is jealous?

People can go to such lengths. Some people have no boundaries. None at all. Nothing they won't do.

I scroll through pages for news, clicking and re-freshing. Nothing. Nothing, except repetitions of the unconfirmed reports. Nothing concrete.

And no pictures of Enola there. That's a good thing, surely? If this guy who claims he saw Enola and Max in the jewellery shop really had done, wouldn't he have taken a picture?

Maybe he didn't have a camera? Either way, it's probably not true. He's just looking for attention. Or perhaps he thought the journalist might pay him for information or something like that. He probably made it up. She probably wasn't there at all. He probably said that because he knows Enola is in Paris, like everyone does. Yes. Yes. That will be it. He's probably a fan. Like me. Wants to grab her attention, even if it's in the stupidest way possible.

I log into Breathe Deeply, my favourite fan forum.

Enolasbestfriend: Anyone heard about the crash in Paris do we think Enola is really there?

Croissantsandchocolate: I've been to that shopping centre . . . it's a v nice one. Pricey. The kind of place you could imagine her going.

Enolasbestfriend: Might someone be targeting her? I'm worried.

Chorizo72: You're always such a drama llama. Why would anyone target Enola? Everyone loves her. Calm down. Chances are she's fine.

Redlight: Babe let's wait and see. Fingers crossed for her. That's all we can do for now

Enolasbestfriend: Anyone going to the Paris concert?

I wonder if it'll go ahead? Maybe if anyone's there they can find something out if they're on the ground? I'm so scared for her

Croissantsandchocolate: I am. I'll let you know if I hear anything but I can't go to the shopping centre – I'm not getting to Paris till later today.

I log off. No help at all. I'll check back in later and see if anyone's come up with anything.

I wonder about going and standing outside Enola's place, which is usually what I do when I'm worrying about her safety, but there's no point, I know she's not there.

I don't have any money to get to Paris – I'm totally broke after buying the concert ticket. And I wouldn't be able to get near Enola anyway with all that's going on.

All I can do is wait. But it really, really hurts.

22

November 2008
Paris
Enola

'Honestly, I'm fine,' I say. I'm in a private hospital which is so luxurious it's more like an upscale hotel, except for the familiar plugs above the bed for oxygen masks and whatever else they might need. I don't want to think about it too much. 'I don't know why they've brought me to hospital at all. This is all a lot of fuss about nothing.'

Max is by my bedside, holding my hand and periodically stroking my forehead. It's actually quite annoying and I kind of wish he'd leave me alone, but I know he means well so I don't say anything. And it is reassuring to have him here in a way – his French is no better than mine so he's no help there, but even though most of the staff speak to me in near-perfect English, when they are talking among themselves, I don't know what they are saying and it's surprisingly disconcerting.

'You passed out,' Emery says. Fucking hell. Why is he here? 'So they're worried in case you inhaled some smoke or hit your head or anything. They want to run a few more tests to check everything's ticketyboo.'

I roll my eyes. Ticketyboo! Emery must be properly concerned – he never uses words like that. But I'm under no illusion that he's worried about my health – it's the tour and his profits that he's bothered about.

'OK, whatever,' I agree. 'If it's really necessary. But I'd still like to get out of here as soon as possible.'

I pause, realizing that even though I might be physically OK, as I'm sure I am, something utterly horrific has happened today, and there will have been plenty of people other than me involved.

'Did everyone make it out of the shopping centre?' I ask.

'I'm afraid there were a few casualties, Mademoiselle Mazzeri,' says the doctor in near perfect English, though with a strong accent, 'but they are in the very best hands and, miraculously, as yet, no fatalities, we believe.'

I nod. 'That's good news. Do they know what caused the crash?'

'That will be a matter for the police,' he says. 'But I think they don't yet know. The driver is, I believe, not in the best condition, sadly, and not ready to hear questions. So we may need to wait.'

Tears come to my eyes for someone I don't know. I'm not sure why. Perhaps I have been more affected by what happened than I thought. 'I hope he'll be OK.'

The doctor pulls a face. 'You are very kind. But as far as I understand there is a possibility that . . . well it's not my place to say, but sometimes when these things happen, it is not always an accident.'

'You mean they think it might have been terrorism?' Emery interrupts. 'Christ. That's all we need.'

The doctor shrugs. 'Perhaps. Or it is even possible that . . . well, I shouldn't make guesses. We should wait until the investigation is done. But we have a policeman waiting outside the room – he wants to talk to you when I tell him that you are fit enough. So if you feel you are not too tired, can I tell him you are happy to talk to him?'

I feel a lurch of alarm. 'Me? Why does he want to talk to me?'

'I mentioned those letters you've been getting,' Emery says. 'The ones which have been a bit threatening. They interviewed me while they were checking you over.'

I frown. 'Everyone in the public eye gets those kind of letters don't they?' I pause, suddenly realizing what he and the doctor might be talking about. 'It doesn't mean the sender is going to take a truck and plough it into a shopping centre!'

Emery and the doctor look at each other before Emery continues: 'You're probably right, but as far as I understand, the police simply want to make sure they look at all possible angles.'

I suddenly feel breathless and panicky, like I might throw up. 'They don't really think this is about me, do they?' I squeak. 'I don't think I could live with myself if people were injured because some nutter took it upon themselves to do something like this because they've got some strange obsession with me!'

Max squeezes my hand tighter and I snatch it away. I don't want to be touched right now.

'I don't think it's a very likely scenario,' Emery says, 'and as far as I understand, neither do the police. Like I said, they just want to rule it out. But you don't need to talk to them yet if you don't want to. I can tell them you're not up to it.'

'Thank you. I would appreciate that. I don't think I can face it right now. In fact, I'd kind of like to be left alone to sleep for a while, if you don't mind.'

It takes some persuading to make Max leave, but as soon as I manage to get everyone out I burst into tears.

No one would do this on account of me, would they? And even if they wanted to, none of it makes any sense. They couldn't have known we were going to be there anyway, could they? Unless . . .

We'd had some rare time off the day of the crash and slept late in our beautiful suite. 'I've got a surprise for you,' Max said that morning. 'Put something nice on and let's go out.'

I'd mentally planned celebrating our day off in the lush hotel spa, maybe with a massage, but Max was almost leaping around with excitement so I couldn't quite bring myself to say 'no' to him.

I assumed he was planning a special lunch or a trip

up the Eiffel Tower or something, but instead he eventually revealed that he was taking me to a jewellers in some posh shopping centre not far from the hotel.

Oh God. He wasn't going to propose, was he? Things had been good between us since he'd joined us on the tour, but I wasn't ready for anything like that, and I also knew that, Max being Max, he wouldn't take a 'no' or even a 'maybe but not now' well. I decided to head it off, just in case.

'Are we choosing my birthday present?' I asked nonchalantly.

An expression I couldn't quite read crossed his face before he agreed, 'Yes! Anything you like. It's also almost our four and a bit year anniversary too, so I wanted to get you something special.'

'Four and a bit. Is that an anniversary?'

He took my hand and kissed it. 'Every day with you is worth celebrating, Enola,' he said.

I laughed. It was nice to remember that things between us were often good. When he was in this kind of mood, I absolutely, definitely loved him.

Even so, I knew I wasn't anywhere near ready to commit to marriage.

'That's so sweet Max!' I said. 'What did you want to get me?'

'Well, that's the thing,' he replied. 'Unfortunately I've got appalling taste in just about everything as you know, so I figured it was better you choose your birthday, anniversary, whatever-it-is present yourself. But come on, we need to go. I've booked an appointment before the shop opens to the public at midday so we can browse in private and not be bothered by the normals. Not that you'll get that many normals in the kind of shop I'm taking you to though, they couldn't afford it.'

I flung my arms around him and kissed him on the cheek, actually in relief more than anything, but thankfully he wouldn't have read it that way. 'You are absolutely the best boyfriend,' I said. 'Thank you.' Thank God. Jewellery. Just a present. Not a proposal. That would be the last thing I needed.

But after that . . . I don't remember. The doctors said it's normal after something traumatic, and the memories might come back in time, but it's weird and I don't like it.

Max told me that he made an appointment at the shop before we arrived, so they would have clearly been expecting us.

And if he'd done that, other people might have also known we'd be there. He might have told Trixie. Could there have been a photographer lurking? Or perhaps he told Liam. Or any number of other people. Sophie. Angel. Whoever. He might have said something in passing, in a 'what are your plans for tomorrow?' way. Or he might have wanted people at large, the public, the press, to assume that we were getting engaged, as I had, initially. Maybe he thought if it was all over the gossip columns it would be too hard for me to back out?

No. No. Push that thought away, Enola. Max might be jealous, but he is *not* that manipulative. He is not. Things are good between us at the moment. I'm just not ready to get married, that's all. One day, maybe, because I love him, and he is certainly devoted to me, I never doubt that. He would probably be a brilliant husband once he's got over his possessiveness, which surely he'd grow out of. One day, I could see us being together for ever. Just not now.

But back to what I was actually thinking about – if someone *had* wanted to hurt me that day, they might have known where to find me. Because Max had obviously planned the trip. Who might he have told?

For the first time, I wonder if I should be taking some of those letters I've been receiving a little bit more seriously.

23

November 2008

Press statement released by Brilliant Records:

Breathe and This Way Up band members Enola Mazzeri and Max Heaton were in the Galeries Monique shopping centre today when it was hit by a truck at 11.37 a.m.

Enola was taken to a nearby hospital as a precaution where she was checked over by doctors and later released.

She is currently resting at her hotel, and we ask that her privacy is respected.

Brilliant has decided to cancel tonight's concert as a mark of respect to those injured in the incident. Ticket holders will be contacted with details of how to claim a refund. The rest of the tour is expected to run as scheduled.

24

26 June 2024
Las Vegas
Angel

There is a stunned silence around the table as we all look at Max in horror.

He drains his glass and slams it down on the table. 'Oh come on guys! It was a joke! *Of course* I don't know what happened to Enola!'

The music in the restaurant suddenly sounds very loud as the table remains silent. Max gives us all a bewildered look and then sighs deeply.

'Seriously! I loved her with all my heart, you know that, and it took me many, many years, and a lot of therapy, but I managed to move on. I didn't do that by pretending she never existed though, like you fuckers seem to be doing. Enola liked a laugh, she'd have found that funny.'

He stands up from the table. 'But it seems I misjudged

my tone, I apologize. I'm going to absent myself long enough to get another round of drinks in and by then hopefully you can all have found a sense of humour and we can interact like normal human beings. Same again for everyone?'

He weaves a little as he storms off towards the bar and I see now that he is even more drunk than I realized.

'That was in extremely poor taste,' says Sophie quietly, so softly I can barely hear her.

She seems to wipe away a tear. God. She needs to get a grip. Enola's been gone for a very long time. Nearly two decades. Get over it.

'Right, on that cheery note, I'm off for a wazz,' says Liam, getting up from the table and stalking off, leaving me and Sophie alone. She looks like she is trying to hold back tears and I can't think of anything I want to say to her so I get my phone out, have a quick scroll and take some selfies. I'll post them later. Sophie appears to be simply staring into space.

I put my phone down as Max approaches with another tray of drinks, when suddenly a woman walks straight into him, sending everything he's carrying flying everywhere with a noisy crash as the glasses hit the tiled floor and shatter.

'Whoa! Watch where you're going!' Max cries as a couple of staff rush over with napkins and dustpans and start sweeping and dabbing. 'What's the hurry?'

'Sorry, sorry,' the woman mumbles, offering a hand and helping him up. 'Let me get you some more drinks.'

He gives her an unnecessary look of disgust. 'No, that's all right love, don't bother yourself.'

She shakes her head. 'I insist. Tell me what you ordered.'

'Erm . . .' Max is wasted and has clearly forgotten already, so I answer for him.

'Gin and tonic for me, elderflower cordial for her,' I say with a disdainful glance towards Sophie, 'a pint of lager for Liam and, given the state of Max, I think a Coke.'

Max shakes his head. 'No. No. A whisky. Single malt. None of that blended shite. Thank you.'

She turns on her heel and scuttles away. Poor woman, it was totally Max's fault he dropped the drinks because he's pissed and wasn't looking where he was going.

Max sits down at the table, seemingly struggling to focus, and Liam comes back from the loo, drying his hands on his trousers.

'Right, what were we talking about?' Liam says. 'Oh yeah. Enola. As usual. That was it.'

'Can't we talk about something else?' Sophie bleats. 'I've done everything I can to leave that part of my life behind, and it's a time I find it extremely distressing to think about,' she continues. 'Sometimes I feel I will never entirely be free of the past. I only hope that wherever she is now, Enola's at peace.'

Max taps his hand on the table and nods his head sarcastically. 'Right. So that's your line is it? Well with respect, Sophie, that's utter bollocks. It's not fear for the good of Enola's soul you're feeling there, is it? Or even sadness at her passing? It's guilt. Guilt for how you made her miserable, before she disappeared. You and Angel. Now that she's gone, you can never atone for that, and I can see why that would be a difficult thing to deal with. *Emotionally.*'

Sophie stands up abruptly from the table. Tears are glistening in her eyes. 'You're drunk, Max. I'm not listening to any more of this. You know as well as I do that if anyone was making her life a misery, it was you. Your jealousy, what they'd call coercive control these days, probably forced her to go into hiding. Or worse. Just because it wasn't really talked about back then doesn't mean that you weren't guilty of it.'

Max chuckles and shakes his head. 'Don't be ridiculous, Sophie. You've got it all wrong. Sure, I was jealous sometimes, but Enola and I, we loved each other. We were going to get married, thinking of having a baby together even. You and Angel were nasty to her, sure, and I'm not surprised you feel guilty about that, as rightly you should. But there's no way she'd have taken off, leaving not just me but those cats she adored, because of someone like you. Not when we had so much great stuff going on between us. She had so much to look forward to.'

He pauses and his expression turns sombre. 'She didn't run off anywhere,' he continues, 'there's no way she would have done that. We were in a really good place at the time, *she* was in a really good place. When she was taken, and, although I hate to say it, being realistic, probably killed, things were better than they'd ever been for us. If that hadn't happened . . .'

'*Taken?*' Sophie screeches, so loud that half the bar turns to look at us even though the music is pretty loud.

The woman who Max barged into reappears with a tray of drinks, places them down on the table and mumbles, 'Sorry again', before scuttling off.

I wonder if anyone here recognizes us, if this conversation will end up in the papers tomorrow. Or online, as is more the case now. I cast a glance around to see if anyone is obviously taking pictures of us or, even worse, filming, but as far as I can see everyone has gone back to their own conversations. This is a hip, high-end hang-out and they will be used to much bigger and more current celebrities here than us; apparently Taylor Swift was in a few days ago. Hopefully the music is loud enough to cover most of the content of the conversation, even if it wasn't quite enough to hide Sophie's sudden outburst.

We're not the big names we used to be by any means, but stories about us (or more particularly, Enola) still crop up in the press from time to time when some crazy comes up with a new theory about her disappearance or claims to have spotted her on a beach in Thailand or whatever.

'Of course she wasn't *taken*,' Sophie hisses, thankfully at a more moderate volume. 'Stop being so ridiculously melodramatic, Max. This is real life. Not Netflix.

'Enola left of her own accord,' she continues. 'We probably all played a part in our own way, I would argue you more than anyone else, Max, but . . . at the end of the day it would have been her decision. I try to hold onto the hope . . . however unlikely it might

110

seem given the amount of time that has passed, that she has been in hiding somewhere. Her passport was never found, remember? I hope she's taken on a new identity and she's living her best life somewhere far away, somewhere far from you, and far away from all the toxic nonsense which goes with the so-called "lifestyle" of the music industry.'

She swipes at her eyes and sniffs. 'That's why I moved to Ibiza and set up my retreat. To escape all this. I wanted no part of it any more. In fact I'm starting to wish I'd never agreed to these stupid legacy concerts.'

'Oh for God's sake,' Liam interjects. 'Listen to you all. We all know that Enola living a secret life on a remote island or whatever is an extremely unlikely scenario, and we all know what the most likely thing is. Enola had had enough and decided to check herself out once and for all. It's the only thing that makes sense. God rest her soul and all that, but Christ, let's all get over it and move on.'

25

November 2008
London
Charlie

Enola's alive! Oh my God I am so relieved.

My jubilation at learning that she is alive from the statement put out by the band quickly turns to horror as I continue browsing the internet and find a fuzzy picture of Enola and Max which has been posted on a French showbiz site. I can't understand the text but more searching finds an English version which appears to have nicked the photo and says that they were snapped browsing in Bee Jus – a high-end jewellery shop. I feel a lurch of alarm. They're not getting *married*, are they? Enola absolutely can't marry Max. He's quite clearly toxic. She wouldn't get it so wrong, would she?

If I was her best friend, this wouldn't be happening. We would talk it through and I could help her see sense. Look after her. It's so frustrating. If only I could get close to her, she could get to know me, I'm sure she would realize this.

I zoom in to the photo as far as I can, though the quality isn't very good. It was clearly taken at some distance. It might even have been taken on a phone.

Enola and Max are both looking down at something – a tray of rings? I can't see clearly. I feel another wave of nausea. She can't marry him. She mustn't. She is pointing at something towards the top left of the tray and he is resting his hand lightly on her waist as she looks. I wonder what they are saying. I wonder if she's saying 'I like that one best' or 'Oh my God look at how hideous that one is?'

It's difficult to tell, but I think they are both smiling. I can just about make out Max's hideous goatee beard he's been sporting lately.

And Enola . . .

I actually leap up from my chair and move my face as close as I can to the screen.

Something isn't right here. Something is very, very wrong.

26

November 2008
Paris
Enola

I am discharged from hospital later that day and allowed to go back to the hotel thankfully. They have cancelled tonight's concert, not because they are worried about my health, but as 'a mark of respect' to the injured and to the poor truck driver, who sadly died a few hours after I asked the doctor about him.

It was apparently the venue rather than Emery who made the decision to cancel the event, not that that is what Trixie put out in her press statement, and he is fuming. Personally, I don't care either way about whether it goes ahead or not. A man died – our concert is entirely unimportant in the scheme of things.

Investigations are still ongoing, but from what I am told, it looks more and more like what happened was simply a tragic accident. It's still awful, of course, but it's also a huge relief. I simply couldn't cope with something like this being on my conscience. Being my fault.

The driver was a French guy in his late 50s, no criminal record or signs of radicalization. Overweight, a smoker. It hasn't been released to the press yet, but we've been told unofficially that they think he had a heart attack. He leaves a wife and two grown-up sons. The police will apparently be looking into his finances in case it's possible he was bribed, but now that I'm out of hospital and able to think a little more clearly, I can't imagine this was anything to do with me, with Max, with the publicity team, or indeed anyone else we're involved with. It's too big a thing, surely? It was just me over-thinking and the people around me putting the ridiculous idea in my head.

I've a vague idea that there was some crazed stalker in the past who shot a US president to try to impress some actress or other, but . . . even taking into account those horrible letters I've been receiving, I'm sure that what happened with the truck was nothing like that – no more than a tragic accident that Max and I happened to get caught up in. Things like this happen all around the world, every day. People find themselves in the middle of something unexpected and this time, it happened to be me and Max. That's all.

I'm almost embarrassed that I thought even momentarily that this was about me, that I put myself at the centre of it, like I am the only person that matters.

I am trying to lie and relax on the sofa in the hotel

suite, but Max is fussing around me and fretting to a ridiculous degree and it's getting on my nerves.

'The thought that I could have lost you . . .' he whines, yet again. 'I couldn't bear it.'

'You were never going to lose me,' I remind him. 'From what the medics said, I might have passed out briefly. It was probably a panic-related thing. As far as I understand, the truck was nowhere near me. I don't really remember anything about it, but I'm quite certain there was no need for them all to make such a fuss. I'm sure I didn't even need to go to hospital. I'm more worried about the family of that poor man. Do you think we should do something for them? Go and visit at least?'

He shrugs. 'Why? It wasn't our fault. It's sad for them, but . . . there's nothing we can do for him. It might even be seen as inappropriate. We can ask Trixie.'

I smile weakly. Everything is always about whether or not what we do is good for our image and by extension, for sales. That always comes before everything else, and it's not OK. I'm sick of it.

'OK,' I agree, because I'm too tired for a row. 'We'll ask Trixie. But I'm also going to ask her to try to find out who the injured in hospital are. We could take signed photos and presents. That kind of thing.'

Max has turned on the TV and is flicking through the channels, quite clearly not listening to me any more. I much prefer that to him fussing though.

'If you like,' he says, distractedly. 'For now, though, you should rest.'

27

It's not her. I'm sure it's not. It's not Enola in the picture in the jewellery shop.

I grab some magazines and flick through to compare what I'm looking at to recent images of her and Max. This latest one in Paris . . . it's all wrong. Even though the two of them are bending over the jewellery rather than standing up straight, and Max is closer to the camera than she is, their heights look all out of whack. In real life, they are about the same height. Enola is tall and willowy, model-like, and Max a short arse. This woman is definitely smaller than him.

Her face is partly obscured by a hat, but the line of her jaw looks different. Enola has a kind of strong, determined jaw, this one is weaker. They've probably put whoever this woman is in a hat to try to make it less obvious it's not her, to obscure her face, but Enola almost never wears hats! I grab my scrapbook where I keep pictures of her in all the outfits I like the best and flick through, and no, not a single one. Not a single hat.

Brilliant Records put out that statement saying she was OK, but it was just a statement – that doesn't mean it was true! If Enola had been injured or even – tears spring to my eyes at the thought of it – killed, they would want to cover it up. For all I know, this photo could even have been staged *after* the crash.

I look at the picture again, leaning in closer. It's frustratingly blurry. The woman, the stand-in, has obviously been chosen and dressed carefully, the way she holds herself is similar to Enola, standing with one knee bent, granted. The decoy, whoever she is, has probably studied Enola. Been coached in her poise and mannerisms even. Practised behaving in a way Enola would behave. Moving like her.

But why would they do this? I wonder what I should do. I lean back in my chair and exhale loudly. Should I tell someone? Tell the police, even? Let them know that someone is impersonating Enola?

Or perhaps Enola is in on the deception? She might have her reasons. I wouldn't want to get her in trouble.

I go on to Breathe Deeply and post a message, but I decide I need to be careful. I don't want to let anyone know about my suspicions, at least not yet.

Enolasbestfriend: OMG I'm so relieved Enolas OK. I wish she'd spoken on camera rather than the band just putting out a statement though, so we could see for ourselves.

I stay in my seat for several hours as replies to my message drop, but no one seems to think there's anything odd about the picture. Or at least, if they do, they don't say anything.

Croissantsandchocolate: I'm sure she's fine. I hope they were choosing a ring! Love a wedding. Enola would be a beautiful bride.

Enolasbestfriend: I dont think she knows Max well enough.

Chorizo72: Unlike you, of course, who has probably never met either of them in your life . . .

Redlight: Let's not jump to conclusions. It's her birthday soon – they might just have been shopping for a present.

Enolasbestfriend: So no one thinks there's something a bit off? That there's something we're not being told?

Chorizo72: Like what? You're just jealous.

I know from experience it's better to keep some things vague in these forums to avoid a pile-on. But I am sure that something is up.

I won't tell the police. They won't believe me, especially given what happened last time, when I got all upset before and ended up with the restraining order. And it could be unsafe, if I have found out more than I should.

I don't mind about my safety, but I need to know for Enola. For now, I will investigate by myself. Find out what they are doing and why.

I feel tears form and start to flow. Where was Enola when this picture of this stand-in, whoever she is, was taken?

Could it be her twin? But why?

Oh God. I hope Enola is OK.

28

27 June 2024
Las Vegas
Angel

Urgh. That was the worst night I've spent in a long time.

I got back from the somewhat fraught dinner with the others late and wasted – drinking a lot seemed to be the only way to get through it for most of us once Max had felt the need to bring up Enola again rather than letting us enjoy the perfectly pleasant evening we'd been having up until then. I barely remember falling into bed. Then an hour later, I woke up knowing I was going to vom and have been basically chucking up about every hour since then.

I can hold my drink – this was nothing to do with that. That bloody restaurant. I'm sure the seafood wasn't quite as 'fresh out the water today' as the signage claimed, in fact, a quick Google shows that the nearest coast is about five hours away. Fuck's sake. If only I'd bothered to listen in geography lessons at school.

I'm finally starting to feel better, thank God, but there's no way I can make rehearsal today. My throat feels like it's been grated, my stomach punched by a giant, and I've barely had a wink of sleep. I send a message via the tour WhatsApp group.

Sorry guys, I can't make rehearsal today. I'm sick. Think it must have been something I ate.

Immediately Liam pings back:

You too? I've never felt so awful. Those mussels must have been dodgy.

Followed by Max:

Dirty bastards. I'm sick too and I didn't even eat mussels. Sophie?

But there is no reply. Perhaps she's still asleep. And she definitely didn't eat the mussels – she was on about her seafood allergy, wasn't she?

Sounds like you lazy fuckers had too much to drink. Emery cuts in, sympathetic as ever. Stay in bed if you must but anyone who isn't at rehearsal tomorrow 10 a.m. sharp will have me to answer to. You have been warned.

I'll put out a press release.

Trixie adds, God knows why. We ate some dodgy shellfish, who cares?

I go back to sleep for an hour or two and then wake up feeling like I could finally actually eat something, so I phone down to order some breakfast to my room. Around twenty minutes later there is a soft knock at the door, someone calls 'room service' and brings in a trolley of white and brown toast, with little pats of both salted and unsalted butter, three different pots of jam, a bowl of honey with one of those weird wooden things which looks like some kind of miniature sex aid, and a huge glass pot of fresh mint tea – I can see the leaves floating around in the water waiting to be plunged.

'If you could leave the trolley here by my bedside that would be great,' I say. The woman nods and brings it over. I know I should tip, but I can't be bothered to get out of bed to find my cash, if I even have any, and after all, these people are paid, aren't they? She slopes out, closing the door behind her a little more loudly than was strictly necessary, quite possibly due to the lack of tip.

I ease myself up in the huge round bed to rest on the enormous plump pillows and look around the suite. If I'm going to be ill, there are certainly worse places to spend it, and on the plus side, at least I will actually get to have some time enjoying the facilities of the hotel, a rarity when I have a concert coming up.

This suite is incredible – I'm used to luxury, but even

so, I'm sure it's the biggest I've ever been in. The ceilings are double height and the walls are glass – I'm on the fiftieth floor, and when I look out I can see almost the entire length of the Strip. Some people hate the Strip and think it's the ultimate in tackiness, but I love it – plus I can go to about a million different fabulous shops and restaurants without even going out in the open air. What's not to like? Give me some neon lights over olde-world charm any day.

While I eat the toast I flick on one of the suite's five TVs – this one is almost the size of a cinema screen. There's a news report about our arrival in town which gives me a little thrill until I notice that it's on the hotel's internal channel. Never mind. I carry on flicking through what seems like hundreds of channels until I find another programme with a report about us.

'Breathe and This Way Up have arrived in Las Vegas to rehearse at The Cube for its inaugural concert,' says a besuited reporter with slicked-down hair, 'but so far things have been marred by a series of unfortunate incidents. At Breathe's first rehearsal at the venue, a large gantry fell and narrowly missed lead singer Angel, while today, the band are apparently laid up with food poisoning. Tazu Tazu, the celebrity hang-out where the band ate last night, are strenuously denying the accusation.

'A spokesperson for the restaurant said: "Our hygiene and supplier standards are second to none, and we have had no reports of other diners similarly afflicted. We are, of course, extremely sorry to hear that the band mem-

124

bers of Breathe and This Way Up are unwell, and wish them all a speedy recovery."'

I tut. So typical of the restaurant to be covering its arse like that. I guess Trixie must have got straight on to sorting out the press release she mentioned. You have to admire her I suppose, managing to get coverage for us out of something as mundane and frankly as unpleasant as food poisoning. Though all publicity is good publicity, isn't that what they say? Maybe less so for the restaurant in this instance though.

'Tonight we are asking, are the two bands cursed?' the reporter continues. 'And if so, what can be done to lift it?'

I sigh and switch the TV off. A curse! Ridiculous. What century are we living in?

Apart from the gantry thing, the rehearsal went OK – I'm excited for the concerts. It's a long time since I've played in a venue anything even approaching the size of the one here.

I am feeling much better now that I've managed to eat, but I haven't showered since before we went out last night and I smell rank. Now that I can stand up without wanting to pass out, I think a shower will make me feel human again.

The bathroom here is on the same gigantic scale as the rest of the suite, with a huge round bath/Jacuzzi, easily big enough for four, and the same enormous glass walls as the rest of the duplex suite, which turn opaque at the touch of a button. The shower is also big enough for at least two people, and fat ones at that, with twin rain heads and various other nozzles that spray in all sorts of directions.

I strip off and throw the pyjamas I'd put on to be decent for room service on the floor. I know it's bratty, but when I'm away now I like to make full use of the typically excellent housekeeping services they offer in these places.

Just like everything else in this room, the shower gel, shampoo and conditioner dispensers are enormous, refilled with the in-house spa's own-brand products in accordance with the 'no individual use plastic' ethos of the hotel, as a cheery sign by the double sink unit tells me.

I eventually manage to locate the right handle to get the water to come out of the overhead nozzle after being squirted with freezing cold water from all the side-angled ones (really, why are hotel room showers always so overly complicated?) and once I manage to get it to the right temperature, the powerful jets are a welcome joy.

I squeeze some shower gel into my hand and almost instantly feel like it's been set on fire. I scream, scrubbing frantically at my hand, but the running water seems to make it worse and now that I've touched it with my other hand, both feel like they are being blow-torched. I stumble out of the shower, my skin already blistering and reddening, more patches appearing on my legs where I must have flicked the gel trying to get it off me, and now I feel a burning patch on my face too, shit! I try to bat it off, but nothing seems to help.

I stumble to the bathroom phone by the loo and stab at 0. It rings and rings and I slide down to sit on the heated floor, my head is spinning and I feel like I might pass out.

'This is reception, Miss Williams, how can I best serve your needs today?'

'Something's burning me,' I manage to force out. 'I need a doctor. Urgently.'

29

November 2008
Toulouse
Enola

I much prefer it when we travel by bus than by plane. Our bus isn't like an ordinary bus in the same way that the private planes we use aren't anything like normal planes. It has these massive comfy seats and the outside is all painted with our logo, colours and even our faces. People spot it and send pictures in to the papers and post pictures on social media – the fans seem to love that. We travel separately from our stage, set and entourage for security, and also because we would pretty much block the road – there are ninety-four trucks in total. Ninety-four! Just for us. Utter madness.

We have to have a police escort with the bus now because there were incidents with people driving dangerously around us, following us, going too fast et cetera. It was Emery's idea, travelling around on most of our tour by bus rather than plane to show how eco-friendly and caring we are. Obviously Emery doesn't give a shit about that kind of thing, but it goes down well with the fans and gets us in the papers more often because everybody loves to see the bus out and about.

The boys and Sophie are playing cards. Angel is having a lie-down on one of the upstairs sleeping pods – it's all kitted out for us, but it's still a bus obviously. We don't all have our own rooms or anything like that, and we're never on it overnight, but it's nice to be able to have a proper nap on the road when we want to. We have had so little time to ourselves on this tour. Sometimes I go and hide in a pod when I simply want to be away from everyone else, and pretend I'm sleeping when really I'm just taking some time out. Sometimes I read, but often I don't. There is always so much happening, both around me and inside my head, that it's nice to literally do nothing at all for a while. Everyone needs time out, and I for one certainly don't get enough of it.

I am staring out of the window, still thinking about the poor man who crashed his lorry. I don't remember much about the actual day it happened at all. I remember being in the hotel suite with Max, him suggesting we go shopping, and then the next thing I remember is being in that hospital room.

I haven't told anyone except the doctors in case they think I'm going mad or that I'm not up to performing or anything else like that. I don't want to make a fuss. Apparently, it's not that unusual to lose a bit of memory in the wake of something traumatic, according to what they said in the hospital. I imagine it will come back in time.

Eventually we turn off the motorway onto roads that become smaller and smaller and windier and windier before we drive through some enormous gates and up a long, straight drive towards something that looks like Sleeping Beauty's castle.

'After what happened in Paris, we figured there might be more press around than usual,' Trixie says. 'And given there seems to still be some, erm, speculation about exactly what happened in the more pointless sectors of the internet, we thought it might be better that you guys lie low between performances for now as the fans and the paps are likely to be hassling you even more than normal. Staying here you won't have flashguns going off in your face the whole time because this place has grounds, as you can see, so you can also get some time out in the fresh air without being bothered for a change if you'd like to. And most importantly, we can try to control what coverage is out there a little more.'

'What kind of speculation?' I ask. I hate this kind of thing.

'Silly stuff,' Trixie says. 'Things like that you were actually badly hurt in the incident and we're covering it up so as not to ruin the tour. Absolute nonsense.'

I frown. 'In that case wouldn't it be better if the paps *did* see me? To see that I'm OK?'

'We talked about that, but there's a possibility it might make things worse, fan the flames. Everyone will see you onstage tomorrow, and by then all this will probably be forgotten. We don't want to pander to them, that way, madness lies. It'll be fine, honestly. Nothing to worry about, just a couple of online nutters with nothing better to do. Most important is that you can get some rest without having microphones and tape recorders thrust in your faces the whole time. It's always better if we can control the narrative and what pictures and interviews come out and when.'

30

Letter delivered to Brilliant Records:

I am thinking about you Enola and praying that you are OK wherever you are. I know what they are doing. But I am here for you. Never forget that. Love you love you love you.

31

November 2008
Toulouse
Enola

The hotel in Paris was nice in a kind of bog standard five-star way – it had the luxe spa, the marble floors, gilt fittings, fluffy robes, logoed slippers and handmade chocolates on the pillow at turndown – things that before Breathe was formed would have been out of my league and I'd have been bowled away by, but in all honesty, have become a little blasé about these days. I make a mental note to myself not to become entitled about these things, I don't want to end up a spoilt bitch like Angel or Sophie.

This chateau, however, is like nothing I've ever been in before. The enormous wooden double doors are opened by a uniformed butler into a huge hallway with a central staircase that sweeps upwards and outwards to galleries on the first and second floors. I look up to the ceiling high above, where a vast chandelier twinkles.

We are shown to our rooms by women wearing black and white French maid uniforms who speak immaculate English with almost comically sexy French accents. Liam is already in full charm mode, but hopefully this is too classy a place for them to be allowed to offer any extras like that. Sometimes he can be a real sleaze. And I should know.

Mine and Max's suite on the first floor has a four-poster bed (of course) with heavy brocade drapes all around it. Once the French maid lady has finished demonstrating how the various light switches work (everything looks old, but it turns out the tech at least is all thoroughly modern) and how to summon someone if we want anything, I leave Max to tip her while I open the doors that lead out onto an elevated vast stone terrace. I step out to get some air – the journey was several hours, but it feels more like we've been on the bus for days.

There are low stone balustrades all around the edge and I sit down on the knee-high wall – it's one storey up, a kind of roof terrace on top of a room below, I guess. I stare out across the grounds at the setting sun. Suddenly I feel a shove on my shoulders, a huge surge of sickening adrenaline as I pitch forward and am yanked back.

'Saved your life,' Max says, chuckling and letting go of me. But I am not in the mood.

'Don't do that!' I snap. 'I was scared.'

He rolls his eyes, sits down on the balustrade and lights a cigarette. 'Oh, please. You know I'd never hurt you. Don't be so silly.'

'Did it not occur to you that I might be feeling jumpy after what happened in Paris?' I spit.

I know I am being tetchy and unreasonable, but I don't care. I've felt on edge and tearful all day and the last thing I need is Max winding me up.

The doctors in the hospital warned that I might find myself feeling jittery after what happened, and I almost wish I'd accepted their prescription of something to calm me down if I needed it. But I hate taking drugs of any sort – I don't even take painkillers for a headache if I can possibly help it, so my natural instinct was to say 'no'. Perhaps I should have thought about it more carefully.

Not for the first time I wish I'd made an excuse for wanting my own suite on this tour. I adore Max, but sometimes he can be exhausting. I'd love nothing more right now than to have a nice hot bath in the claw-foot tub I spotted in the bathroom and sink into the no doubt cloud-like pillows, burrow into the thick duvet and close the heavy drapes around me. Alone. Not having to talk to anyone or even think about being touched or having sex. But there is no chance of that tonight.

Max gets up and moves to the other side of the terrace under the darkening sky. 'Always about you, isn't it, Enola?' he sneers. 'I was there too, at the shopping centre, remember? It was me that made sure you got out OK when everyone was panicking after hearing the big bang. Including you, I might add. But no one's bothered about *me* are they? As long as you're OK, precious Enola, that's all that matters.'

Oh God. I can't deal with this. Not now. I'm too tired. I'm already feeling fragile. I need to shut this down before it escalates. I get up and move towards him. 'I'm sorry. I was overreacting. Of course it was upsetting for you too. And I'm very grateful that you helped me get out. You're my hero.' I go to touch his arm but he yanks it away.

'I'm not upset about the shopping centre, Enola, for fuck's sake,' he says, seemingly directly contradicting what he just said. 'Everyone seems to be making a big deal of it, but really, if you think about it, not much happened. Some poor guy had a heart attack in the cab of his giant truck and lost control. It blew up. He died, but chances are, by the sound of it, he'd have died anyway in the not too distant future, given the state of his health. A building got damaged, it will be fixed, it's no doubt insured. A few people went to hospital and then went home. You and I happened to be nearby, you had a shock, passed out for a few seconds, Trixie got a few headlines out of it, but no real harm done. *Blah blah blah.* What I'm *upset* about, Enola, is that you no longer seem to give a shit about me.'

Not this again. 'Max! That isn't true. Why would you say something like that?'

He sighs, looks up at the sky and stubs his cigarette out. 'Do you honestly not remember what happened that day? The day in the shopping centre? I thought you

136

were just saying that because you don't want to talk about it.'

'Well, I remember being in a jewellery shop and . . .' I don't remember that. I've been told that that's where we were when it happened. I saw a blurry picture of us, which, to be honest, looked like it was probably me but in reality could have been almost anyone. But I don't want anyone to know quite how little I remember. That the whole thing is a blank. The doctors might say it's normal, but it makes me feel like I'm going mad.

'You don't remember what happened before the truck hit?' Max presses.

'Um, we were looking at jewellery. I think you wanted to buy me something for my birthday? Or our anniversary?' I vaguely remember talking about this in the hotel suite. My birthday is soon. The jewellery shop is a famous one. Max would see shopping together for a bauble in Paris as a romantic thing to do.

He nods and lights another cigarette. 'Almost. But not quite. We were looking at jewellery. You chose a ring. I asked you to marry me. And you said "yes."'

32

November 2008
London
Charlie

The next stop on the bands' tour is Toulouse – they will be arriving right around now, I imagine. I don't sleep, waiting for the first photos of Enola to pop up online or the earliest snippets of gossip on the forums. The true fans often manage to find things out before the papers do. But so far I've seen nothing since Paris.

The bands are travelling mainly by bus this time and I am worried about that – I have looked at the statistics in detail and they would be much safer travelling by plane. Pilots have to be properly trained, vetted and qualified, but you can have any old lunatic on the road – I mean, look at what happened with the truck! Though I'm still not convinced that that was simply a random accident like they are now saying. I mean, really, what are the chances? It's not as if things like that happen very often, and with two famous people in the building? I don't think so.

I am working on several theories right now.

One, the publicity people for the two bands arranged the 'accident'. Breathe are doing brilliantly of course thanks to Enola, but This Way Up, not so much. Since the thing at the shopping centre happened, there's been way more in the papers about both bands, especially because it has put Max back into the limelight with speculation about what he was doing in a jewellery shop with Enola, who is quite clearly the bigger star. The papers love a celebrity engagement, so there's a lot of commentary in the showbiz columns about whether that was what was happening when they were apparently caught on camera.

Enola hasn't been seen in public again since, but Max has given an interview to some French music site, telling the world that she's OK and how well he's looking after her. Making himself out to be the brilliant boyfriend which I know he isn't. Loving all the attention, I'm sure.

Maybe Enola didn't want to go along with the charade that she and Max were a happy couple out jewellery shopping. Maybe her management sent someone else out with Max that day as a stand-in while it all happened because she refused. Were they going to pretend she'd been killed? And then something went wrong?

Perhaps she didn't even know anything was going to happen – maybe the publicity people set it all up and felt that her actually being there in person was too risky. That she might not agree to it. Or even that it was a risk to her safety. I peer in again at the picture. The more I look, the more convinced I am that it's not Enola, and while I'm almost sure that's Max in the shop, I guess there's still a small possibility that it's not. Perhaps they are both body doubles. The photo isn't very clear.

Where was Enola while this was happening? Hopefully in the spa, having a nice massage, oblivious. Or back in the hotel room. Is she complicit? Did she know this was going on? Or . . . oh God . . . have they done something to her? Got her out of the way? Maybe something had already happened to her before this! Perhaps she's already dead! And this picture is simply the first stage of whatever narrative they're planning to present. That she and Max are a happily engaged couple, while all the while . . .

I squeeze my eyes tightly shut and rub my forehead. All the while what? This is all so confusing.

Option two is that this scenario was set up by Max, the truck driver, the explosion, and everything. I read somewhere that Max's dad was in prison years ago, he's probably got some dodgy contacts who could arrange this kind of thing. Maybe Max arranged it so that he could play the hero, rescue Enola, prove to her that she needs him.

But I don't know. It seems like quite an elaborate gesture, the kind of thing that happens in films and not in real life. But, given how special and utterly unique Enola is, and what a lowlife Max is, maybe he felt like this was the only way. She is completely out of his league of course, and he probably knows that. But that doesn't fit with it not being her in the picture I'm looking at. There would be no point him doing all that if she wasn't even going to be there. So if that's the case, then I'd need to accept that I'm mistaken about that. Which I'm not sure I'm willing to, because I don't think I am.

Option three is that the truck going into the building simply didn't happen at all, or at least not in the way that it's been presented. After all, has anyone heard from the 'truck driver'? Has he even been named? No he has not. Or at least not that I know of, but even if he has, how would we know if he is actually a real person?

Of course there have been pictures of the 'accident' in the media and even some videos on the news, but they could have been staged, plus hoardings went up around the shopping centre pretty quickly and now they are saying that the driver is dead. Isn't it strange that a truck went into a busy shopping centre and no one was killed, except the driver?

Somewhat convenient! This could be a huge publicity stunt – I wouldn't put it past them.

However, if something really had happened to Enola, puppet master Emery wouldn't countenance losing his golden goose. He will know that without Enola, none of this works. Without Enola, Breathe is nothing.

I have a lot of work to do. Most importantly, I need to get close to Enola.

I go back to Breathe Deeply and have a scan through the new messages. No one has said anything significant but there must be other people who noticed that it wasn't Enola in the picture? Surely? I want to know if I've got any allies out there, anyone who can help me find the truth. But I also need to be careful not to put her in danger – if her management finds out that I know the truth then who knows what they might do? To her – or even to me? I've always suspected that there are moles in the forums, keeping an eye on what's been said, as well as the genuine fans and people who are simply complete bitches like chorizo72.

So I keep my post vague.

Enolasbestfriend: Did no one think the picture was a bit weird?

The replies come in quickly.

Angelfan: I thought Enola looked rough as f*ck

Breatheforeva: The picture was rubbish – you could hardly see anything. I want to see what ring she chose!

Enolasbestfriend: They werent choosing a ring

Chorizo72: how would you know?

Enolasbestfriend: I just do, OK?

I decide to test the water again, putting a bit of a clue in my wording this time in case anyone is thinking the same thing and might message me privately if they don't want to post publicly.

Enolasbestfriend: I'm worried about Enola. I thought she didnt look like herself in that picture. I hope shes going to be OK for the concert

Croissantsandchocolate: Shes got Max looking after her she'll be fine. I wouldn't mind him looking after me!

Fuck's sake. Utter waste of time.

33

I try and clearly fail to hide the astonishment I feel at Max telling me he proposed. Wouldn't I have remembered something like that? It's true that I don't remember anything that day until waking up in hospital after we left the hotel, but . . . before he joined me on the tour, Max and I had hardly been in the best place. True, it's been up and down, and things have been good the last few days between us, but I think that's mainly because we currently spend pretty much every hour of every day together so there's no time for him to be worrying that I've been away from him doing something I shouldn't. Even before we left we still had our good moments, but overall, things were not brilliant.

But then . . . we'd had a good night before that day when it all kicked off with the truck, and just before we went shopping I was feeling like perhaps things between us could be all right after all. Max had ordered champagne from room service and then we messed about together in the huge bath with a view of the Eiffel Tower. It was like something from a film. He'd touched me in the ways he knows I like to be touched and asked for nothing in return. There were no sudden tangents into why had I been talking to so and so for so long, or why had I chosen to wear a low cut top when I went to whichever meeting or event. It was all good, and for the first time in ages I could fall asleep with him spooned into my back without wondering if he was about to accuse me of desperately wanting to bed someone I'd barely even noticed.

I had been so content in our little bubble that I didn't want to break it, so we ordered room service again instead of going downstairs for breakfast and didn't hold back at all – eggs benedict with smoked salmon, vast *cafés au lait* and freshly-squeezed orange juice which we enjoyed wrapped in the hotel's huge and uber-soft robes. It was so madly perfect and so far removed from anything I could have ever imagined for myself growing up that doing anything to jeopardise it would be incomprehensible. This is how my life can be, I thought to myself, if only I don't set Max off. It isn't that hard. Then we had sex again, got dressed, and Max said he had a surprise for me. We left the hotel, and then . . .

'So you don't remember me proposing?' he presses. 'Nothing about it at all?' Oh God. Up until now things had been going so well between us since we've been away from home. This could set everything back again.

I try to take his hand, but he snatches it away. 'Brilliant,' he says. 'I wanted it to be one of the most special moments of your life and you don't even remember.'

'I'm . . . sure it was amazing,' I say, falteringly, 'but I don't remember anything about that morning, you know that. And I'm sure that's not because it wasn't special, but like the doctor said, the trauma. The mind does weird things to block it out. They said that at the hospital, remember?'

He nods, biting his bottom lip. 'I'm sorry to hear that my heartfelt proposal was so *traumatic* for you,' he says, sarcastically. His voice is tight and for a horrifying moment I think he might cry.

'Max! That isn't what I meant at all. The truck, that poor man dying . . .' I realize that now is the time to be honest about quite how little memory I have of that time. 'I don't remember anything of being in the shopping centre that day. It's not just your proposal which has . . . gone. It's the whole thing. The whole time in the shopping centre.'

He looks up at me and, oh God, I see that tears are gathering. But sometimes tearful Max is easier to deal with than angry Max. Usually blows over more quickly and is easier to calm down. He takes my hand. 'I'm sorry Enola,' he sniffs, swiping at his eyes. 'I forgot how upset you were by the whole thing.'

He gets down on one knee. Oh God. 'If you can't

remember, then the right thing to do is for me to ask you again. Enola Mazzeri, I have loved you from the first moment I saw you. Will you do me the honour of becoming my wife?'

34

27 June 2024
Las Vegas
Angel

It takes me a few seconds to work out where I am when I wake up – huge bed, high ceiling with twinkling lights embedded in it which look like stars, several people around me.

My hands hurt. I lift them up and see they're covered in bandages. I seem to be naked except for a large white towel which someone has draped over me, and then I remember. I'm in the hotel. I was in the shower. The burning. What the fuck happened?

'What the fuck happened to me?' I ask, repeating my thought out loud. I'm not shy, but I'm suddenly quite uncomfortable about all these people being in my bedroom while I'm naked, none of whom I recognize apart from, oh yes, Trixie. Great. 'And who are all these people?' I ask, turning towards her. 'Aren't I entitled to some privacy?'

'They're here to help you,' Trixie says. 'To make you as comfortable as possible. Now that you're awake and your . . . um, situation has been attended to, I'm sure they'll be leaving. This is Dr Lainez, the hotel physician, and this is Mr Greenwood, the hotel manager. The two ladies in your bathroom are part of the housekeeping team ensuring that everything is clean and that there's no residue left of whatever it is that you reacted to.'

'Do you have any allergies of which you are aware, ma'am?' the doctor asks.

'Allergies? No! Look at me,' I say, lifting up my hands, but they are bandaged so I can't see anything.

'That wasn't caused by an allergy!' I snap. 'There was something in that dispenser which shouldn't have been. Acid? Bleach? Something like that. I've never known pain like it.'

What kind of doctor would think this was an allergy? Suddenly I realize – one who is in the pay of the hotel. Fuck's sake. It's my hands which really hurt, but I can also feel a throbbing on my face. 'It didn't burn me anywhere else did it? Can you hand me a mirror?'

The two men look uneasily at each other before the doctor delves into his bag. Oh God. There's a large square white plaster stuck on my cheek and the skin underneath feels like it is trying to explode.

'Fuck!' I say. 'If this has scarred my face . . .' I feel

149

tears come to my eyes and fight them back. 'Can you take it off so I can see?'

The doctor clears his throat. 'Allergies can sometimes cause a burning sensation,' he mansplains. 'It will be better for your recovery if you leave the dressing in place, Miss Williams, to prevent you scratching and further aggravating the skin.'

'What the fuck?' I turn towards the hotel manager. 'You can expect to hear from my solicitors very shortly. Whatever did this to me, it was something that your people put in the shower. I fully intend to sue the pants off you.' I glance at the doctor. 'Probably both of you.'

'We will be testing the shower gel of course,' says the hotel manager, 'but there have been no similar complaints from any other guests, so we can only assume that whatever happened to your skin is something specific to you.'

He pauses and gives me a look which is somewhere between sympathetic and deeply irritated.

'I have to say though, it is highly unusual, as the spa products we use in these suites contain all natural ingredients. Though, clearly, allergic reactions can still occur and we will be looking into how we distribute information about product ingredients in future to avoid such an unpleasant occurrence happening again.'

What?

'For now,' he continues, 'we have emptied your room of all our house toiletries to avoid any repeat incident, and if you can let us know which brands are your favourites, we will send someone to source them immediately.'

'I would recommend using plain, unscented soaps for the next few days,' the doctor interjects, 'to avoid aggravating the skin further.'

'Fine. Perhaps your staff can get me something like that?' I snap at the wank-stain of a hotel manager, who clearly doesn't give a shit about what has happened to me and is only bothered about covering his arse. 'Whatever the so-called *doctor* recommends, I don't know anything about those kind of brands. But in the meantime, like I said, you can expect to hear from my lawyers. Whatever did this to me, it's your fault. The thing that burned me came from your dispensers.'

'You are clearly upset, ma'am,' the hotel manager says, smarmily, 'which I entirely understand. We will leave you to rest now. I hope you will reconsider your position, and in the meantime, please do let us know if there is anything at all we can do to make you more comfortable.'

'And I will be back tomorrow to check on you and change your dressings,' the doctor says. 'It's important you take care to keep your skin covered.'

'And what about the concert?' I ask. 'Will I be able to perform?'

The doctor frowns. 'We will have to see how you are doing tomorrow. You might find too much movement tricky for a few days, and you'll certainly have to be careful with any costumes which might rub or scratch the affected areas.'

'And do you have any idea what might have caused it?' I press. 'It was something other than shower gel which did this to me. Believe me, I know. I was there. I've never known pain like it.'

'Impossible to say at the moment, I'm afraid.' He glances at the manager. 'Allergic reactions can sometimes be quite severe,' he adds, both patronizing and gaslighting me in one single phrase. 'But while the skin is a little blistered, I'm hopeful it won't scar. Whatever the irritant was doesn't seem to have penetrated too deeply. We've bandaged you as a precaution, mainly to avoid you scratching in your sleep, and the dressings should be able to be removed within a few days.

'I would advise you to drink plenty of water and rest as much as possible,' he continues. 'I have already given you some painkillers intravenously, and will leave you some more which you can take in the night and over the next few days if you need to. But please be careful not to exceed the recommended dose, they are somewhat stronger than the ones available over the counter.'

'We'll get out of your way now, ma'am,' the hotel manager adds. 'I will arrange for those replacement toiletries immediately and wish you a speedy recovery. Please call us if you need anything at all or if there is anything we can do to make you more comfortable.'

The two cleaners emerge from the bathroom and exit my suite with the two men, leaving me alone with Trixie.

I lift my bandaged hands and look at them helplessly. 'Fucking hell,' I say. 'What are we going to do?'

Trixie is already on her phone and doesn't look up

as she taps out messages frantically. 'For now, nothing. I'm just keeping Emery up to date on what's happened. If you can't do the concert though, shit the bed, that would be a disaster.' She finally looks up from her phone. 'How are your hands feeling now?'

I know this isn't an enquiry about my well-being, in fact, the way she's phrased it could barely make that more plain. All she's bothered about is the likelihood of me being able to perform as planned.

I feel a stab of loneliness as I realize how little any of these people care about me.

'They're OK, I think,' I say, 'but as they've given me the painkillers it's kind of difficult to know.'

She nods earnestly. 'And in yourself, how do you feel? Like, do you feel like you could stand up? Dance?' She frowns. 'I'm wondering how we should play this. I mean, if you feel like you could, let's say, sing but not dance, for example, perhaps the better thing to do would be to sit you on a stool and make a plus of it?'

'What do you mean, a plus?' I hiss. 'I've just suffered what I'm pretty sure are chemical burns which might leave me with permanent scarring. I don't see any *plus* in that. Please, enlighten me, do.'

I can see she's not really listening. 'Perhaps we could put out that you're hurt but you're soldiering on because this reunion concert means so much to you,' Trixie suggests, clearly warming to her theme. 'How you want to make sure it goes ahead as a tribute to Enola. People love that kind of thing. We could get some guitar gloves made with sequins or something like that so that you can still play the guitar.' She goes back to her phone and taps something out. 'Though we'd have to make sure you don't end up looking too Michael Jackson. I'll get someone to find out what's available that we can get at short notice.'

She *tap tap tap*s for a while and then looks up at me again. 'Or, if you need to keep the bandages on, you can sing as usual and we can get someone else to do your guitar bits. Yeah. That could work. What do you mean, chemical burns?' she asks, seemingly only just registering what I said.

'This is nothing to do with an allergy,' I say, 'I'm never allergic to anything and what happened wasn't just itching or something like a wasp sting, it was properly burning. I'm no snowflake, but I passed out from the pain. Did you actually *see* my skin?'

She shakes her head. 'No. You were already bandaged and patched up by the time I got here.'

'I could show you? It was blistering as soon as whatever it was touched it. I dread to think what it looks like now.'

'No. You might disturb the skin, make it worse, like the doctor said. You need to give yourself the best chance of recovery. Wait until he comes to change your dressings tomorrow.' She pauses. 'So, if you don't think it was an allergy, what do you think it was?'

'It's obvious isn't it?' I snap. I am tired and have had enough of this. I think the painkillers are wearing off as my hands are starting to throb – I can feel my heartbeat in the tips of my fingers. 'The cleaners must have put something caustic in the containers by accident. Maybe bleach? Some kind of cleaning agent? I don't know. They're paid a pittance and some of them probably don't even speak English. It's hardly surprising if their minds aren't always on the job. That said, the manager should have taken responsibility and at least apologized properly, and he didn't, so I fully intend to go ahead and sue. Whatever the doctor said, it's early days and those burns might even scar, which could affect my future career. I deserve compensation.'

Trixie is looking pensive. 'You don't think . . . it's a possibility that . . . someone might have done it deliberately?'

I laugh. '*What?* You think the cleaner thought I didn't leave her a big enough tip so she decided to teach me a lesson? No, I don't think so.' I pause. True, earlier I'd wondered if the room service lady banged the door on the way out because I didn't bother to tip, but this is a totally different level. 'You need to take a step back, Trixie, it looks like the stress of working for Emery is finally getting to you.'

She shakes her head. 'No,' she says, more gently now. 'I didn't mean the cleaner did anything deliberate. That wouldn't make sense. But this is hardly the first thing that's happened on this trip, is it?' she continues. 'I meant . . . maybe someone else. That gantry falling, nearly killing you.'

I shrug. 'That kind of thing happens sometimes, especially when the sets are put up and taken down so quickly. We're only doing a couple of nights, and the venue is brand new – it was built quickly and there are bound to be things that weren't finished off quite right. Plus it could have hit any of us realistically – it would be a dodgy way of trying to hurt me, which it didn't. I don't see how it can be related to what was put in a soap dispenser.'

'It's not just that though, is it?' Trixie persists. 'There's also the food poisoning. All of you struck down with it, even though you didn't eat the same foods. You have to admit that that's weird.'

I frown. 'Not really. Like you say, that was all of us. Not just me. Probably the restaurant being lax about their hygiene. I read somewhere that more cases of food poisoning come from contaminated salad than from oysters. Or something like that, anyway.'

Trixie nods. 'Maybe. But there's a possibility that someone is trying to hurt you. Or even the entire band. I think we should step up security.'

35

November 2008
Toulouse
Enola

Oh God, Max is still kneeling on the terrace, looking hopefully up at me. The sun has now dipped behind the horizon and it's freezing cold. A light drizzle is starting. I want to rub my arms in an effort to warm up but he's still holding my hand and it would feel like I was snatching it away if I did.

I can hear someone moving about on the terrace next to mine and rack my brain to try to remember whose room is there, but I can't. Maybe Sophie's? Probably better her than Angel, though neither of them are remotely likely to be discreet if they overhear anything. I glance at the wall between the two terraces – I can't see anyone, but I can tell someone is there and they'll no doubt be able to hear everything we say. I bet whoever it is heard our row earlier. I hear light footsteps and then the door close – hopefully the rain has sent them inside.

Did his proposal in the jeweller's even happen? Surely I'd remember something like that? I stare at him, open-mouthed. 'God Max I, um, so much has happened in the last few days and this is the last thing I expected and . . .'

I see his expression cloud. 'I mean, obviously I'm thrilled,' I continue, babbling, trying to buy time, 'but, wow, this is so out of the blue and my head still hurts a bit and . . .'

He drops my hand and gets up. He rubs the knee which was on the ground – his trousers are soaked. It's raining harder now.

'Fine,' he says, tersely. 'You told me in Paris that you wanted to be my wife. But if you've changed your mind, maybe we should call it a day. End this now. No point in continuing this relationship if you're not even sure how you feel about me.'

I feel panic rush through me – that isn't what I want. When things are good, they're really, really good. I don't want him to leave me. I need to fix this. Quickly. Now.

'No!' I shout, and then clamp my hand over my mouth. I glance at the terrace wall again but hopefully whoever it was out there has gone in. But I don't want to take any chances – I'd rather be inside where we can be more private. Rain splashes onto my face. 'No,' I repeat. 'That is, I don't mean no to your proposal. No to us finishing. That's the last thing I want. Let's go inside and talk about this.'

He turns his back and disappears through the patio doors. I follow him inside and close the doors behind me. He looks at me, his wet hair and damp clothes making me think of a bedraggled puppy. I don't want to lose him.

I take his hand. 'I'm sorry I can't remember the time in the jewellery shop,' I say. 'Hopefully the memory will come back eventually.' I pause. 'Of course I want to marry you. How could I not?' His face brightens.

'But I still feel tired and confused after the truck thing,' I continue, 'and seem to feel more and more exhausted. So yes, let's get married, but let's not tell anyone our plans yet, hey? Get the tour over at least first. Maybe after that we can go on a holiday together, just you and me, announce it then. I just can't deal with any more . . . stuff right now, and the press won't leave us alone if we announce it now. Plus isn't it kind of more special if it's our little secret for a while?'

He takes me in his arms and buries his face in my neck. I can't tell as he's already soaked, but I've a feeling he might be crying.

He lets me go and looks at me, his hands still gently on my arms.

'You've made me the happiest man alive, Enola,' he says.

I smile back at him.

I don't want him to leave me.

And at least I have bought myself some time.

I can put off getting married until I feel ready. Until I am sure.

At least, I can, unless he ever finds out about what happened with Liam.

There'd be no question of marriage then.

He'd kill him.

Or me.

36

Letter delivered to Brilliant Records:

I'm so worried about you Enola I hope you are OK. Please let your fans know you are alright we are looking out for you. Dont marry Max though he isnt worthy of you please please please

37

Even though I had decided I had no money to get out to
Europe to check on Enola, I then found I couldn't sleep,
eat or basically do anything for worrying about her,
so I needed to find a way. I couldn't simply do nothing. I needed to investigate. See for myself. Enola might
need me.

I'll have to sell my concert ticket – it's the only thing
of value I have. It's more important to get out there and
help Enola than it is to see the show.

A few days later, the money is in my account. I've had
a good look at the concert schedule, and the bands move
almost every day. It's not the easiest, combined with not
having much money, so I need to pick somewhere with
cheap flights. I decide on Barcelona as the flights aren't
too bad and the concert is only a few days away. I don't

want to wait any longer – I need to do this now. And to save money I'm flying to Girona which I don't think is really Barcelona at all but I can hitch a lift once I get there – I'm not worried about that.

I've never been on a plane before. I've only got a passport because of, well, the last time, when I was making plans I thought I might need to go abroad, but then I was given that restraining order and by the time that expired, I'd moved on – I'd found Enola.

Booking the trip and working out what I could take with me is much more complicated than I'd expected. I have to throw away my shower gel at the airport because it's too large for their rules and that's upsetting because I'm certainly not going to waste money replacing it. I've booked the cheapest hostel I could find vaguely near the stadium they're performing at so I doubt there will be things like shower gel provided. Hopefully I can steal some soap or something, I don't know. It doesn't matter. There are more pressing things.

I leave the airport and hitch to Barcelona. Eventually, after a lot of walking, I find the hostel which is about as grim and grimy as I was expecting but never mind, I'm not here for a holiday. I have at least got my own room as I don't want anyone poking their nose into my business and who knows what might become necessary?

I have a soapless shower in a not-that-clean shared bathroom but it's better than nothing. Then I sit down on the narrow bed with my computer and log on to the free Wi-Fi, which was the one facility I ensured the hostel actually had, and see if I can work out where the band are.

It doesn't take long, browsing some of the showbiz sites, to work out which hotel they are in from a picture of Angel entering somewhere called Hotel Amanti carrying what looks like dozens of designer shopping bags.

I don't give a shit about Angel or where she is, but it's likely that the band will all be staying in the same hotel so hopefully Enola will be there too. I put on a suit – it's not the kind of thing I'd ever wear normally but it's come in handy loads of times over the years when I need to blend in at posh places and I wore it to court too which probably helped me avoid jail according to my solicitor.

I add sunglasses and leave my backpack here, putting the bits and pieces I might need in my pockets.

I look up the hotel and work out how to get there. I need to get up close to Enola whatever it takes.

38

November 2008
Barcelona
Enola

Max holds my hand almost all the way on the bus to Barcelona and keeps giving me stupid little 'I know our secret' looks. It's quite sweet and, for now at least, I'm glad I said yes to him.

I am wondering what would happen if he ever found out about the Liam thing. I can't imagine he would take it lightly. Sometimes I worry about it coming out unexpectedly, whether he would react better if I told him myself. Wouldn't a husband want to know everything about his wife? Max my husband. Such a weird thought.

Perhaps I should simply 'fess up. It was a long time ago. Before we even got together. I was very young and didn't know any better. It was actually my first time ever, not that I told Liam that. But I know what Max is like, and I don't think he'd think it was OK that his girlfriend had slept with his bandmate, even if it was just once and even if they were both deeply embarrassed about it and neither of them have ever spoken about it since.

At least, I assume Liam is as embarrassed as I am, probably more so. Although for me, I no longer think 'embarrassed' is quite the right word for me and I wonder if, for Liam, a better word might be ashamed.

Looking back on it now, a few years on and being a bit older, I can see how entirely inappropriate what he did was. I was young (legal, yes, but barely) and starstruck, and he took advantage. I wasn't exactly unwilling at the time – I couldn't believe someone like him was interested in me – but it isn't the kind of thing I would do now, even if I wasn't with Max, and it's always made me somewhat wary of Liam.

I'm sure he must know that what he did wasn't exactly great behaviour, and that he was taking advantage of the situation. So he wouldn't tell Max, surely?

Or would he? Boys like to brag about that kind of thing, don't they? Or he might allude to it to wind Max up if they've had a row about something as they do – they're always having little spats.

Maybe the best thing to do is have a conversation with Liam about it. Yes. I'll do that. Make sure we're on the same page. It's Liam who did something wrong here, not me, but if Max doesn't know, then there's no harm done. It's not like I've been unfaithful to him. I'd never do that. Then again, I'm not sure if Max will see it that way. He'd be bound to blame me, say I must have fancied Liam and that I probably still do.

'Penny for them?' Max says, stroking my hand.

'What?' I ask, a little flustered as he jerks me out of my reverie, not really understanding what he's asking.

'It's something my grandmother used to say. You were looking thoughtful. It means penny for your thoughts. I wondered what you were thinking about.'

I smile. 'Oh. Yeah. Of course. I was wondering if we'd have time to see the Sagrada Familia when we're in Barcelona,' I lie. 'What do you think?'

He frowns. 'The what now?'

'Sagrada Familia. It's a massive cathedral which is still unfinished even though they've been building it pretty much forever. Look . . .' I flick through one of the tourist brochures which have been left on the bus for us, find an image I saw earlier and show it to him. 'See? Looks cool, doesn't it?'

He takes it and gives it a cursory glance. 'Yeah. Guess so. If that's what you want to see, we'll make sure there's time for it.'

A text message notification pings on my phone. 'Who's that? he asks.

'Just Mum.' I open the message.

Hi darling. Surprise! I'm in Barcelona! Dom decided to surprise me with a minibreak and thought it would be fun to come and see you too! Hope you can meet us for lunch today? Bring the gorgeous Max of course! Will call later to arrange where and when.

I'm surprised to feel a little lift in my spirits. Normally Mum interfering and wanting to get too involved in my life is a total pain in the arse, but I've been surprised at quite how lonely touring is making me feel. Things have been so up and down with Max, I don't have anything in common with Sophie or Angel, and there's barely time to do anything for myself or call my friends at home.

Even if I have any left, that is. I think of Becki with a pang. I'm going to call her right now, while I have time, before I forget. Even if the signal cuts out because we're on the coach, at least she'll know I'm thinking of her. I know it's been years, but I still send birthday and Christmas cards and try to call her now and again. I still miss her.

I make the call and it rings and rings. As usual, she doesn't answer.

'Well, this is very lovely,' says Mum. We're in Mimosa, a new restaurant owned by some hot celebrity chef which normally you can't get into unless you book months in advance, but when I told Trixie that Mum was turning up she said she'd get us a table here and sort a photographer. 'Dinner with Mum and the boyfriend – exactly the kind of nice, wholesome scene which is perfect for your brand,' she enthused. 'Leave it with me.' Given that apparently every table is booked every day and night

I don't know quite how this is achieved – I hope they don't cancel someone else's booking, but I've a nasty feeling they probably do. I hope it wasn't their birthday or anything.

Absolutely everything in the room is white, it's so bright I'm tempted to wear sunglasses, but everyone knows that wearing sunglasses inside is absolutely the height of wankiness. Nonetheless, Mum's 'man' Dom, who is more of a boy than a man and doesn't look that much older than me, is wearing his Ray-Bans anyway. It's the first time Max has met him and I'm kind of embarrassed for both Mum and Dom. Them being together is inappropriate and weird and I've never really liked or trusted him.

I'd actually rather have gone for tapas and a massive jug of sangria in a cosy bar than somewhere flashy like this, but as usual, no one asked me. However I don't want to spoil it for Mum, who loves this kind of showiness so I lamely agree, 'Yes, isn't it lovely?' as a waiter flicks an enormous white napkin out over my knee.

Dom is wanging on about how he's a musician too (bass player, apparently) and all he needs is his big break, and Max is listening politely, agreeing heartily and making helpful suggestions. I feel a little pang of love for him as I watch – he is brilliant in these kind of situations, making conversation with the most tedious of people in a way that makes them feel like he actually cares.

'But you'll meet him tomorrow at the after-party,' Max is saying. 'You can ask Emery yourself.'

'Ask him what?' I ask, having tuned out.

'If he has any openings for a bass player anywhere. Dom plays bass.'

I nod. 'Oh right. Yeah.'

I'm pretty sure there won't be, but Max is always good at saying the right thing. 'Should be a fun party,' I add.

39

28 June 2024
Las Vegas
Angel

I barely sleep that night, mainly because my hands still hurt however many painkillers I take, but also because I am thinking about what Trixie said.

Trixie is hard as nails, never one to catastrophize, so if she thinks there's something going on here in Vegas, I need to consider the possibility that there actually might be.

But who would do this? Max, Liam and Sophie aren't exactly my friends, but neither do I think any of them actively hate me, at least not enough to do something like this. We all kind of know each other's secrets and tolerate each other largely because of that, and that seems to work fine.

A crazed fan? There have been a few issues along those lines over the years of course, but usually they're deranged saddos who would be too scared to step out from behind their computer screens and actually do anything. And also, it was usually Enola who attracted them, I'm not entirely sure why. She always seemed to find it tiresome and upsetting, while I was always mildly offended that they didn't tend to find me interesting or attractive enough to stalk online. There were unwanted gifts, of course, letters and the odd dick pic, though pre smartphones they were less of an issue. But nothing I couldn't handle, or which ever felt particularly concerning.

So I think Trixie's wrong. It's much more likely that whatever it was that burnt me was a simple accident, the hotel housekeeping staff not paying attention, unlinked to the other things which have happened since we got here. I take yet another painkiller and push it out of my mind.

40

November 2008
Barcelona
Charlie

I see Max and Enola leaving the hotel just as I arrive, getting into an enormous limo with blacked-out windows. Fuck! I missed them and have no way of knowing where they're going. I could cry.

I quickly compose myself, put my shoulders back, head up high and walk in through the glossy black doors as if I have as much right to be there as everyone else. Which I do.

I sit down in the lobby as far away from reception as I can but making sure I have a clear view of the door while I think about what to do next.

A man in a black suit comes over and says something to me in Spanish. I feel a jolt of alarm as I assume he is chucking me out. 'I don't understand,' I say, over-enunciating everything. 'I am English.'

'Ah, excuse me, Señorita,' he says. 'I simply wanted to ask if I can get you anything to eat or drink.'

'Oh.' I wonder if I can get away with simply saying 'no thanks' and that I'm waiting for someone, but I figure they're likely to leave me alone for longer if I order something. Looking around the prices are going to be eye-watering I'm sure and I wonder what the cheapest thing I can order is. I can always do a runner if need be. 'Maybe a cup of tea please?' I say, because it's the first thing I think of and now I come to think of it, I could kind of do with one.

'Of course,' he says, 'I will bring you the tea menu so you can make your selection.'

I choose the cheapest tea possible, drink it slowly and let a couple of hours pass, but there is still no sign of Enola coming back. I start to think about leaving because I've been here ages and I'm starting to get strange looks from the people at the reception desk and I don't want anyone to remember me.

And then Max and Enola walk through the lobby! They are laughing and giggling together and fortunately pay me no attention at all. I try not to stare because I don't want them to notice me but it doesn't seem like natural behaviour for them and 'Enola', if it is actually her, definitely looks smaller than usual I'm sure.

But they are past me and in the lift before I know it and I didn't see enough to be sure. I need to get closer, to find out more.

The tea wasn't that nice especially given what they were expecting me to pay for it and the milk tasted weird so I decide that I'll just slip out of the door when no one is looking. I need to get back to my laptop to see if I can work out a better way to get a longer and closer look at Enola.

41

November 2008
Barcelona
Enola

'She's all right, you know, your mum,' Max says, as the lift heads up to our floor and we return to our suite. 'She's great fun.'

'She just fancies you, is all,' I say, and he laughs. It's been a good afternoon. Max was on top form and apart from one brief side eye when he thought the handsome waiter was being a little bit too attentive towards me, I don't seem to have done anything to upset him.

'What did you think of Dom?' I ask.

He shrugs. 'Seemed OK. Reckons himself though. Thinks he can play bass.'

'Bit young for Mum, no?'

'She's a good-looking lady. If she wants to have her fun then, well, why not?'

'I guess. Though also, *eww*. They've been together

quite a while now, but I hope he's not with her because he thinks she's a route in to Emery.'

'Enola! I'm sure he's not. You always think the worst of everyone. He seemed really into her.'

'He also seemed really into the idea of meeting Emery. He used to try to get me to engineer an introduction when he was first around, but quickly realized that I wasn't interested in helping. You're fresh meat to him though.'

'I think you're reading too much into it – almost everyone is interested in Emery, aren't they? He's just one of those people. Even if you're not a wannabe musician, everyone wants to meet him because he is who he is and because he's on the telly. I wouldn't worry.'

I frown. 'You don't think Dom's a bit . . . creepy?'

'Not really.' He pauses. 'You know, I've never asked you, what happened to your dad?'

'I don't know. Mum never wants to talk about it. She's hinted at him being someone famous, but to be honest, I think she's making that up.' I shrug. 'She was very young when we were born – only nineteen.'

'Wow. That must have been . . . hard. Especially with two of you arriving at once.'

I feel a pang. I probably don't appreciate enough how much Mum did for us. How much she gave up for us. But especially for me. I am now living her dream, and I probably don't think about that often enough.

'Yeah. I'm sure it was very hard. I'm now older than she was then obviously, and I know there's no way I could cope with even one baby on my own like that, let alone two. Her family disowned her – I've never met any of them. But she managed. Amazing, really.'

'And she never talks about who your dad is at all?'

I shake my head. 'Not in any concrete terms. My guess is that maybe he was older, married, or basically someone who shouldn't have been with her.' I don't really like talking about this. It feels disloyal and, if I'm honest, a little seedy. 'Or maybe it wasn't as complicated as that,' I add. 'Perhaps Roxie and I are the product of a fumble at a club which got out of hand. Maybe Mum doesn't even know who our father is – she's made no secret of the fact that she was quite a party girl before we arrived. Perhaps one day it'll be like in that ABBA musical and my various possible dads will assemble on my wedding day, ready to claim me.'

He laughs and takes my hand. 'Speaking of weddings, have you thought about what you'd like to do yet?'

I feel a lurch of unease and concentrate on not allowing it to show. I fix a smile on my face. 'Not entirely sure. But I think it might be nice to slide off to a beach somewhere sunny or something like that and do it there, don't you? I don't want to wear a big meringue and I feel like I'm the centre of attention enough already. I'd like something maybe just me and you, simple, barefoot. No press, no magazine deal. Perhaps we can ask a couple of waiters to be witnesses. And some little local kids to be flower girls. That might be cute.'

He pats my hand and lets it go. 'Whatever you want, Enola. As long as we're together. That's all that matters.'

42

28 June 2024
Las Vegas
Kimberley

I'm keeping a low profile while I'm here in Las Vegas – I'm not planning to spend any time with the bands. I don't know if they even know I'm here – they certainly wouldn't care. I tried to persuade Roxie to come with me but she refused – said she wasn't being cooped up on a plane with all those people and she wasn't interested in attending a concert where Enola wasn't anyway. I worry more and more about that girl – I'm not sure she even ever leaves her flat any more. I should have paid her more attention as a child, but I was always so busy making sure that Enola was making the most of her talents. And now Enola is gone and Roxie is a hermit with whom I have almost no relationship at all. It wasn't exactly the outcome I was hoping for when my two little girls were born.

I've got the access all areas pass I asked for from Trixie and I've been along to a couple of the rehearsals to have a look, making sure I couldn't be seen and really, the band are nothing without Enola.

Some might think it a bit mad coming along to the concert, or even somewhat masochistic, like probing a wound, but I wanted to see them all together, get some closure. Things like that. I was due a holiday anyway and there are worse places to be than here. Plus there were a couple of things I wanted to do, should the opportunity arise.

When Enola disappeared, Max was the only one of the actual band members who even bothered to get in touch to pass on their condolences in a way which actually felt like he might mean it. Emery and Trixie sent flowers and offered to pay for counselling, which I didn't take them up on because that's never been my kind of thing. Then after a couple of years had passed and it seemed likely that she was not going to reappear, they arranged to sort out Enola's 'estate' as they called it so that I didn't have to.

Estate! She was a child. A rich child, admittedly, but still a child. Her 'estate' consisted of her beautiful penthouse, where I now live, a few designer dresses which I gave to Roxie, not that she ever goes anywhere, and of course, future royalties for the songs. So far they have not been inconsiderable, and I imagine these concerts might give those a boost. 'Loud and Proud' has always been the biggest seller, followed by 'All The Way', which was written by Enola and Liam for *The Chosen* and annoyingly, rights reverted to him.

So while the record company sorted out everything that needed to be sorted in the main, I got my own lawyer in too, to make sure it was all done fairly, and that I got what I was due. What Enola would have been due. I gave up a lot for her, and it was all over far too quickly. For both of us. So I needed to make sure it wasn't all for nothing. One day Roxie will inherit it all, but her being the way that she is, I thought it was better that I hang onto the lion's share until the time comes. I make sure she's provided for, but she never seems to want much for herself.

When it all happened, I had all these big plans about setting up some kind of foundation in Enola's name, I was never sure quite what, maybe something for deprived kiddies or battered women or victims of domestic violence or whatever it is they call them now, I don't know. I haven't done it yet. Maybe one day I will. It would be nice to have Enola remembered properly. Though there's already the songs for that, so perhaps doing something else as well isn't all that important.

We have never had a funeral or a memorial service because, at least in theory, it remains possible that Enola might turn up again. But much more than seven years have passed now, and she has been officially declared dead. I for one know she is not coming back.

Some say it's creepy that I still live in her penthouse. But why not? It's beautiful. Her success was, to a large degree, down to me. In some ways, I feel like I'm close to her because it was her place. Getting rid of it would feel too final, for me, for Roxie, and probably for some of the mad fans who still think she is coming back.

I moved in not long after she went – initially to look after the cats, as I'd done so often when she was alive. They were everything to her, and I'd kind of grown fond of them too. They had everything they needed here while I lived on a busy road. At least that's what I told myself was the reason, and other people, not that it was any of their business. And then once I was in, I got used to all the light, the space, the lack of clutter and the high-end furnishings, and it seemed pointless to move out.

Thanks to Enola, it's true that I will never have to worry about money again, but as far as I'm concerned, that's only down to all the effort I put into training her up as a child. Making sure she was in a position to make the most of her talents.

There have always been whispers about me profiting from her success, and even from her disappearance, but fuck them all, they don't know any of it. What I gave up for her. That could have been me! If only I hadn't got pregnant. I was on track for good things, I'm sure I was.

I didn't even tell the father about it. No point – he wouldn't have been interested. He would have made me get rid of the babies. Wouldn't have wanted the responsibility, wouldn't have risked the scandal – while I was legal, I was still a child really – he was older. And even though I was only nineteen and frightened, I knew I didn't want to do that.

And then I found out, it wasn't just one baby. It was twins! Double the work. Double the expense.

Looking after them was much more difficult than I'd expected. Not simply like looking after a pet or a live action doll as I'd somewhat naively imagined. Or I'd heard about this thing where in some schools they get teenage girls to look after an egg all day to represent a baby and try to scare them away from getting up the duff, but really, how easy is that? An egg is just an egg – it doesn't cry or need feeding or its nappy changing. And if gets broken, you can get another one.

Looking after two real live babies was hard. As I was so young I could just about cope with the sleep deprivation, but it was the constant demands of the two of them and the loneliness which I found the most difficult. Alone, with no one, in some God-awful high-rise council flat, with drug addicts in the corridor and the relentless arguing of the couple upstairs through the thin ceiling, followed by their making up afterwards, which made the light on my ceiling shake. Grim.

I wanted to be a good mother, I really did. I read all the books, I breastfed (mainly because formula was so expensive, but even so), and then made purees to freeze rather than buy jars (again, cheaper, and it helped pass the time), I tried my absolute hardest for them and I think on the whole, I did OK. I wasn't playing them Mozart or teaching them sign language like I've heard they do with babies these days, and they weren't dressed in designer clothes, but they were clean and fed.

But loved? I'm not sure. I always provided for them.

I did my best. If I'm honest with myself, I never stopped resenting what they'd taken away from me, even though I hated myself for it – they were innocent babies, it wasn't their fault. I tried to love them, but I'm not a hundred per cent convinced I ever quite got there.

I hated being in the flat – it was damp, manky, dark and most of all, boring and claustrophobic. So simply to get out of the house I'd take the girls to every possible class I could find which I could afford, before they could even walk. Luckily if you hunt around enough and are on all the benefits like I was, there are quite a few which are as good as free. So both Enola and Roxie were banging tambourines before they could stand, pretty much singing before they could say a word. Like in that old ABBA song.

I told myself I was doing it all for them, but really, a large part of me was doing it for me. Brain-fogged by lack of sleep, covered in stretch marks, my pregnancy weight not falling off in spite of my youth because I was eating so badly, and perhaps, now I look back, I had a bit of undiagnosed post-natal depression and was simply not looking after myself – I felt my chance at stardom had come and gone. But the twins, they were brand new. I could live my dream through them. It would be almost as good. Even better maybe.

But from the outset, it was obvious that the two of them were very different. Enola loved to perform, even when she was tiny. But Roxie, not so much. In fact, not at all. While Enola would dance and clap along to the music whether at home or in the classes we went to, always loving an audience and eager to please, Roxie would lie face down on the floor, refusing to engage. To start with, I found it embarrassing, but there was no way I was going to sit and stagnate in my horrible flat, and anyway, Enola clearly enjoyed it. So Roxie had to suck it up and learn to live with it. It would probably be good for her anyway, bring her out of her shell, I reasoned, as well as being a good life lesson. Most people don't get everything they want all the time.

Once the girls went to school things got a little easier, I got a job and could afford to rent somewhere nicer. I signed Enola up to even more lessons while Roxie went to afterschool club and I started exercising. I got my body back. Had my hair cut. Bought some new clothes – they might only have been cheap, but it was way better than still slobbing around in my maternity joggers. I met a man and we lived together for a few years. We split up when I found out he wasn't really a travelling salesman but actually had another family which he lived with half the week, but I can't deny he helped me get back on my feet financially, even if he did leave me heartbroken and even more distrustful of men. And indeed, people in general.

By then, the twins were eight or nine and it was already clear that Enola had proper talent. Her singing voice was incredible, I entered her into every local competition I could find, and she always won. Roxie would usually have to tag along if I couldn't send her to a friend's house, spending most of the time on her Gameboy computer thingy with a packet of sweets while Enola did her thing and I watched with pride and wonder.

Enola also did beauty pageants for a while with some success too, but she hated them and would cry and rub her eyes to deliberately ruin her make-up, so it wasn't long before I decided to ditch them and concentrate on where her talents really lay – with singing and dancing.

However brilliant I had thought I was when I was nineteen or so, I could see that Enola's talents way surpassed mine. So I fully committed to directing all my energies into her. Sacrificing myself. In the end, it would be for the greater good for both of us – I was sure of it. Roxie seemed content to be in her own little world with her computer games, so by and large I left her to it. In retrospect, our relationship suffered badly for it, but I couldn't be everything to everyone. I am only one woman.

When Enola was little, she was more than happy to share in my joy when we won a competition. We'd have our picture in the local paper, and even be on the local TV news sometimes! She loved that to start with, almost as much as I did.

But as she got into her teens, things changed. She didn't want to do the competitions any more, she wanted to hang out with her friends. Or do her homework. Sometimes when she was feeling like being particularly hurtful she'd ask why couldn't I leave her alone to live her own life like I did Roxie, why did I always have to interfere with everything she did?

Or if she was in a better mood and didn't want to

start a fight, she'd say something like, 'Why don't you enter, Mum? It could be fun for you. I'll come and watch. I've got a big history project on, I don't want to waste time practising.'

But I'd missed my chance – I could see that. Enola – she was our future. If only she could see it herself.

Ungrateful bitch.

43

November 2008
Barcelona
Charlie

Inwiththeincrowd: So, word on the street is that the after-party is at the aquarium tonight. Anyone planning to go along and watch them go in?

Croissantsandchocolate: I wish! Long way from me though.

Chorizo72: My cousins working there tonight, she had to sign an NDA and everything. I'm going to ask her to try and steal something Angels touched

I give an inadvertent little squeal as this conversation which I have been waiting for finally drops on Breathe Deeply.

Inwiththeincrowd is always going on about how close

they are to the band and while I have always thought they were a complete bullshitter and had initially written this info off as them simply showing off like they always are and pretending they know more about the band than they actually do, chorizo72 is actually Spanish, lives here in Barcelona and, while he or she is always mean, they have so far shown no sign of being a huge liar (it is sometimes hard to tell, though after a while you generally start to get a feel for people, even online). So with two of them basically saying the same, I start to think it might be true.

It's the only lead I have to go on for now anyway as I think the party is my best chance of getting close to Enola or the person pretending to be her if I can manage to crash it. The concert is sold out, and even if it wasn't, going along would be pointless – I wouldn't be able to get close enough to have a proper look at her.

There is no time to waste. I go to have a look at the aquarium and there is a sign outside which says it will be closing early for a private function tomorrow so that makes it seem even more likely that the party will be there so I decide the best thing I can do is assume it is and work with that.

As long as it turns out to be true, it is brilliant news for me because even though no doubt security for the party will be strict, during the day the aquarium is a public place. Shame the tickets are so extortionate, but I don't want to risk drawing attention to myself by trying to get in without paying and if I can manage to do what I want to do it will all be worth it.

But I don't have anything remotely suitable to wear, I don't think the suit I brought to wear in the hotel lobby will work for a party so the next day I go into a few shops, first checking out the changing-room situation. In the third one I go into, a massive building with clothes spread over three floors, the two staff at the entrance to the changing room are flirting with each other and not bothering to check people going in and out properly at all as far as I can see, so I find a dress that looks like it's probably the right kind of thing to wear to a party like this one from the pictures I have seen, stack loads of other items on top at random and head in. The attendants don't pay a blind bit of notice.

The dress is plain black and stretchy which I think is ideal, I don't go to parties but as far as I can tell from pictures this is the kind of thing a lot of the girls wear to that kind of thing and I want to be unobtrusive and normal-looking – I don't want to draw attention to myself by being dressed in anything memorable. I check the dress carefully for any of those tags which set off alarms and there don't seem to be any, put my jeans and sweatshirt on over the top which is easy to do because the dress is so tiny, and walk out of the changing room, dumping the rest of the clothes on the counter in front of the two employees who don't even look at me this time. Pathetic. On the way out of the shop I help myself to a little silver bag which is so small as to be almost totally pointless and drop it into my rucksack. And then I have everything I need.

* * *

Back at the hostel, I have a lukewarm shower, keeping a careful eye on the time as I need to be back at the aquarium well before closing time to make sure I can get in like any other member of the public. I dry myself with the thin, rough towel supplied and put the dress on. Often forgetting to shop for food and not bothering to eat half the time means that I'm thin, what some might call skinny, so it might not be particularly healthy but it does mean clothes tend to look good on me.

I glance at my watch. It's 5.30 p.m., only an hour and a half till last entry tickets at the aquarium, better get a move on. I pick up my bag and . . . shit! I forgot shoes! I'm not used to dressing up and it simply didn't occur to me, but I know I'd stick out like a sore thumb at the party in my manky old trainers.

There's no time to go back to the shops and find somewhere suitable to nick stuff from – if I rush, that's when I mess up, that's what happened before, so I slip into one of the dorms which has been left unlocked and I can see is empty and it doesn't take long to find a pair of black heels which are only slightly too small for me under one of the beds. Honestly, some people are so careless with their stuff.

Fucking hell though how do people walk in these things! I go back to my room, put my trainers back on and put the black heels in a plastic bag. There's no way I can get all the way across town wearing shoes like that. I then put the trousers and T-shirt I like the least on over my dress so that I'll look less conspicuous going into the aquarium – I'd look weird among the tourists in their jeans

191

and jumpers in skimpy party clothes – plus I'd be freezing cold. I'm aware I might have to leave without them after the party which is why I pick my least favourite to wear but it will be a small price to pay to get close to Enola.

I queue up for what feels like hours, by now barely able to stand still I'm so excited, and eventually get my ridiculously priced ticket. I'm not particularly interested in fish at the best of times and this place is absolutely heaving, plus there are too many children who freak me out with their weird short limbs, high-pitched voices and snotty noses. I push through the crowds, scoping out the place as quickly as I can, looking for somewhere I can hide between the time the aquarium closes and when it opens for the party. I have already thought about it and think my best option is likely to be in the toilets – just need to select the best ones, I imagine in a place this size there will be more than one set.

A buzzer sounds and there's an announcement in several languages that the place is about to close. I increase my pace as I continue my tour of the building. I figure they'll have the party in the large round room surrounded by giant tanks, so it probably makes sense to hide out close to that in case they section off the building and do anything like lock internal doors.

Or is that actually the best plan? Should I head to the far corners of the building where they're possibly less likely to be so thorough in their checks? I mean, how do they even check everyone is out in a place like this? I've no idea. I'm kind of banking on the fact that they don't do it very thoroughly.

The buzzer sounds again. The crowds are starting to thin out. Security guards and other staff members are starting to move people towards the exit so I panic and duck into the first set of loos I see. I cast around and go into the furthest cubicle, leaving the door half open and climbing up onto the ledge thing above the loo where the flush button is so that no one will see my feet. I push myself as far into the corner as I can and hold my breath.

There is less and less sound outside and soon it fades away to nothing. But I know I need to wait longer to be safe so stay where I am. Eventually I hear footsteps approach and the door opens but as far as I can tell they don't even step inside. Really? Is that it? Pretty lame as far as checking goes.

I wait a little longer but nothing else happens so I get down from my perch, slip off my trousers and T-shirt and stuff them in the plastic bag. I put it down the back of the sanitary bin and will try to come back for it later. Waste not, want not.

It suddenly occurs to me though that there might be cleaners – do they clean last thing at night or first thing in the morning somewhere like this? I'll need to find somewhere else to wait just in case. Carrying my stolen shoes – I don't want to put them on until the absolute last minute – I head out into the dark.

44

28 June 2024
Las Vegas

Online news report:

Breathe lead singer Angel was rushed to Sunrise Hospital this morning after apparently taking an overdose of prescription painkillers.

'Angel appears to have suffered a mild allergic reaction last night to something in the hotel shower gel,' tour publicist Trixie explained at an impromptu press conference at the Jupiter Hotel where the band members are staying ahead of their much-awaited reunion concerts. 'She was attended by a doctor at the hotel and prescribed painkillers. When she did not arrive for rehearsal and failed to answer her phone, her room was checked and she was found unresponsive.

'She was treated in hospital and is now awake and in good spirits. The overdose was accidental as a result of the pain caused by the allergic reaction and a misunderstanding about the correct dosage. We are confident that Angel will perform at the next concert as planned. In the meantime, she would like to thank all her fans for their kind wishes.'

45

November 2008
Barcelona
Charlie

In the end I lurk in a dark corner just outside the loos
I'd left, figuring that if anyone finds me I could rush past
them or pretend to be a confused tourist who had got
lost as really, what are they going to do? I paid my entry
fee, I haven't done anything wrong. Not yet, anyway.
But in the end, no one comes.

It's boring, waiting so long, and I slip the stupid high-
heeled shoes off to make myself more comfortable as my
legs begin to ache. I start to wish I'd chosen something
easier, but this party seemed like a good way to get up
close to Enola and actually get a good look at her. If
I'd just waited outside the stadium she'd go past in a
car or limo which would be no use at all, and the hotel
lobby turned out to be next to useless because she went
through too fast.

I hear another set of people start to arrive very shortly after the final tourists leave, shouting in Spanish to each other, words that I can't understand, doing what sounds like clattering tables and chairs around, probably staff and caterers, decorating the room, bringing in the food and drink I imagine. My stomach rumbles and I remember than I haven't eaten all day.

The shouting gradually ramps up and becomes more urgent before dying down again at about 11 p.m. when the music is switched on. Fucking hell I have been here hours and am desperate to move, I feel like my legs might have totally gone to sleep. But obviously I don't want to be one of the first into the room as I don't want anyone to notice me so I need to stay where I am a bit longer. Except I can't because by now I am absolutely desperate for the loo (why didn't it occur to me to go when I was actually in there?) but I think I can risk going in now if I'm quick.

Once I've done what I need to do, I stand in front of the mirror and pinch my cheeks. I'm not someone who has ever worn make-up. I feel like it's too late to learn now and I saw someone doing this in a TV programme I watched years ago. I run my fingers through my hair which hasn't been cut for several years but likewise, it'll have to do. I think I look OK. When I have done this kind of thing before I have learnt that getting away with being in a place you shouldn't be is mainly about poise and confidence. That got me pretty far last time but then I got caught out and everything happened and I got the restraining order but I won't make the same mistake this time. By now I can hear that what was a low hubbub of conversational noise barely audible below the music has increased, so it's clear to me that the evening's guests have started to arrive. I pull myself up tall, put my shoulders back, smile, and head out to join the party.

It's easier to look confident with something in your hand so I grab a glass of what I imagine is champagne from one of the passing waitresses but then I notice that another one has bottles of beer on her tray so I take one of those instead and put my glass down on a random table. I take a swig of the beer and it's lovely, ice cold and incredibly refreshing, I am feeling quite dehydrated after standing around for so long as I didn't think to bring any water with me. I must be careful not to drink too much even though I am nervous as I need to keep a clear head and not slip up. Also I am absolutely starving and I need to eat something otherwise I will probably pass out. I look around for something like a buffet table but there doesn't seem to be anything like that, however just then someone comes by with a tray of tiny burgers so I take one and shove it into my mouth whole. I notice a woman near me give me a look and say something to her friend and I look around and see that other people with the burgers are eating them in dainty little bites so that's what I will do next time. But that waiter has gone now, another passes with oysters but however hungry I am I can't bring myself to eat something like that which looks and probably feels and tastes like a giant bogey. Burger man comes back again so I take another and this time eat it more slowly. While I do that, I look around and my heart gives a little leap as I see Enola on the other side of the room.

If, of course, it really is Enola. I need to get closer to check.

46

November 2008
Barcelona
Enola

A lot of our parties are in cool places but I have to admit that the aquarium is a particularly good shout. Trixie and Emery seem to want to make sure we are in the press today judging by the longer-than-usual walk to the entrance from the limo and the banks of photographers. Or maybe it's simply that for whatever reason, we're really popular in Spain – I lose track.

'Enola! Enola!' they are calling, the Spanish accent giving my name a weirdly exotic sound with short-ened vowels giving it a different emphasis than usual. En-OH-la. I like it.

'Are you and Max getting married?' shouts a voice which sounds very English among all the Spanish. I look over to see who it is – one of the main showbiz corre-spondents from one of the UK tabloids.

Fuck. How does he know? Is Max leaking stuff? Or has someone else found out? Someone has been feeding little stories to the press about me for ages – my bet is Angel. But as far as I'm aware, she doesn't know anything about his proposal. Or, at least, I hope she doesn't. Shit. Unless it was her in the room next to us at the chateau? All this reminds me that I need to speak to Liam about what happened too – make sure he doesn't say anything to Max before this goes any further.

'That'd be telling mate!' Max shouts, putting his hand in the small of my back and steering me inside. I keep my face arranged in a fixed, forced smile and hope I'm not giving anything away.

'You haven't said anything, have you?' I whisper as soon as we get inside and away from the flashbulbs. 'I thought we agreed we were going to keep this to ourselves?'

'Not said anything, I promise,' he says. 'They're just taking a punt because of seeing us out shopping for jewellery that day. Don't worry about it.'

The room is already full and the music is too loud. I suddenly wish I could have gone straight back to the hotel and gone to sleep or had a nice bath and watched some TV on my own or even read. When did I last have the time to read?

Max takes a couple of glasses of champagne from an impossibly beautiful waitress and hands one to me. He's immediately cornered by a woman I vaguely recognize – I might have seen her on a poster. Maybe she's a model.

Mum rushes over with creepy Dom, bright-eyed and

201

already clearly pissed. 'Darling! You were SO amazing tonight! The a cappella version of "Loud and Proud" was absolutely fantastic.'

I smile. 'Thanks Mum. I'm glad you could make it.'

'Listen,' she leans in confidentially, 'do you think you could introduce Dom to Emery? Like we talked about the other day? He'd be ever so grateful and so would I.'

I cast a glance at Dom who is standing awkwardly a few paces back by a pillar, nursing a cocktail and glancing around, probably wondering who is worth talking to. I can see Mum's attraction to him, he's very good-looking, but also ridiculously young for her to the point that it's embarrassing. And I can't quite put my finger on it but there's something a little off about him too.

'Yeah, I can do, I guess, but Mum, don't you think he's a bit—'

'Young for me?' she snaps, her eyes somehow both fiery and glazed. Definitely drunk, and I've clearly touched a nerve. She leans in further and I feel her spit fleck my face as she speaks. 'No I don't think he's *too young*,' she spits. 'I look after myself. I look good. He and I are having fun together. He's lucky to have me. And after I missed out on so much as a single mother,' she looks me up and down with an expression verging on rage, 'I think I deserve some me time. Don't you?'

I step back from her, a little shocked. While she's often alluded to what she missed out on by us being born when she was so young, she's never sounded quite so bitter about it before. What with Max on about marriage and the thing that happened in the shopping centre I feel like I've got a lot going on at the moment and this is the last thing I need. I know she's given up a lot for me, but at the same time, I didn't ask to be born.

'I'm sorry our arrival inconvenienced you in that way,' I say, trying to keep my voice even. 'Of course you deserve time for yourself. And if you're happy with Dom, then I'm happy for you,' I add, not even trying to hide my insincerity. 'Personally, I don't trust him, and he seems more interested in being introduced to Emery than anything else, but I would, of course, be absolutely delighted to be proved wrong.'

'I didn't mean . . .' Mum starts to say but we are quickly interrupted.

'Enola!' Trixie says, barrelling up to me. 'I need you to come and speak to the journalist from *Gala* please. Sorry to intrude,' she says as an afterthought, turning to Mum. Obviously she doesn't apologize to me as I am nothing more than a commodity, but right now I don't mind. It's probably the first time I've actually been pleased to see Trixie because she gives me the perfect excuse to end this conversation with Mum.

'Emery is over there,' I say to Mum frostily, pointing. 'Dom is a big boy, I'm sure he can introduce himself.'

47

29 June 2024
Las Vegas
Liam

'Well, happy birthday to me,' I say, raising a glass. 'Can't say any of you would be my first choice of birthday companions, but here we are. It is what it is.'

We're in the 'VIP bar' at the top of the hotel which is reserved for those in the most expensive suites, which at the moment means just the band and our entourage because we have all the best suites booked.

'Oh I didn't know it was your birthday,' Sophie says. 'We should have got you a cake or something.'

I shrug. 'Not to worry. I'm happy with all this free booze I'm enjoying on Emery, to be honest.'

'This hotel is the last place I'd choose to spend my birthday,' Sophie says. 'It isn't my kind of place at all.' She shudders. 'Too modern, too glitzy. It's the kind of thing I'd have loved when we were first touring, I'd have been blown away by the opulence, but now, ugh. All this shininess and ostentation does no one any good, I'm sure. The energy is all wrong.'

For fuck's sake. Who cares? It's free luxury accommodation, with food and drink and everything done for us and all on someone else's dime – which I plan to take full advantage of.

'Could be worse,' Max chimes. 'I quite like it. Though I'm looking forward to some time on my yacht in the Caribbean after this. More privacy. Quieter.'

Nice. A quick dig to remind me that we didn't all have an acting career and property portfolio to fall back on after This Way Up. Admittedly if I hadn't gambled most of my money away and put the rest up my nose I might have a mansion in LA too, but, yeah well. Too late to change things much now.

'What do you think about all this stuff with Angel?' I ask, changing the subject. I don't want to hear any more about Max's wealth or Sophie's chakras. 'Forever needing to create a drama around herself. It was always like that,' I continue. 'Back in the day, when Enola was the star attraction, she was constantly livid. Hated Enola for it. But I don't understand why she still has such a chip about it now that she's gone. Angel's getting to be lead singer for the concerts, isn't she? It's what she's always wanted.'

'You're not saying Angel took an overdose for attention are you?' Sophie asks. 'Or burnt her own hands? Why on earth would she do that? Trixie said she looked like she was in real agony. Wasn't she, Trixie?'

'Yep,' she says. 'I only saw her once she'd been bandaged and sedated but she said she'd never known pain like it.'

I down the remains of my vodka Red Bull and indicate to the barman to bring me another. I don't know why I've bothered with rehab so many times – it never works.

'She was always trying to upstage Enola since the day Breathe started,' Max adds. 'Used to wind me up even more than it did Enola. This is probably her way of making sure that any headlines about the concert put *her* at the forefront rather than any of the rest of us. Or Enola, for that matter. I wouldn't be that surprised if Angel did that stuff to herself to make sure she got the most coverage.'

'Don't be ridiculous; Angel wouldn't do something as extreme as this for attention,' Trixie interjects, 'but equally, there is absolutely no suggestion whatsoever that she wanted to kill herself. She was in a lot of pain due to her skin and took too many painkillers to try to ease it. That's all. And I would remind you that in any forthcoming interviews, that is the line we are taking, as it is also the true and correct version of events.'

The waiter brings a new drink and I down it in one.

'Angel is back in her suite now and says she will be perfectly fit for the concert,' Trixie continues, 'and she will tell you the same herself when you see her I'm sure. She's quite embarrassed about it all, though, so I would thank you not to bring it up, please.'

I totally get why that's the line Trixie wants to take,

that the overdose was accidental. A suicide attempt is rarely good publicity, however you spin it.

But I don't think she's telling the truth. I think there's much more to this than meets the eye.

48

November 2008
Barcelona
Enola

After I have as brief a conversation as possible with the *Gala* journalist, I plaster a fixed smile on my face and excuse myself as graciously as I can manage. Fucking hell. I've been so looking forward to this party, marking the end of the tour, which has been so exhausting and eventful in the worst ways, and Mum has to come along with her creepy boyfriend and spoil it all. I've had enough, I'm so sick of them all, I just want to go home and be alone.

I don't want to do any of this any more.

I feel tears coming to my eyes as I storm through the party towards the loos, not because I need to go but because I want to get away from everyone for a while and I'm not really looking where I'm going when suddenly:

'Whoa!' I feel a splash of something wet on my arm –

I've walked into Liam and spilt his drink. 'Watch where you're going!'

'Sorry,' I mutter. God. Could this evening get any worse?

Then I remember that there was something I needed to say to Liam – might as well get it out of the way now. 'Listen, Liam, while you're here . . . you've never told Max about what happened . . . with us, back when I was on *The Chosen* did you?'

His face softens briefly and then transforms into an unpleasant leer. 'No, darlin'.' He leans in closer and adds: 'I think about it often though. Usually with my hand in my boxers. A great night that was, wasn't it?'

I feel a wave of revulsion and lean away from him. The more I've thought about it, the more he – what he did – turns my stomach. He shouldn't have taken advantage of me like that and tonight more than ever I'm not in the mood for his lechery.

'Liam, you know what Max is like. It would really help me if . . . you could promise not to say anything.' I pause. 'Please.'

'You can rely on me.' He looks me up and down, his eyes unashamedly lingering on my boobs. 'As long as we don't rule out a repeat performance one day.'

He lightly touches my waist and I spring back from him. Fuck's sake. He is pissed and I can't tell if he's joking or not, but either way, I can't be bothered with his sleaziness tonight in any shape or form.

I lean in close. 'Might I remind you,' I say in a low voice, 'that you didn't exactly cover yourself in glory that night. I was very young, inexperienced and you were there on that show with me in a position of trust. Now that I look back on it, you very much took advantage of your being a hot-shot celebrity while I was a wide-eyed and easily impressed no one.'

I pause. '*If* I was ever to tell anyone, Emery, the production company, or the papers even, about what happened then, I don't think you'd come out of it very well. There might even be questions raised about whether you are the right kind of person to be in a band like This Way Up, beloved of so many prepubescent girls. What do you think?'

I step back as his face darkens. 'Steady on, Enola,' he says. 'I was only joking. I'm not going to tell Max anything. But you . . . you wouldn't, would you?'

I'm surprised to see he genuinely looks worried. But I don't give a shit. Let him worry – he deserves it. I turn on my heel and stalk off without a word.

49

November 2008
Barcelona
Charlie

I wasn't planning to speak to Enola when I set off for the party tonight – I didn't think I would have the nerve and I don't want to draw more attention to myself than necessary because, well, I don't yet know what I'm going to need to do next. But I know I need to do something. If she's been hidden away somewhere while this stand-in, whoever she is, takes her place, the real Enola might need my help! I choke back a sob. What if I'm already too late?

When I start heading across the room towards her, the plan is to simply hover and watch. But as I approach she darts off towards the loos and before I have time to think too much about what I'm doing, I follow her.

I open the door quietly and creep in – I can see that only one of the cubicles is occupied – coincidentally, the one I had hidden in earlier. But of course I know that there are no coincidences and it is yet another sign that Enola and I are twin flames, even if she doesn't know it.

I try not to be weird by, you know, listening, but it is silent in the room, absolutely silent, and I get the impression that she isn't actually using the toilet, but hiding too, like I was earlier.

I can't go into one of the other cubicles for fear of missing her leave while I am in there but equally I can't stand here doing nothing as it will look suspicious when she comes out. I wonder about washing my hands but I don't want to alert her to the fact that I'm here as it might put her off coming out so I just stand facing the mirror trying to breathe as quietly as possible and not make any sound at all. I pretend to be checking my eyes with my fingers in the mirror like I've seen girls doing in public loos in the past, although I think they are probably actually putting up make-up when they do that. I should have stolen some mascara or something which would have at least given me something to do but I had no idea I was going to end up in this situation.

Eventually I hear a flush and the woman who may or may not be Enola comes out, standing at the mirror a couple of sinks along from me. I try not to look directly at her, unsure of how long I can stand there without it becoming obvious what I'm doing, until eventually she says, 'Hi.'

For a second I think I might wet myself, Enola speaking to me! It wouldn't be quite true to say that that has never happened ever even in my wildest dreams, because in my wildest dreams we are best friends, going on holiday together, drinking wine in her penthouse, she's confiding in me about Max, but even her saying 'hi' to me is something I'd found quite hard to imagine actually happening in real life.

'Hi, Enola,' I reply and then instantly wonder if that was the wrong thing to do – should I have pretended I didn't know who she was? But no, that would clearly be ridiculous, even though there may be some people who wouldn't recognize her, I get that not everyone is a huge fan of Breathe like me, surely people at this party should know who she is? It's fine, I tell myself. Just fine.

'How are you enjoying the party?' she asks, pleasantly. Oh my God. I knew she would be a lovely person as well as being beautiful. I knew it. Some people say you shouldn't meet your idols but I somehow knew that when it came to Enola, it would be fine. It would be amazing.

'It's really nice,' I say, and then before I can stop my myself, 'I'm so excited to meet you!' gushes out.

I feel myself go red. *Argh, argh, argh.* Now she will think I'm just a fan like anyone else and not the person destined to be her best friend.

But then she says it's lovely to meet me too and asks my name! I can't believe it! I almost tell her my real name but then I remember why I am there – to investigate, I don't even know if this is actually even the real Enola, after all, so I need to rein in my excitement. If my suspicions are correct I don't want whoever this is to know who I really am, and I say the first name that comes into my head, Maisie.

And now that I am looking at her straight on, I can see that she looks sad. Strained. I'm sure I'm right about things with Max. That he's unkind to her.

But then I give myself a little mental shake and remind myself again why I am here. To check on her welfare. She does look different. Smaller than usual, like I thought the other day when I saw her in the hotel lobby. Her voice is softer than when I've heard her speaking in interviews.

Granted, there are similarities but . . . it's not her. I'm sure of it.

'Listen, can I ask you something?' I continue, without having thought it through and now, well, what the fuck am I going to say?

She smiles graciously, though she suddenly looks a little wary. 'Of course. But I must be getting back to the party in a minute. They'll be wondering where I am.'

Shit! She's about to leave! This is my only chance. What can I ask?

'How are you, um, feeling now? I wondered if you were OK after what happened at the shopping centre?'

She smiles weakly. 'That's kind of you to ask. It was quite a shock.'

But it's the thing she says that makes me absolutely certain.

'I haven't really been myself since then,' she adds. 'But I'm sure it'll pass. Listen, it was lovely to meet you, Maisie, but I'd better get back.'

She gives me a tight smile and opens the door, leaving me standing staring at myself in the mirror in disbelief.

This woman, whoever she is, is trying to tell me something. She hasn't been herself. She is not Enola.

Something has happened to her.

Where is she?

50

30 June 2024
Las Vegas
Sophie

To everyone's relief, especially Emery's, Angel's skin is deemed to be healing well, the overdose a simple accident with no lasting effects and she is proclaimed fit enough to perform in the concert. None of us ask directly about the overdose and Angel doesn't say anything, other than that it was all a silly misunderstanding about how much she was allowed to take and that she just wants to get on with things now.

Her bandages have been taken off and some glittery guitar gloves sourced to protect her hands while she plays. So all in all, it's pretty much business as usual.

Angel doesn't seem to have been cowed at all by the events of recent days and has been her usual cocky self today, strutting about the place before the concert, making demands of runners for various drinks and very specific snacks she fancies while I am simply waiting, doing some breathing exercises and trying to tune out everything around me. It's more than fifteen years since I have performed and I am really, really nervous. If it wasn't for the financial issues with the retreat I would have said no to these concerts, and I'm starting to wish that I had.

The keyboard starts up the iconic intro to 'Loud and Proud' and from my box suspended high above the stage I can hear the crowd already starting to pay more attention, to whoop and to cheer. I feel weirdly nervous, in spite of having done this loads of times before, it's been a very long time and I am a totally different person. At least, I think I am. Back then, I was vain, selfish, only out for myself. But also, weak and easily manipulated. And now . . . now I run my retreats to empower other women, and at the same time, I have worked hard on myself. I do good in the world, I tell myself. I am a worthy person.

I wish I could make myself believe that.

The guitar, bass and drums join the keyboard, and the cheers ramp up. I look over at Angel who I can only just see on the other side of the stage. She is in short white robes with wings and sequinned white knee boots, I think the idea is she's some kind of sexy angel but she looks a bit country and western to me. It's almost an exact replica of what she wore for the Out There tour which we did just before it all happened with Enola. I'm in a red trouser suit with a demon's tail, a nod for the long-term fans to what I wore on the same tour for this song, thankfully they didn't try to persuade me back into a red PVC catsuit. I'm thin again these days, thanks to the gastric band, but no one would want to see me in anything too tight even so.

The final bars of the extended intro play and the shouts from the crowd reach a crescendo. My faux-balloon basket starts to lower and on the other side of the stage, the one holding Angel does the same. The crowd goes mental. The boxes gently settle down onto the podiums and two bare-chested men in tight silver trousers take our hands as we walk down the few steps to our waiting microphones.

'Good evening Las Vegas!' Angel yells, taking her vintage Fender off the stand, the one she's always played that apparently used to belong to some rock legend – I forget which one. 'Are you ready to party?'

The crowd roars even louder and we launch into 'Loud and Proud'. And almost instantly I'm transported back to the old days, when I used to love this. When I still loved myself. The way I looked. The way my body felt. The way performing made me feel. Why did I let all that slip away? I look over at the extra microphone notionally left out for Enola, with the hideous LED yellow ribbon lights to make sure that no one can miss it or its significance.

That was why I let this all go. Enola was why – and all that stuff that happened. When did I last feel good about myself? It's been a very long time.

Since then I have done what I can to atone, helping the women who come to my retreat, donating to charity when I can. But it's a poor and only temporary fix, the feelings of self-hatred never really go away.

After this concert, I can donate more money. Free places at the retreat to those who need it. Yes, I'll do that. Definitely. That's why I'm doing this, I remind myself. The more I help people, the further I can be from what happened before.

Though sometimes, in my darkest moments, I feel like I'll never be free, and that's when I'm most afraid.

Angel finishes her solo and we launch into the chorus, with new lyrics:

> *Loud and proud, we're here*
> *We're back*
> *Like we never went away*
> *We're here*
> *We're back*
> *We're here to stay*

Angel shouts, 'We miss you Enola! Wherever you are, we hope you're happy!'

Then there is a loud bang, and everything goes black.

51

30 June 2024
Las Vegas

Online news report:

We are receiving news of an incident at the Breathe and This Way Up concert at The Cube, with reports of the concert being abruptly terminated and ambulances rushing to the scene. As yet, it is unclear what has happened.

More to follow.

Two weeks after the Out There tour

221

52

Sunday 7 December 2008
London
Sophie

I open my eyes. Ow. My head hurts. For a second I don't know where I am and then I realize I'm at home in my bedroom, like usual. But something is different. Someone else is here. In my bed.

It's a man, snoring softly. He's got his back to me and I have no idea who he is.

What is the last thing I remember? We won! The Ultimate Starz People's Choice Award. That was it. What a result that was! Though also, it was probably never in doubt. And then after the awards ceremony, what did we do? There was a party. At a club. A lot of drink. Some drugs, maybe. Hope Emery didn't notice. I don't remember leaving. How did I get home? I glance at the sleeping body next to me. God. Not again. I guess that should be how did *we* get home?

I wonder about waking him up, whoever he is, but that would mean talking to him and admitting I probably don't know his name and I just can't face it. Not again. Not yet at least. I need to stop doing this at some point. It's getting embarrassing and if I'm honest, a little bit depressing. Half the girls I was at school with are in long-term relationships and some even have babies, while all I have to my name man-wise is a series of one-night stands.

I slide out of bed and tiptoe across the bedroom and down to my kitchen. I love my little house near Waterloo. The rest of Breathe and This Way Up live in glitzy new apartments by the river or in gated developments up in North London, Enola's penthouse being the showiest of all, but I love my cosy little cottage. It's only a stone's throw from the river and the West End, and it feels way more private than those enormous cookie-cutter monstrosities.

I make coffee in my shiny Gaggia coffee maker which gives me a thrill every time I use it. Growing up in various children's homes, I never expected to own anything like that of my own.

I hear the loo flushing and steel myself, whoever was in my bed has clearly got up and is no doubt going to reveal themselves to me. I'm tempted to rush out to my little terrace and hide, but that would be ridiculous – I'm a grown woman in my own house. I need to stay here calmly and face the music. The worst it can be is a few embarrassing moments, surely? Then he'll leave, hopefully not sell his story to the papers, and we can all forget about it.

Oh God, I think to myself, as I hear footsteps pad down the stairs and he comes into view, wearing nothing but a pair of boxer shorts.

'Hey,' he says.

Fuck.

'Max?'

Oh shit.

53

30 June 2024
Las Vegas

Online news report:

Breathe lead singer Angel Williams was tonight rushed to the Sunrise Hospital following an accident in which she appeared to have been electrocuted during the opening night of the much-anticipated series of Breathe and This Way Up concerts.

'I've been excited about this concert for months,' said Hayley Anderton, a Breathe fan who had travelled from England to see the bands' first performance in more than fifteen years.

'It happened during "Loud and Proud", the first song. It was all going fine, and then there was a huge bang and half the lights went out onstage.'

'There was a lot of screaming – maybe people thought it was a bomb at first and there was a kind of crush and panic as people started running for the exits – but then if you actually looked at the stage like I did you could see that Angel was lying on the ground. She wasn't moving – it was horrible – I burst into tears. And then some medics came in and took her away on a stretcher.

'I hope she'll be OK. So much has happened to her in the last few days it's like the band are cursed or something.'

Former lead singer Enola Mazzeri disappeared in mysterious circumstances in 2008. In a bizarre twist, conspiracy theories are now circulating around some sections of social media that the star is not in fact dead, but is in some way responsible for the things which have happened to Angel and other members of the band since their arrival in Las Vegas.

The band members have suffered an unexplained bout of what was initially thought to be food poisoning, strenuously denied by the high-end celeb hang-out Tazu Tazu. Miss Williams narrowly avoided being struck by a falling gantry during rehearsal, and then suffered what is believed to have been a serious allergic reaction to toiletries in her hotel room, as well as taking an allegedly accidental overdose of prescription painkillers.

Along with the conspiracy theories, some of a more superstitious nature are putting the unfortunate incidents down to a curse, claiming that The Cube is built on an ancient burial ground.

'There was no love lost between Enola and the other band members, that was never a secret,' says showbiz reporter Dan McKenzie. 'But Enola was one of the biggest stars around back in 2008, at the height of her fame, and there has been no confirmed sighting of her since then. It's extremely difficult to disappear when you are that well known. I wouldn't want to speculate on how she died or why. But one thing I'm ninety-nine per cent certain of is that she is sadly no longer alive, however much her fans might wish she was. Someone as famous as Enola cannot simply disappear from public life and remain undetected for almost two decades.'

So far there has been no news as to whether the remaining concert, scheduled for Independence Day July 4, will go ahead.

54

30 June 2024
Las Vegas
Sophie

'While obviously our concerns and thoughts are with Angel,' lies Trixie, 'we need to decide as a matter of urgency what is going to happen about the remaining concert. Angel is apparently responding well to treatment following her electrocution, but it sounds like she is lucky to be alive. It's possible that she will be able to perform, according to the doctors, but we need to have a contingency plan in case she is not. It's only fair to the ticket holders.'

Emery is pacing up and down in the VIP bar where we have all assembled, having been summoned by Trixie once the concert venue was cleared out.

'Fuck. This is a lose–lose situation,' he says. 'If we go ahead, we look like insensitive fuckers and the fans will hate us, and if we don't, the fans will all hate us anyway and we will lose millions. Literally millions.'

'I don't think I feel comfortable performing if Angel is too unwell to do so,' I say.

Emery stops pacing and glares at me. 'I don't give a flying fuck what you feel *comfortable* with, Sophie,' he sneers. 'You will do what's best for the band. And the concert. As defined in your contract, I think you'll find.'

I shrink back into my chair. I haven't read the small print in any great detail, but it's hardly beyond the realms of possibility that he basically owns all of us for the duration of the concerts. It was always the case back in the day anyway – he owned us then too. He made sure of it.

'Though if Sophie doesn't want to perform without Angel, we could make that a selling point,' Trixie interjects. 'Sophie pictured by Angel's bedside in solidarity with her friend. The boys could do the concert anyway. Put This Way Up at the forefront for a change.'

'That *would* be a refreshing change,' Max says, 'in that it has literally never happened before in our entire histories.'

'I'm a better guitarist than Angel anyway,' Liam chips in, entirely inappropriately. 'Although, to give her credit where it's due, it's probably partly down to that ridiculous antique piece of shit she insists on playing. Chances are that's what caused this problem in the first place too. The old guitars, they aren't . . .'

'It's hardly the point though, is it?' I interrupt. Not only is it totally inappropriate, though entirely unsurprising, for Liam to be boasting about his musical prowess right now, he's also even more tedious than usual when he gets on to guitar spec. 'Should we really be carrying on as if nothing is wrong when we don't even know if Angel will live or die?' I add.

'Of course she'll live!' Trixie says. 'Don't be so melodramatic. She's expected out of hospital tomorrow or the next day, all being well.'

I nod. 'Right. Well, it would have been nice if someone had told us that.' Fuck's sake. We are barely even treated as real human beings by Brilliant.

'Sorry. I thought you knew,' Trixie says, distractedly, going back to staring at her phone, scrolling and stabbing. 'So she will be OK, as in she's not going to die, but we don't yet know if she'll be ready to perform,' she continues. 'I made some notes about what the doctor said earlier. She has some minor burns and it's apparently possible that the shock could cause some muscular issues in the short term at least, plus there's the trauma of what actually happened. Whether that affects her state of mind remains to be seen, but given quite how Teflon Angel is, I can't see that being a problem.

'At the end of the day it is not up to us, but up to the doctors who may or may not sign her off as being fit to perform,' she adds.

'And when will they let us know?' Emery asks. 'The final concert is only a couple of days away. People have travelled from all over the world to be here – we can't leave them hanging. We need to put out a statement one way or another as soon as possible. Everyone saw what happened at the concert tonight and it's already in the news, we can't just fudge it.'

'I think what makes sense is what Trixie suggested earlier,' Max interjects. 'Sophie said she doesn't want to sing without Angel. I'm sure Liam and I would like to take centre stage for once. It's been a long time coming, after all. We tell the fans that we're doing the concert without the girls. That way, almost everyone gets what they want; Liam, me, Sophie, Emery and at least the This Way Up fans, if not Breathe's.

'You can put out pictures to the media of Sophie at the hospital in Angel's room or whatever, so it would even be good press-wise, and maybe if Angel's feeling well enough the girls could record a message for us to play out on the big screens at the concert. Maybe even sing a line or two. If she . . . can. You know.'

Max speaks nonchalantly, as if he doesn't care either way when he is quite clearly desperate to finally get what he seems to feel is his fair share of the limelight. As his voice trails off, I see his cheeks colour slightly. I glare at him, but he seems to be deliberately avoiding my eye.

'Liam? What do you think?' he asks.

'Sounds good to me,' he says. 'If Angel can't do it. I'm happy to help out in any way I can,' he adds, clearly insincerely. 'Whatever's best for the concert.'

Is this what this is about? Even back in the day Max never made any secret of the fact that it irked him that when Breathe arrived on the scene and knocked This Way Up off the top spot. While he might have thought he loved Enola in his coercive and controlling way, he also hated the fact that she was a bigger name than him. I think that was probably a big part of the problems between them. It only came out in jokes and little digs in public, but we all knew that there was a lot of truth behind it. And while I have an inkling of what might have gone on in private, for all I know, there might have also been much worse happening behind closed doors.

Max would love it if This Way Up was the headline act for our final concert. It's what he's been gunning for forever.

Could he really have set things up to hurt Angel? To put himself and Liam at the forefront?

He'd have had access to her room – he could have been in to chat and made the excuse of needing the loo. Put something in the shower gel then. He knows his way around a guitar, and probably knows how to set one up to give her a shock, especially that ancient Fender of hers.

But no. My imagination is running away with me. Surely he wouldn't go that far? Either way though, I owe it to Enola's memory, and to Breathe, and to fighting the patriarchy for that matter, not to let him have his way.

'No,' I say, louder than I mean to and sounding more confident than I feel, even to my own ears. '*We* are the headline act. Breathe. Not This Way Up. If Angel isn't ready to perform, I will stand in for her. I've changed my mind about not wanting to perform without her. One of the backing singers can be me, it won't take much extra rehearsing, they know all the songs and the dance moves. Enola is already long gone, there is nothing we can do to change that sadly, but you, Max, you are not wiping me and Angel out as well.'

I catch Max's eye and his expression makes my heart leap into my mouth. It is one of pure hatred.

Fuck. I'm not putting myself in danger, am I? If he was willing to hurt Angel, would he do the same to me? No. No. Surely not. I am overreacting, catastrophizing. I take a deep breath and try to steady my nerves.

Perhaps it is a mistake being so insistent on something that I don't even really want – I don't really care if Breathe front the concert or not as long as I get paid – but it's too late to back down now. I'm not particularly looking forward to the concert, but I don't want Max to win, and I need the concert to go ahead to bail out the retreat. All that stuff I said about funding places for poor women, I *would* like to do that, one day, but more pressing is simply paying off my debts, otherwise the retreat goes under.

When I made the decision to leave Breathe, it wouldn't be true to say I came away with nothing, but I did take quite a financial hit. Emery had made sure our contracts made it very difficult for us to leave of our own accord – we were his until he had finished with us.

I should have taken more advice when I set up the retreat in Ibiza. I realized too late that I am not much of a businesswoman, and have made a lot of bad decisions over the years.

'That OK, Emery?' I press. 'I think it's important. It's what the fans have come here for.'

Emery frowns.

'Trixie? What do you think?' he asks.

She is scrolling through her iPad and I'm not sure if she's really listening, but she looks up when he speaks. 'Yeah. Sorry, lads. I'm having a look at the socials and, with respect, Sophie's right, it is mainly the girls that most people want to see.'

'In that case, Sophie should lead as Angel if it turns out she can't perform,' Emery says, 'and I'll line up probably Aleysha to take Sophie's part.' He pauses. 'But Max, I like your idea of playing a film of the two girls in hospital on the big screen too if it turns out Angel can't make it. In fact, maybe you should all be in that film to show what a caring, sharing group you all are,' he adds, sarcastically.

'I'll go and see Angel first thing,' Trixie says. 'Talk to the doctors. See what's possible.'

'I'll come with you,' I say. 'I'd like to see how she's getting on. Show my support.'

Angel and I have never really been true friends, and especially not after Breathe. Even back in the day, while we'd go out on the town and mess about together, it was mainly for the paps and to bitch about Enola, and I never trusted her further than I could throw her. And after the business with Enola, it seemed better all round that we stayed away from each other.

But right now, visiting her feels like the least I could do. And if I can get a moment with her alone, I'd like to get her take on with all these strange things that have been happening since we got here. Perhaps there's something she knows that I don't.

55

November 2008
Barcelona

Newspaper report:

A 22-year-old British woman was arrested after causing a disturbance at the Breathe and This Way Up after-party at the Barcelona aquarium.

The woman was apprehended by security staff and taken to Port Vell police station.

There were no injuries and it is believed the party continued without incident once the woman in question was removed.

56

1 July 2024
Las Vegas
Sophie

'How are you feeling?' I ask.

Angel smiles weakly. 'It's nice of you to come in,' she says.

Already she doesn't seem quite like her usual self. It's not like her to say thank you, even obliquely, for anything.

Once Trixie found out that I wanted to go to the hospital she decided she was too busy and had other things to do, and she'd delegated the task of asking the doctors what was likely to be possible around Angel performing.

'I hate hospitals,' Trixie had said, shuddering. 'All that antiseptic smell creeps me out. That and the fact that I know that somewhere on site there will be dead bodies. *Ewww.* If you're going, no point in me coming too. I've got about a million things to sort out anyway.'

The boys also found they had sudden other 'urgent' tasks. 'I think it would be better if we spent the rest of the day rehearsing, in case Angel can't make it and we have to move things around,' Max had said, clearly hoping that that was going to be what would happen.

While it's not exactly surprising that none of them could be arsed to come in and see how she is, I imagine it's still somehow a little hurtful for her.

But there's no way Angel would admit anything like that to me. 'I'm OK,' she adds. 'I got them to send a runner in with some nice pyjamas and my make-up and stuff. Don't want to look like a total minger,' she says, with a half smile. 'There are standards to maintain, even if just for the nurses.' She pauses. 'And for you, I suppose.'

'And, does it . . . hurt?' I ask. For a moment I wish I hadn't come. I don't know what I was thinking. I'm very aware that I am probably little comfort, and now I'm here, I've no idea what to say.

'I'm not in pain, exactly,' she says. 'More like a bit achy. As if I've done loads of exercise even though I haven't.' She adjusts her position in the bed, wincing slightly.

'It's not that bad,' she continues. 'Could have been a lot worse, apparently. They're saying I've been lucky – if I wasn't so fit, I might not have survived. So my personal trainer was right – exercise is more than about just looking good.'

She forces out a laugh and then sighs. 'If I'm honest,' she says hesitantly, 'don't tell anyone this, but today I've been feeling quite freaked out by the fact that I nearly died.'

I nod. I can totally understand that. It's something that crops up fairly often on the retreats. Women who have been through something traumatic almost always find that it leaves a trace of some sort – coming close to death will leave a big one. But it feels weird coming out of Angel's mouth – it's not the kind of thing she'd usually admit to, or even the kind of feeling I'd have thought she'd be capable of.

'It's so hard to get my head around the possibility of simply not existing any more,' she continues, seemingly warming to her theme. 'What would have happened had I died? Who would mourn? A few fans maybe. My mum and dad. A handful of random men I've hooked up with in the past might think a passing "oh that's a shame" if they read about it in the news, but I don't think any of them would *mourn* exactly. I'd just become a slightly more macabre party anecdote for them, a dead notch on the bedpost. Some of them might turn up to the funeral in case the press or any interesting celebrities might be there. Which, to be honest, these days, they probably wouldn't.'

'I, um, I . . .' I don't know what to say. What she says is bleak, but probably true. Probably true of me too, except with fewer random men (at least since I went to Ibiza) and no parents. So possibly even worse. Since Breathe was wound up, I've cut myself off from most people. It's easier to live much of my life online, at a distance. Hosting the retreats suits me – people don't come for long – and I have an on-site therapist who does all the emotional stuff – I can't get involved in that. I stick

239

to organization, admin and acting as hostess in a more general sense.

And most importantly, being away from London, and being away from this showbiz world I've suddenly been thrust back into, has helped me keep a distance from everything that happened. Helped me not to think about it. Agreeing to do these legacy concerts was a mistake. It's brought everything back, reminded me exactly why I needed to get away from it all in the first place. How toxic it all is.

'If I died,' Angel continues, 'it wouldn't be anything like when Enola . . . went – almost a national event. It's almost impossible not to compare the two.'

I nod gloomily and we sit in an uncomfortable silence for a few beats.

Angel sits up straighter, wincing again. 'Fucking hell! This isn't like me!' she adds, sounding much more like herself. 'I've got to pull myself out of this. I had an accident, whatever. I need to get over it. The docs did warn me that electrocution can cause mood swings and depression, or even PTSD, so maybe that's it.'

I manage a smile, though I am now feeling thoroughly depressed at how alone and unloved we have both ended up. I mean, if you look at us and the boys too, none of us has a stable relationship or any kids. Angel's marriage lasted about five minutes and she's the only one who's even got that far. In some ways, it's perhaps unsurprising, but in others, it's tragic.

Probably best to try to move the conversation on. 'That's the spirit,' I say, lamely. 'Positivity. It can make an

240

incredible difference, you'd be surprised. Do the doctors think you can perform?' I ask, eager to change the subject.

'They haven't said yet, but I don't see why not. I might not be able to dance, but my voice is fine. I'm going to insist they let me. I'm a grown woman after all, not a child.'

I nod. 'Emery and Trixie must be pleased?' Trixie will be delighted she doesn't have to bother to come here herself and visit Angel, apart from anything else.

'I haven't told them yet. I thought I'd let them sweat a bit longer. Their fake concern is getting on my tits. All they want is me back on the stage so the concert can go ahead. Other than that they don't give a shit whether I live or die.'

'I'm sure that's not true,' I lie.

She raises an eyebrow. 'Really?'

I laugh. The doom and gloom of a moment ago seems to have lifted and it looks like we can return to our usual superficial relationship, thankfully.

'Yes, well maybe you have a point,' I agree. 'This whole reunion thing has been a disaster from start to finish so far, so personally I'm not that bothered if we perform or not,' I say. Another lie. I need the money, and I haven't read the contract closely, but I can't imagine we'll be paid in full if we don't perform. 'Though I'm glad you're feeling better.'

I cast my glance around the private room and lean in closer. 'But are you not worried that . . . all these things happening to you. Do you think it's to do with . . . with Enola?'

She stares at me with what looks almost like

241

incomprehension. 'What? No. Of course not.' She pauses. 'None of this has anything to do with her. It's not possible. That's a ridiculous thing to say.'

'But what if—' I protest.

'None of this is anything to do with Enola,' she interrupts, faux-patiently, as if talking to a somewhat dim child. 'It's simply a run of bad luck. My guitar was faulty. I love it, but it's old. It electrocuting me like that was probably an accident waiting to happen. The gantry . . . yes, in theory someone could have pushed it over, but, really, is that very likely?' She pauses. 'You know how quickly they put up and take down the staging for concerts. It's a brand new venue, it's entirely possible that not all the fixings have been entirely finished off. *If* someone pushed it over, and that's a big if, it could have hit either of us. Any of us on the stage, or even someone nearby if they were unlucky. And the thing with the shower gel, well, that was no doubt housekeeping being careless.'

'Someone might have put it there deliberately,' I counter.

Angel shakes her head and then winces again. Is she really up to performing? She seems determined to get back onstage and claims the doctors say she's OK, but I can't see her dancing any time soon if she can barely make small movements comfortably while she's still in bed.

'But how would anyone get into the room?' Angel continues. 'I really think it was a simple accident. And I'm still planning to sue the hotel.'

The room is silent for a few moments and I feel my

face grow hot. Again I wish I hadn't come, I'm no doubt making both of us feel worse.

But I can't help myself. I need to share my worries or suspicions or whatever you might call them with someone.

'And the food poisoning?' I add. 'Maybe it's not just you being targeted. Maybe it's all of us.'

She shrugs. 'That was just that, as you say, food poisoning. It's hardly uncommon is it? Especially when you're eating out. That restaurant might be famous and expensive, but you've no idea what the kitchen looks like, or how often the staff might wash their hands.'

We sit in silence for a few seconds. Maybe I shouldn't have bothered coming at all. Angel remains a bitch and is clearly not interested in listening to me.

'I've been thinking about it though,' I continue in a low voice, 'if anyone is doing these things, if anyone wants to harm the bands, it's most likely to be Enola's mum. Did you know she's here in Vegas? I heard she went a bit loopy after Enola's death, and no one has heard much from her since.

'She still lives in Enola's penthouse though – isn't that creepy? And then she decided to come out to see our final concert, even though Enola's no longer here, in spite of not being interested in being with us at all – Trixie said she wants to keep her distance. Don't you think that's weird?'

Angel sighs. 'No, I don't think it's weird. Coming here to Breathe's final concert is probably some kind of closure for her. I don't know. I don't know much about that kind of therapy speak, that's more your area than mine. But I can see why someone might want to do that.'

'Maybe,' I concede. 'I can understand why she doesn't want to spend time with us. I've never spoken a word to the woman, it's not like we're exactly mates, is it? I passed her in the corridor and pretended I hadn't seen her because I didn't know what to say.'

'Perhaps she even thinks Enola might turn up, like some of the fans apparently do,' I add. 'Maybe she's here in case that happens – you wouldn't want to miss that as a mum, would you?'

'I really think you're overreacting,' Angel snaps, as if she is trying to be firm and resolute, but I'm sure I detect a light wobble in her voice. 'The things which have happened are nothing more than a series of unlucky coincidences. Nothing to do with Enola, her mum, or anyone else. In fact, I don't want to think about this any more,' she continues. 'Can we talk about something different?'

'Then again, it could be Max, doing all this stuff,' I continue, ignoring her. 'He loved Enola, or at least he'd have seen it that way, I'd say he wanted to possess her, but same thing as far as he'd be concerned, I imagine. I heard them talking on the terrace, when we were in Toulouse on that tour. He was controlling, yes, but they were going to get married. I heard him propose to her, though admittedly before that they were having a row. But she said "yes" to him. And then she went missing before they got the chance to get married, or even

244

announce their engagement. Perhaps he never got over her loss. Perhaps he wants to avenge her death.'

'Have you heard yourself?' Angel asks, sarcastically. 'Avenge! We're not living in a Shakespeare play or an opera. Get a grip.'

'Then again, perhaps this isn't about revenge,' I continue. I want to get all the options out there. I want Angel to think about them. Something is going on here, someone is trying to hurt her, or possibly even all of us, and I want her to pay attention. 'Perhaps all the *unfortunate incidents*, as you would have them, are about the business, the tour. I wouldn't put it past Trixie to set up these things for the publicity. Obviously she wouldn't get her hands dirty, but she could arrange it. Then again, it could be . . .'

Angel physically puts her hands over her ears, as if she's five years old. 'Sophie! Please. Stop. You're letting things run away with you. No one is trying to hurt me, or any of us. None of this is anything to do with Enola or what happened to her. Sometimes these things just happen. Now, go back to the hotel, help yourself to a nice big drink or go and meditate or chant or whatever it is you do instead of that, try and calm down, and let me rest so that I am in the best shape possible for the concert.'

57

Sunday 7 December 2008
London
Sophie

Oh God. No, no, no. Surely not. Why is Max here? We didn't . . .

'Please tell me nothing happened between us,' I say, though a large part of me simply doesn't want to know. Perhaps if no one says anything out loud, it won't count. Shit. Enola is going to kill me.

'I'm rather hurt you don't remember,' he says, with a wink.

'We didn't . . .' I ask. Please no.

He laughs. 'No. Though I'm somewhat offended you look quite so repulsed by the idea. Most girls think I'm quite the catch, I'll have you know.'

'Yeah.' I breathe a huge sigh of relief. 'Well . . . yeah, but . . . you and Enola?' Thank God nothing happened.

Assuming he's telling the truth, that is. 'So in that case, why are you here?'

'I thought I should make sure you got home OK – you were wasted. Do you not remember?'

Small flashes of last night come back. Champagne. Shots. White powder. Something else. Shouting. But it's all hazy, indistinct. Whatever it was, I guess I did a lot of it.

'Um, no. I was wasted, remember?'

He makes a sarcastic laughing gesture, putting his hands on his stomach, lifting his shoulders up and down, throwing his head back and mouthing *ha ha ha*.

'Funny,' he says. 'I'll remind you then. We were all at Enola's. Then you and she had a big row about something and she screamed at you to get out. You don't remember that?'

I put my hand to my head. That must have been the shouting I have a vague sense of. We had a row? 'Did we? I don't remember. Do you know what about?' We're not exactly great mates, but we usually stay out of each other's way rather than argue. She's boring, a suck-up when it comes to Emery and quietly up herself in my opinion – she loves that all the fans like her best even though she pretends she doesn't care about the fame at all. But that's about as far as my thoughts about her go. If anyone starts an argument among us it's usually Angel.

Max shakes his head. 'Dunno. But you both seemed pretty upset about whatever it was. You were so wasted,

Angel asked me to make sure you got back OK, and I'm under strict orders not to crowd Enola at the moment so I don't stay over there unless I'm expressly invited – you know how she gets sometimes.'

I nod. Max tries to hide his jealousy and his controlling nature, but in my opinion, he doesn't do it that well. It's kind of an open secret although Emery and Trixie do their utmost to keep it out of the press, on the whole, pretty successfully.

'I was going to go on to mine after dropping you off,' he continues, 'but you fell over when you got out of the car and I wasn't convinced you'd get up here without passing out on the stairs or something. So I brought you up here and then figured I should probably stay as you were in such a state.'

I nod. Really? How embarrassing. Normally I can hold my drink, and none of this rings any bells at all. I guess he spots I'm looking a bit dubious about it as he adds, 'I dropped Enola a text to let her know I was going to stay and look after you – it was all above board I promise. She probably wasn't pleased, but I knew neither of us would want it on our conscience if I left you alone and you ended up drowning in your own puke.'

I feel nausea rising. 'God Max, do you need to be quite so graphic?'

'I was going to sleep in your spare room,' he adds, 'but the bed was covered in clothes, and the sofa downstairs is tiny so . . . I figured you wouldn't mind.' He raises his hands. 'Absolutely no funny business, I promise. No sneaky touching. Not even looking.'

I tug the over-sized T-shirt I seem to be wearing a little further down over my thighs and wonder how I came to be wearing it. Did I get changed by myself or did Max help me? God. Probably better not to know. 'And Enola . . . she was OK with it, was she?' I ask, tentatively.

He pulls a face.

'She didn't reply last night, I think she must have fallen asleep, but she knows we left together so I could look after you and she's fine about it – she messaged me this morning – I'll show you.'

He keys through his phone and shows me a text.

It was nice of you to look after Sophie even though she was being a bitch. I am lucky to have a boyfriend like you. But I feel like shit now and am going 2 spend day in bed, then spa day tomorrow. See u at rehearsal on Tuesday. Luv u xxxx.

I nod. I wonder again what we rowed about. 'OK. Well, thank you, I guess. And I don't mean to be ungrateful or anything, but I'm tired and hungover and need to have a shower quite urgently so perhaps it's best if . . .'

'Understood,' he says. 'Do you mind if I have a quick shower before I go though? It was quite a long night in the end and I wouldn't want to gross out the taxi driver too much on the way home.'

'OK. Guest bathroom is through the spare room,' I say. I feel a bit weird about the fact that he slept in my bed, but it's true that my spare bed is covered in clothes. I need to get some wardrobes built but haven't got round to it yet.

'There should be towels in the cupboard and some disposable toothbrushes and stuff in there too,' I say. I know it's silly, but I can't help but help myself when they're on offer in hotel rooms or when we're flying – it always seems like such a luxurious thing to have. I've got stacks of the free washbags you get on first class flights as well. If anyone ever wants an eye mask, I'm the girl they should come to.

He gives a salute for some strange reason and heads off up the stairs. Relieved that he is finally out of my way I find my phone and switch it on. As soon as it comes to life it starts pinging and vibrating with notifications and messages. I smile to myself, thinking that it's probably about the awards, everyone congratulating us on winning.

Until I have a closer look. There are too many missed voice calls, all from Angel. Five or six, a couple of hours ago. No voicemails. No messages from her. The rest are, as I imagined, mainly congratulations from other people.

What was she calling about? I'm not sure Angel has ever called me even once. Occasionally she'll send me bitchy texts about Enola, but that's usually about the limit of our communication. Perhaps they were pocket dials.

But even as I'm staring at the phone it rings again and this time I answer. 'Hello?' I say, somewhat suspiciously. 'Angel? Is everything OK?'

'No,' she says, her voice tense and strangulated. 'No,

things are not OK. I'm at Enola's. You need to get over here. Now. Don't talk to anyone about it. Don't let anyone see you. Don't come in a taxi. Call me when you're here and I'll buzz you up. Just come.'

'Why?' I ask, but there is no answer, she's already hung up.

Why is she even there?

58

1 July 2024
Las Vegas
Charlie

I couldn't believe it when I saw that Angel had been electrocuted. What the fuck? Could that really be an accident? Or is there someone else out here to harm her? Who?

Could it even be Enola?

I made the decision to come to Vegas as soon as I saw the reunion concerts announced. Being here, doing what needed to be done, is something I'd been thinking about and planning for a long time. Not as a fan, but because I knew they'd all be in one place. I could finally get my revenge on those who had wronged Enola. I stole a few things to sell to pay for the flight and booked a cheap hostel away from the Strip – there's no way I was paying the price of the hotels around here.

I wasn't planning to pay good money to go to the

concert after having to find the money for the air fare and come all the way out here – the prices they're charging too! Back in the day I went to as many of their concerts as I could but without Enola in the line-up I'm not interested. I'm amazed anyone is. The rest of them, they're just like anyone else really. Good-looking, at least in their day, I'll grant them that, and they can just about carry a tune if the wind is in the right direction. But a fool and his money are soon parted, and there are clearly still a lot of Breathe and This Way Up fans who are complete fools.

I started off small, almost a spur of the moment thing, pushing that gantry over after blagging my way into the rehearsal initially just to have a look. So many people scurrying in and out, all dressed in black, it was easy enough to pick up a black case (speakers? Instruments? I don't know) from the road outside where all sorts of things were being unloaded and carried through by all manner of people and walk purposefully in. I'd checked them out the day before, seen what they were wearing and dressed the same. I got lucky as they were still setting up and hadn't secured everything properly and I didn't really care who the massive metal structure holding up the light hit, as far as I'm concerned, all of the band members have a part in what happened to Enola.

Next, I gave the band what they thought was 'food poisoning' in that restaurant. They were all wasted and blamed Max when I bumped into him, spilling their drinks. The cost of replacing them was eye-watering but it gave me the chance to add some antifreeze to each one which I'd brought along in a perfume bottle and could drop in with a discreet spray – you don't need much to make someone quite sick and antifreeze tastes sweet, so they didn't notice.

But I wanted to do more. First on my list, Angel.

The brilliant thing about hotels is that even though important and famous people stay in them, they are also public places. And in a hotel of this size, with 5,000 rooms, not only was there likely to be a huge staff turn-over, but there was no way the staff were all going to know each other.

Here, because of the sheer scale of everything, it is all much easier than when I wanted to get close to Enola in Barcelona. That time, there was only so long I could hang out in the lobby of the boutique hotel they were staying in which is why in the end I had to crash the aquarium party. It was tricky, but it was worth it, even though I got arrested when I started trying to alert people to fake Enola and got another restraining order slapped on me. But here, in a hotel this size, I can lurk in lobbies or bars or casinos and walk the many corridors as much as I like – it's so huge and sprawling that the chances of being noticed are minimal as long as I take care.

I figured housekeeping was the best way to go, having access to the rooms would be key to doing what I wanted to do, to getting what we had discussed done. In this hotel the housekeeping staff wear a simple black uniform with a tabard, so when I felt ready, I dressed in black and followed one of them through a 'staff only'

254

door looking like I had every right to be there. They didn't bat an eyelid and I'm not surprised – when I was looking in to the best way to do what I need to do I found out they probably have more than 300 chambermaids to service the 5,000 rooms, working around the clock.

Unsurprisingly, it was very different down in the basement staff quarters to the glitz and glamour of 'above stairs'. I walked in through what must be the staff canteen – it was incredibly noisy with no soft furnishings to dull the sound of the clatter and the many different languages being spoken between the staff. There were no windows and it stank of fried food. I headed on through to the other side to some kind of lounge where people were mainly slumped in worn-looking chairs, scrolling on their phones, chatting or flicking through magazines. And then once I passed through that, I got to a huge room which smelt of feet and body odour but was the one I was looking for – the changing room.

As I had guessed there might be, there were banks and banks of lockers but walking along the rows, I could see that many locks were broken and some doors were hanging open. It wasn't that surprising, while people are at work they would want to lock their valuables away but no one's bothered about protecting their uniform are they? Who would want to steal that?

The answer, of course, is me. Several of the open lockers had tabards on hooks, so I grabbed one and slipped it over my head. Then I looked like all the others down here.

I had thought that one of the master keys I needed might be in the lockers too but as far as I could see, they weren't. *Arse!* After a brief few moments of panic, I took a deep breath and gave myself a good talking to. I had come this far – to the other side of the world – there was no way I was giving up now.

I walked slowly back through the stinky canteen, casting an eye around for the piece of white plastic I'd seen them using to open doors when I've been doing my many corridor recces. I spotted one on the tray of a woman who was queuing for food so I queued alongside her and quietly pocketed it while she was reaching for a strawberry yoghurt. She'd probably get in trouble for losing it later but that wasn't my problem and what I needed to do was more important. She should have been more careful anyway.

I had already noted where the cleaning trolleys were kept, and that was where I headed to next.

I held my breath as I placed my stolen pass against the black keypad and heard a satisfying click. I knew I was in the right place as I'd seen the cleaners come in and out of here with their trolleys many times but what I wasn't prepared for was the size of the room, it was vast.

I took one of the trolleys which already appeared to be loaded up with everything a cleaner might need, sheets, towels, bottled water, large hoppers labelled shower gel, conditioner and shampoo, as well as a big bucket of cleaning products and a box of turndown chocolates.

I had only learnt about turndown since I'd been here

watching the chambermaids, working out their routines, listening to their chat, checking out a few YouTube videos and looking up anything I didn't understand. Apparently guests who stay in this level of hotel can't get into bed unless someone has 'turned down' their sheets, closed the curtains (or, as it is here, made the windows turn black at the touch of a button) and put new towels in the bathroom. Amazing. I had thought the end of the day housekeeping routine would just be putting chocolates on the pillow, but no.

I had already scoped out what time the cleaners usually do turndown on floor 50 where the band's suites are to make sure I'm there ahead of them to avoid raising any questions. Jobs like this are all about preparation.

I was confident that the bands would be rehearsing when I went up but even so, I knocked gently and called 'room service' in my best approximation of an American accent like I'd done when I knocked over the drinks in Tazu Tazu to avoid being memorable in any way. Not that someone like Angel would notice anything at all about someone like a cleaner – simply there to serve, I'm sure. I couldn't imagine my accent would even register.

I waited and knocked again, calling 'room service' a little louder to be sure but there was still no answer so I unlocked the door and went in.

The room was amazing, several worlds away from the nasty hostel I was in where I was sharing a room with five incredibly irritating and loud American girls who were here as a hen party, stepping over winos and drug addicts when I arrive and leave. I'd been getting

The Deuce over here every day, which is what they call the bus here for some reason. Angel's suite was at least four times the size of my flat, and given that there were stairs in the far corner I guessed there must have been another level too. Or maybe it went up to a roof terrace or something like that. I was sorely tempted to have a look but then I remembered that I was there to do a job and the longer I stayed the higher chance there was of me being caught.

I didn't bother with the cleaning products in the trolley because I didn't know what they all were, for all I knew it might have all been eco-friendly bleach-free stuff which wouldn't do anything to anyone.

So I came prepared, and brought along my own stuff which I'd bought in an anonymous supermarket earlier that day with cash. I had thought long and hard about what I should do to Angel as payback for how badly she treated Enola all those years ago, she and Sophie deliberately excluding her, but I always felt Angel was the ringleader. She wanted to make Enola disappear, to drive her away, so she could take the limelight, which, shockingly, she actually managed to do! Until everyone realized that she wasn't that good after all, nowhere near as good as Enola, and she quickly fell into semi-obscurity and her celebrity husband dumped her, which she totally deserved.

Initially I had come to the conclusion that I should kill her, but then when I really thought about it, I realized that the worst punishment for someone as vain as Angel would be to be disfigured. I had been keeping an eye on how much 'work' she has done on herself these days, she clearly can't bear the thought of even looking older, so damaging her skin and hopefully some scarring would be a huge deal to her. Much worse than being dead.

I went into the massive shower, took the canisters off the wall and added some thick, viscous bleach to the shower gel and shampoo. It didn't do quite as much damage as I had hoped, sadly, I'm not familiar with the brands here and should probably have read the label more carefully, bought something a little stronger. Never mind. It will have hurt, at least, and given her a scare. There would still be time – I could have another go.

And, just for good measure, before I left the suite, I took Angel's toothbrush and ran it around the edge of the toilet bowl before putting it back in the tooth mug. She would probably never know, but I would.

59

Sunday 7 December 2008
London
Kimberley

My phone pings.

Really hungover, going to stay in bed today – see you next weekend maybe. Result about the awards hey? X

I smile at the phone – Enola hardly ever bothers to text these days. Nice to know she's thinking of her mum! Perhaps I did something right after all. I tap out a reply.

Total result! Congratulations darling. Let me know where and when for next weekend x

60

When Enola started to make it big with Breathe – wow. At first it was like all my dreams had come true. Not only did I get to see my daughter's name in lights and feel all the pride you'd expect which went with it, but there was also more than a certain amount of reflected glory for me.

I made a big show in public and to any journalist who asked on the rare occasion any wanted to speak to me of how supportive I had always been of Enola, how I basically put my life on hold for hers. I didn't go too much into the single mum stuff for several reasons, and anyway, I'm a totally different person to who I was then. Both mentally and physically.

There were some press interviews with me right at the beginning of Enola's career, after they'd done those camera shots of me cheering Enola on in the audience at the TV show and for the first concert, like they do, but after that, they didn't seem that bothered about me any more. I would remind Enola to mention me in interviews, to tell them how her success was in a large part down to my encouragement and taking her to all the right classes when she was a child, and she said she did when she could, but it never seemed to make the final cut. So I don't know if she did or not.

It didn't take long until I started to feel pushed out, and then Enola announced that she was moving out and not that long after that, buying her own apartment, which hurt as Roxie had already gone. Buying an apartment – and a penthouse at that! She was only twenty-three. When I was that age, I barely had two pennies to rub together – any money I did manage to scrape together had to be spent on my girls. And here she was, swanking off to some uber-smart rentals and then her very own riverside penthouse, not a care in the world.

To be fair, Enola did sometimes try to involve me in her showbiz life. She'd invite me to occasional parties, but it didn't feel like enough after all I'd done. She'd buy me nice presents too – the latest phone and even a car one time – but so what? Money was nothing to her by now. I didn't want trinkets – I wanted recognition.

I got the feeling she was embarrassed by me. After years of being dumpy and dowdy I'd finally got my body back and I liked to show it off. Still do, if I'm honest. Short skirts, high heels, low-cut tops while I've still got the cleavage for it, why not? I'm not even sixty, I haven't gone too crêpey yet. Bit of decent make-up – Enola always said I wear too much. But I can afford the good brands now and I like to look good, nothing wrong with that.

And let's not forget when she got together with Max! That was extremely exciting – she was still at home then, so I got to be properly involved. Her first ever proper boyfriend, and it was Max from This Way Up. Imagine! My little girl with the lead singer of a world-famous boy band.

And he seemed like a really nice boy. When he came round to pick Enola up (I say pick her up like he was some kid in a Ford Fiesta, but they always had a driver and usually a limo as far as I saw) he'd sit in the kitchen and chat to me like he was anyone else at all while she finished getting dressed before they went out. Max Heaton in my kitchen! I could barely believe it.

Enola always took ages getting ready and so Max and I got to know each other quite well. And then even when she'd moved out, sometimes he'd pop round, which I really liked. We'd chat about our days, just ordinary stuff, and he liked to hear stories about Enola when she was younger. Enola seemed to think it showed what a nice guy he was, though she didn't like me talking about her with him, so I tried not to, not that I ever knew anything private about her anyway. I liked having Max round, chatting for no reason, shooting the breeze, as they say, it made a change to have someone paying me some attention.

Their relationship seemed to be up and down, but I only ever heard about it from Max. Enola never confided in me in that way. He would press me for information: what she said about him (nothing, she never spoke to me about him), how I thought she felt about him, what else she'd been up to since last time we'd spoken. I'd tell him a bit and sometimes I'd make stuff up that he wanted to hear to keep him coming round, but I didn't actually know that much about the kinds of things he wanted to know, intimate, private things. She didn't tell me that kind of stuff. Ever.

And then one day . . . well, I'm not particularly proud of this, but they'd had yet another big row about him being jealous and he'd come to see me when I was cat sitting at her place to ask if I'd talk to her about it, try to make her see things from his point of view. The rows about jealousy seemed to be happening more and more. 'I'm not jealous, I just love her!' he was protesting, he was upset, crying, already drunk when he arrived and then we had a couple of bottles of champagne, I was comforting him and, well, yeah, one thing led to another. Like I said, I'm not proud, but no harm done. It was a one-off, it would never happen again. We both knew that. And we didn't do it in her bed. I'm not some kind of monster.

When he got up off the sofa, still butt-naked, and bent over to start picking up his clothes, I took a couple of sneaky pictures on the new phone Enola had bought me. I didn't have any plans to do anything with them, and certainly not to tell Enola, at least not then, but it seemed like sensible insurance, against what exactly, I didn't know.

We never spoke of it again. To his credit, while he stopped coming round for the solo visits, he always acted entirely normally on the few occasions when the three of us met, usually at events with other people around too. Enola would never have guessed, I'm sure. But Max and I, we both knew.

I don't think Enola ever did. God knows what might have happened if she'd ever found out. Sometimes I wonder if Max told her, or if somehow she found out, they had a row and then . . . then . . . but no.

He loved her. He'd never have hurt her. I'm sure of that.

61

I couldn't believe it when I saw in the news what had happened with Angel and the overdose. Was that because of me? If so, then good. I thought the bleach in the soap would give her a scare, hurt, hopefully scar. I hope it got her face as well as her body. For someone like Angel, her perfect skin being blemished is surely a fate worse than death. So maybe that's why she took the overdose. They're saying it was accidental, but I don't think so. It all seems too convenient.

I pushed over the gantry, I caused the 'food poisoning', and of course I put the bleach in Angel's shower gel. But the guitar, the electrocution – that was *nothing* to do with me!

They all deserve to be hurt. My firm belief is that Enola went into hiding because of the way they all treated her.

I'm still hoping that one day she'll come back. Max was the worst culprit of course, but never mind, I still have plans for him. It's most important that he is taken out of the picture. Once he is gone, I'm hoping she'll feel free to come back. That's what I'm doing all this for, after all. To get her back onstage. Back in the public eye. Back in my life.

It's so interesting to see the speculation about this latest event in the press and online. Some reports are saying it was probably a simple electrical fault, they're wheeling out all these old rockers who are going on about how they got electrocuted about every five minutes back in the day because of the way vintage electric guitars were set up, something to do with them not being earthed or whatever, and these youngsters don't know they're born with how safe everything is now, they sucked up minor electric shocks et cetera et cetera *blah blah blah*. Other sectors of the media (and especially social media) are saying that the tour is cursed, that it's something to do with the venue being built on an ancient burial ground, that the concerts need to be cancelled before something worse happens. A few believe that the band is being targeted deliberately, but most of those people seem to think it's the UK or US government or other political groups for various ridiculous reasons, because they 'know too much' or the 'illuminati' wants them gone, whatever that means. And then there are those who think it's Enola causing all this, secretly back on the scene and taking revenge.

I sit back in my chair. Could that be possible? I don't

think so – apart from anything else, she is too sweet and kind. I am convinced that Enola is still alive of course, but even so, why would she suddenly come back again after all these years? Perhaps she feels she's now had long enough to herself, living the quiet life, and is longing for the limelight again. Maybe she saw news of the reunion and for whatever reason, wanted a part of it. Perhaps she's ready to forgive Max and the rest of them for the way they made her feel. Or maybe she couldn't bear the idea of Angel taking the role of lead singer of Breathe because she knows she'd be so rubbish compared to her.

Enola would know her way around a guitar. She'd know that Angel liked to play a vintage one. She could probably set it up to give someone a shock.

The guitar nerds say it was most likely an accident. But personally, I think that's the least likely option. I believe that someone else is out to hurt Angel too, and there's even a small possibility it might be Enola.

My breath catches in my throat as I wonder if Enola might actually turn up at one of the concerts! To finally take the microphone again after all these years! I had thought she would probably keep any reappearance low-key but maybe I've got it wrong.

I feel tears come to my eyes at the thought of her being back onstage. If I could see her again, that would be everything. Everything I have ever dreamed of.

If she is going to reappear, I need to be there. I log on to a ticket resale site, barely able to breathe, and am reminded that the tickets cost an absolute fortune to start with and are even more on the resale sites, and I simply do not have that kind of money to burn. Buying those drinks in the bar totally blew my meagre budget – I had no idea they would be that expensive.

What to do? What to do?

And then it comes to me. How to kill two birds with one stone. Almost literally.

62

Sunday 7 December 2008
London
Max

I love Enola so much. I worship her. She is everything to me. I can't wait for us to be married. She is all I want.

I know I can be jealous. My last girlfriend dumped me because, in her words, it was too exhausting having to account for herself the whole time. She said she couldn't deal with the fact that I couldn't trust her. That I always wanted to know where she was, who with, what she was doing. Check her messages. Know who was calling her and why.

So I am doing my best not to make the same mistakes with Enola. There have been some close run things sometimes – I can feel my jealousy getting the better of me and try to rein it in. Sometimes it works better than others, obviously. Like last night, at the party, when Sophie started kicking off – I wanted nothing more than to take Enola to bed with me and snuggle up with her until the morning. But I listened and paid attention when she said she wanted everyone to leave and I took Sophie home and made sure she got to bed safely even though I don't give a shit about Sophie and neither does Enola, but it makes me look like the sharing and caring boyfriend, fiancé, husband to be, which I know is the kind of person she wants to be with. I am nothing without her. I need her to need me.

When we got back from the tour, Enola said she wanted more time to herself until we announce our engagement, and though it hurts, I am trying hard to respect that. She said because we had spent so much time together on tour, she wanted to spend some nights alone now. 'We've got the rest of our lives to be together,' she said. 'I want a few nights by myself. You understand, don't you?'

I don't, because I would always rather be with Enola than not be with her, but I kissed her and said yes because having to be away from her sometimes is much better than losing her. Once we are married, I can worry about this kind of thing much less. Get her to come round to my way of thinking about how it's always more fun to do things together than separately. I'm sure she'll see that I'm right eventually.

I texted her last night to say that I had taken Sophie home like Angel had asked and I was going to stay over at Sophie's to make sure she was OK with it. If she sent me a text like that I would hit the roof – there's no way I'd let her stay in another man's flat! But I knew it would have the opposite effect for Enola, it would win me extra kudos in her eyes. Enola trusts me, and something like that only makes me look better to her because I am looking after someone else rather than just thinking about myself. She trusts me not to have sex with Sophie and I am faithful to Enola anyway. Apart from that one time, but the less said about that the better, plus it wasn't my fault, I was sad and vulnerable, not to mention wasted, and Kim took advantage.

Even so, I was a bit worried when Enola didn't reply straight away. But then she texted me this morning, to say she was fine with me staying with Sophie, as I knew she would be. I'll wait now to hear from her before I text or call, she prefers that. I can't wait till we're married, living in the same house. Then, I'll never need to worry. I'll always know where she is and what she's doing.

I feel a small pang of guilt at telling her she said 'yes' to me when I'd asked her to marry me in the jewellery shop when we were away. Her losing her memory like that after the truck thing at the shopping centre really worked in my favour.

She hadn't said 'no'. She'd said 'not yet'. So telling her she'd said 'yes' was only a little white lie. And it was for the best. We are meant to be together. I am the only person who can make her happy. I'm sure deep down she knows that. I am what she needs. I know I am.

63

1 July 2024
Las Vegas
Kimberley

I am looking forward to the concert in a way. I got Trixie to get me an access all areas pass. I could have just bought my tickets – I can afford it now thanks to Enola's royalties – but there are many reasons I wanted to be able to go where I wanted, when I wanted. I remain Enola's mother, even if she is no longer here. She was the most important person in the two bands and so I feel it is still my right to be included.

Trixie offered to bring me out here when she got in touch to let me know about the concerts – I don't understand the ins and outs but I think in theory, because Enola wrote some of the songs, they might need my permission to perform them – I have someone who deals with all that side of things for me. I don't pay too much attention as long as the money keeps coming in (it had

273

slowed to a trickle, but perked up again since these concerts were announced), and it means they know it's important to keep me sweet. Enola's success left me very well off, living the life I'd always dreamed of. But I put in a lot of hard work for it – I deserve it. None of this happened by pure luck.

I tried to get Roxie to come out here with me but she wouldn't have it – said she was too busy. You'd think she'd jump at the chance of an all-expenses trip to Vegas, but no. I don't know what she does with her time – she barely seems to step away from her computer, and I'm not sure she even leaves her flat any more if she can help it.

I can see now that when the girls were small, I focused too much attention on Enola and too little on Roxie. And while Roxie and I have built bridges a little since Enola's death, we're not close. Roxie doesn't even like to speak on the phone unless she really has to, but we do communicate by email and WhatsApp now and again. We don't have anything in common if I'm honest. I try my hardest to love her, but she was a strange child and seems to have got stranger and stranger over the years.

I think about Enola before she joined Breathe, how she was then. Maybe I pushed her too hard to perform when she was a child, should have let her get on with her schoolwork and hang out with her sweet little friend Becki like she wanted to. I wonder what happened to her? After the TV show audition which set all this in motion, I don't think I ever saw Becki again. Shame really – she

274

was always around our house before that, and the two of them were very close. Perhaps if Enola had had more friends around her once she got famous, none of this would have happened. In spite of all her success, and her celebrity boyfriend, I think she was probably lonely. Roxie has hinted at that now and again, as if it was my fault, but really, what could I do? I'm just her mum.

I am not socializing with the band or their entourage. Sophie passed me in a corridor the other day and either didn't see me or pretended not to, I don't know, I don't care. They've all got much more important things to think about than little old me, I'm sure. But I prefer that, I don't want to be invited to their dinners or parties. I've got my front row ticket to the last night concert and my access all areas pass for the venue, which is what I wanted. Just to go about where I want unhindered. Seeing what I needed to see and doing what I needed to do. Being here feels like closure, for many reasons.

I always loved going to Enola's concerts. I was proud of her of course, but while I was watching, a large part of me would be wishing that was me up on that stage. Ah well. I may still get my moment – who knows? I look good these days. I can afford tweakments and designer clothes. I've got Enola's lovely penthouse to live in and, while I've never found anyone I want to stay with long term, I do all right with men. Sometimes when the papers remember who I am they take the piss out of my penchant for toy boys. They say they're just after my money. Maybe they are, but they're not getting it, and in the meantime, I get to have a lot of fun. The fun I missed out on when I was young and I had the girls to look after. It's win–win.

I've got a lot of years ahead of me. And I no longer have to worry about embarrassing Enola, or have people saying I'm trying to ride on her coat tails. They may still say that even now she's gone. But whatever, they can say what they like, I don't care.

For now though, here in Vegas, I am enjoying my suite, even though it's nowhere near as lavish as the ones the band are no doubt staying in – I had a look online – but even so, it's pretty good. I haven't gone out except when I've needed to, mainly ordered room service, kept a low profile. I thought it was for the best.

I'm looking forward to the concert. Breathe have always done a good concert, and This Way Up are OK too, if you like that kind of thing. Never the same without my Enola of course, but that can't be helped now.

64

Las Vegas
Charlie

I take a shower, dry my hair and then head out to steal a dress and some high-heeled shoes, discarding my other clothes, including my knickers, in a public loo just afterwards. I've got other stuff I can wear later and this is more important. I call in to one of the huge stores, put on my best smile and pretend I'm interested in buying cosmetics to get a free faceful of make-up like I've seen girls doing when I'm in John Lewis on the way through to nick some socks.

'All done,' the annoyingly fragrant sales assistant says. There is so much perfume around here it's making my throat tickle. 'What do you think?'

She is wittering on about the various products she has used – who knew there were so many pointless things you could put on your face? – and I tune out entirely as I'm not even remotely interested. What the fuck is highlighter for example? Or primer? Why would my lips need a liner? I blink at myself in the round, magnifying mirror she holds up. I never understand why women – and even some men – wear make-up. My lips are now deep red and look much bigger than usual, as if I've been punched in the mouth or stung by a bee. There are pinky-brown smudges on my cheeks, my eyelids have been kind of coloured in and my eyelashes seem to be jet black and twice the normal length. But I asked for 'full on glam' and to be fair, that is what she has given me.

'It's lovely,' I say. 'I'll have a think about it and probably pop back tomorrow and buy a couple of the . . . things.'

Her face breaks into a huge smile. 'Awesome! Let me print you off a list so that you know what I used in case I'm not here when you call by.'

I force myself to sit still and wait for the list which I will chuck away as soon as I leave the store – I'm not at all bothered about being polite because there is no obligation – she's simply doing a job which she is paid to do so I can behave how I like – but I don't want to draw any more attention to myself than necessary.

'Here you go,' she says, handing me a piece of paper with a list of a bewildering array of products on it. 'You have a great day.'

'Thank you,' I say, getting down from the too-high stool and walking away.

Once I get to the bands' hotel I throw away my trainers and put on the ridiculous shoes. I consider sitting in a bar until it's time to do what I need to do, but I've seen what happens to women dressed like me drinking alone and I don't want to spend the whole evening batting off men, nor do I want anyone to remember me hanging around.

During my endless walks around the hotel, I've seen that the best place to be if you want to be unnoticed and unbothered seems to be in the casino at the slot machines. I sit at one and feed in some dollar bills, press a button and watch the wheels whizz around. I don't understand how it works but there are spins and bleeps and electronic congratulations but it doesn't take long until I seem to have run out of turns and I can't afford to put any more cash in the machine so I head to the hotel's conservatory display and nick a wallet from some tourist who is gawping at some wooden brightly-coloured tulips which are about ten metres high. I take the cash, thankfully a pleasingly large wad, discreetly drop the wallet on the floor, head back to the machines, choose a different one and carry on as I was. There's something quite soothing about the press, thunk-thunk-thunk rhythm of the wheels of the machine with occasional fanfares and flashes and now that I'm playing with someone else's money it matters even less whether I win or not.

I know from Max's recent interviews that he likes to go to bed bang on midnight these days whenever possible and I also know from checking the socials and doing my research that the band are staying in and 'resting'

279

ahead of tomorrow's concert. So I hope there's a good chance that he'll be alone in his room by now.

Using the master key I stole which I'm delighted to find still works – I wonder if the woman I stole it from was too scared to tell her boss she'd lost it – I go to the fiftieth floor, check the corridor – empty – and knock softly on his door. 'Room service,' I say, in what I imagine to be a sexy voice, not that I'd know. When I feel like having sex, normally I set something up on Tinder and do it with the least amount of talking and preamble possible. Some of the men seem to find it surprising, but none of them ever seem to mind.

Max opens the door, bare-chested and wearing pyjama trousers but it doesn't look like he's been asleep, in fact I notice that he has a glass in his hand.

He frowns. 'I didn't order anything,' he says.

I've read about something called a coy smile before so I try to do what I imagine is that. 'I'm not that kind of room service,' I purr. God this is embarrassing. So far out of my comfort zone. But if I can do what I need to do, it will definitely be worth it.

He looks me up and down and laughs. 'Oh. I see. Well, thanks darlin' but . . . I don't think you're supposed to be up on this floor propositioning people. So I appreciate the offer, but I'm going to decline.'

He goes to close the door but, panicking, I put my foot out to stop it. I wasn't expecting him to say no! I thought men never turned down sex? That's what people are always saying. I mean I know I'm not as young as I was but I've got a good body and I've made a real effort

280

to look nice tonight. Tight dress, make-up, high-heeled shoes and everything. 'I'm not soliciting,' I say, improvising and trying to keep my voice even. 'My services this evening are already paid for. I was told to tell you that Liam sent me with his compliments. He said to say it's payback time for Liverpool.'

I read an interview in which Liam told a story about Max sending a strippergram to his hotel room for a laugh once, before he was with Enola or perhaps in their very early days, but according to Tattle Life, which obviously didn't exist back then but has had a thread pop up about the bands since the legacy concerts were announced, she was actually an escort and they spent the night. One of the members on there claimed the woman was a friend of theirs.

His face changes and his eyes flicker. 'The dirty devil,' he says. He opens the door wider. 'Well, that changes everything. In that case, it would be rude to send you away. Welcome, come in. Can I get you a glass of champagne?'

65

Sunday 7 December 2008
London
Sophie

Angel insisted I don't take a taxi to Enola's but it's been so long since I've used public transport I'm not sure how to get there otherwise. Is there a bus? If there is, I wouldn't know which number to get or even where the stop might be. But as her place is only a little way along the river I decide to walk. Apart from anything else, I'm hopeful some time out in the fresh air will help with my hangover. Why do I feel so awful? I don't remember drinking all that much yesterday or taking anything too shocking. But that's what happens with drinking – sometimes you don't remember.

I go into my bedroom and pull on some jogging bottoms and a large hoodie – if I put dark glasses on too surely no one will spot it's me? I look around for my watch but I can't find it. Never mind – I probably put it somewhere weird as I was so wasted when I got back.

As I go back into the kitchen Max comes down the stairs, smelling of shower gel and with his hair still wet. Shit. I forgot about him.

'Looking good there,' he says sarcastically. 'You off on a hot date?'

When Angel said 'tell no one', did she include Max? She's probably just being melodramatic, but then again, she might not even know Max is here. Or at least I hope not. God. So embarrassing. No one will believe that nothing happened between us – it's not like either of us has the best reputation when it comes to that kind of thing, especially me, he seems to have settled down since he's been with Enola. Though according to what Max says, we're in the clear with her at least, so that's something.

Even so, probably better I don't tell Max anything until I find out what this is all about. Though it'll no doubt be one of Angel's usual self-created dramas which isn't actually as big a deal as she's making out.

'Thought I'd go for a walk and clear my head,' I say. 'You can let yourself out, can't you? Shut the door behind you when you leave.' I don't especially want to leave him here on his own, but equally I feel like I'll come across as a bit strange if I make a fuss as, after all, what's he going to do? He's hardly going to steal anything, is he?

'Yep, that's fine,' he says. 'OK if I help myself to some toast and coffee first? I'm hungry.'

Fucking hell, anything else? 'Yeah, whatever,' I say. 'Just don't leave a mess.'

I pick up my keys, put on my coat and sunglasses and head out onto the street. It's one of those bright, crisp mornings when the sun almost hurts my eyes. But then again, that could be my hangover. However, it's beautiful along the South Bank, passing joggers, dog walkers, little family groups, tourists taking selfies and couples holding hands. Everything somehow seems weirdly wholesome, like I'm walking through a Disney film, which makes me feel even more ragged and skanky. A wave of nausea rises through me and I manage to swallow it down. Why on earth do I feel so ropey? I never usually feel this bad after a night out, however wild.

I'm not feeling much better by the time I get to Enola's block. Her building is still almost empty – there is still scaffolding around the base and it looks like construction workers are still coming and going, I guess fitting the interiors. Though not today as it is Sunday. Enola has the penthouse (of course, so showy) with its own lift so that she doesn't need to go through the lobby like everyone else – she was going on about what a brilliant feature it is when she bought the place, like anyone cared. It was all we heard about for weeks. Because she writes some of the Breathe songs, and because 'All The Way' which she and Liam wrote together back when we were in *The Chosen* makes a fortune because it was used in an advert, she gets bigger royalties than we do. She'd never admit it, but she likes to remind us of this in not so subtle ways like having the most expensive property of all of us by quite a long way.

I arrive at the building but can't find the stupid

hidden lift so I call Angel like she asked me to and tell her I'm outside.

'Wait there,' she says, 'by where they've parked up the diggers. I'll come and get you.'

A few minutes later Angel appears from behind some scaffolding and beckons me over, looking around uneasily. 'You didn't tell anyone you were coming, did you?' she demands. I feel a lurch of anxiety. She looks pale and her eyes are red-rimmed. I wonder if she's been crying, which seems unlikely as it's Angel – she never cries – or if she's just feeling the after-effects of the night before like me. Either way it's totally unlike her – I've literally never seen Angel without a full face of make-up. She looks like a totally different person.

'Why all the secrecy?' I ask.

She shakes her head. 'Not here,' she says. 'Come up.'

We stand in silence together in the lift as it shoots up to the twenty-fifth floor. There are full-length mirrors on two sides which are doing nothing to make me feel better about myself. I take my sunglasses off and rub my eyes. Angel is jiggling up and down and staring at the art deco-style indicator that shows which level we are at even though there are no stops between the ground and floor twenty-five, the whole of which is occupied by Enola's penthouse. There are also a couple of minus floors indicated though – I guess that's the gym, pool and car park? Something like that. Enola was so excited about buying this place that we all heard a lot about it and saw the artists' impressions and floor plans, whether we wanted to or not.

There is a gentle *ding* as we reach the top floor and we step out into the vast open-plan living room. It's a beautiful space but there is mess everywhere, pizza boxes, bottles, a small mirror on the coffee table with the remnants of white powder. 'Wow. Quite the party last night,' I say, smiling. 'No wonder I feel so awful.'

Angel rubs her hand across her face. 'You really don't remember? This isn't the worst of it by a long way.'

I suddenly feel woozy again and put my hand out to steady myself. 'Can I get a drink of water?' I ask. 'I don't feel so great.'

She nods and indicates the way through to the kitchen, and I note the granite worktops and Bocci lights with a mild stab of envy. I've only an extremely vague memory of being here at all last night, and I certainly wasn't in any state to take in the decor. Until I saw this, I thought I liked my little worker's cottage and its tiny, period-style kitchen with butler's sink and Aga, but today all the light, granite and glass here makes mine feel poky and gloomy in comparison. Or perhaps that's my hangover talking.

Angel grabs a bottle of water from the vast retro-style Smeg fridge and passes it to me. There's no way I could fit something like that in my kitchen. I take a sip. The water is too cold and it makes my head hurt.

'Thank you,' I say. 'So what's with all the secrecy and urgency? Where's Enola?'

'Come with me,' she says. 'I'll show you.'

66

Early hours 2 July 2024
Las Vegas
Charlie

Max closes the door behind me and I walk in, still wobbling on the high heels which I am really struggling with even though I've only worn them since I came into the hotel, during which period I've been sitting down most of the time. Why on earth do women wear these? Why are they even considered sexy? What's sexy about aching feet, bunions, blisters and basically standing on tiptoes all night long?

'Sit down,' he says, indicating the sofa, 'and I'll get you some champagne. Unless you'd like something else?'

'Champagne's great,' I reply. Apart from when I crashed that party in Barcelona which kicked off all the Enola stuff and led to me getting my second restraining order, I don't think I've ever drunk champagne and even then it was only a sip. But in a place like this, the kind of hotel I've never visited before and am unlikely to ever visit again, it seems like the appropriate drink.

I ease myself down into the huge leather sofa – somehow even getting into a sitting position is harder in heels than while wearing normal footwear. With relief, I slip my shoes off and curl my legs up under me. I've seen women do this in films and hopefully Max will think I'm trying to be alluring but really I just don't want to wear those hideously uncomfortable shoes any more. I remember I'm wearing no knickers and surreptitiously pull down my skirt a little as Max takes a bottle of champagne from an ice bucket, deftly pops the cork and pours it into two glasses.

While he is doing so, I look around the suite from where I'm sitting. It's almost identical in decor to Angel's. It has the same colours and knick-knacks and even the same picture above the no-doubt-gas-but-with-real-flames fireplace which is burning away – it's mainly the lack of any crackling sound which gives it away as a fake. But I can see that there is no second floor in this one like Angel has in hers. Interesting. I wonder if that's because Angel demanded the best suite in the hotel – it's the kind of diva-ish thing she'd do whereas Max, for all his many, many faults, I imagine would be less bothered. Or whether the difference in suite sizes is because Angel is still seen as the bigger star. She'd love it if that was the case.

He interrupts my wondering by handing me a glass and sitting down at the other end of the sofa. He lifts his glass and says 'cheers' and I do the same. We don't clink glasses as we are too far apart.

I don't know quite what I was expecting, but it wasn't this. What happens now? Perhaps I should have done some research before I came up here but I was in a hurry and I'm not sure 'How to behave with a client if you are an escort' would have garnered all that much useful information. Is he meant to initiate things, or am I? Perhaps I can get away with not having sex with him at all. Although, part of me would quite like to. I was thinking I could pretend to be Enola and without being crude, he's been inside her and if he's inside me then . . . is that too weird? Maybe it is.

'How has your day been?' he asks, which takes me aback with its ordinariness as a question.

'Um, OK, thanks. How about yours?'

I definitely don't want to talk about me.

'Busy,' he replies. 'Lots going on, as you . . . might have heard.'

'I haven't, I'm afraid,' I lie.

'You . . . don't know . . . ?' I can tell he's desperate to ask if I know who he is but can't work out how to do so without sounding like the absolute wanker he clearly is. I mean, who honestly says 'Don't you know who I am?' in real life. I knew it! Poor Enola. No wonder she was so desperate to get away from him.

'Don't know what?' I ask innocently.

He shakes his head. 'Never mind. That sounds like an English accent you have there – what brought you to Vegas?'

Shit! I didn't want to be memorable in any way and I forgot to pretend to be American this time, like I did in the restaurant and when I knocked on Angel's door. I wasn't worried Max would recognize me from the restaurant, I had tied my hair back then and tonight it is loose, I was in my usual clothes (jeans and T-shirt) before, instead of this hooker dress and full make-up and apart from anything else, he was utterly wasted.

But it doesn't matter much whether I make an impression on him or not, or if he remembers much about me. If all goes to plan, he isn't leaving this room alive.

I smile. 'Have a guess,' I say.

'Actress?' he says.

I nod. 'Got it in one.'

'And how's that going?'

I shrug. 'Well, I'm here, being paid by your friend, Liam, whoever he is, so . . .'

His face falls. 'Listen, it's really nice to have your company. Me and the others, the people I'm here with, well, we're not exactly great mates these days. In fact, if I'm honest, we never really were. This is a business trip for me, so it's a treat to have someone outside of the "office",' he does bunny ears quotation marks with his fingers, 'to talk to. We don't have to . . . do anything physical if you'd rather not.'

What? I wasn't expecting him to be *nice* because I know for a fact that he is not nice at all. And part of me kind of wants to, for the experience. Feel what it was like for Enola.

And apart from anything else, my task will be easier

if we can get physically close. Though there are always options.

I drain my glass, put it down on a coffee table and move closer. I gently touch his bare chest. 'You're the boss. You tell me.' I need to stay here, get the job done. I can't simply have him feel sorry for me and send me on my way!

I go to kiss him but he turns his head away. 'Do you know what I'd really like?' he says, his voice cracking a little. 'I'd like it if we could just cuddle for a while.'

He puts his arm out along the sofa towards me. 'If that's OK with you,' he adds.

God that sounds embarrassing and awkward but I'll have to try to go with it if that's what he wants. I nestle myself into his armpit and try to breathe evenly. He smells manly and musky but also faintly of BO and I can't work out if I'm excited or totally repelled by this. My mind is whirring, thinking about how I can move this along.

He sighs deeply. 'This is nice,' he says. 'I don't know if you know, well you probably don't if you don't know who . . . my girlfriend, well, fiancée, she . . . went missing some years ago. I've had other girlfriends, sure, but nothing that lasted. There hasn't been . . . anyone like her since.'

I feel my heart start beating faster. He referred to Enola as his fiancée! I knew it. They *were* engaged! But why were they keeping it secret? And he might be feeling regretful now but that doesn't mean he didn't make Enola flee because of his coercive behaviour all those years ago. She probably left a few months before they actually claimed she went missing – that's why there were those appearances with the doppelgängers, while her management decided how best to deal with the situation.

Not for the first time, I wonder if they even got her twin in to help? I've tried to track her down in the past to check her out, but always came to a dead end. Would Enola's own sister agree to something like that? She's never seen in public and according to rumours, she's a total recluse. But of course they'd have said that! The band management probably used her while they were working out what to do, what story to tell. Then once she'd played her part, paid her off. If it *was* her, by now she's probably living the high life being a 'recluse' somewhere out of the public eye – like Enola is. Maybe they're even together? I hope they are. Enola always said in interviews that they were close.

I rein my thoughts in. Whatever part her management, twin or body double might have played, Max is still ultimately to blame for taking Enola out of my life.

It's a huge effort, but I take a deep breath and force myself to remain calm.

I sit up and look at him. 'I'm sorry to hear that,' I say.

'Thank you.' I think I see tears in his eyes. But whatever. I don't care if he's sad. Enola left because of him. It's too late for him to feel sorry for himself now.

I touch his arm lightly. I want to hear more about this. 'I've got an idea,' I say. 'I bet there's one of those huge baths in here, isn't there?' There was in Angel's suite, so

I'm hopeful this will be the same. 'Why don't we go and have a nice relaxing soak together? We can have some more champagne and you can tell me all about your fiancée. You might find it . . . helpful to talk about her to a stranger like me.'

He nods. 'That sounds grand,' he says. 'I'd like that.'

'You go and run the bath,' I say, 'and I'll pour us some more champagne and bring it through.'

67

I follow Angel through the living room up a glass staircase onto a landing where she pushes open the first door
we get to. Sun is streaming in through the window and
Enola is lying on the bed, eyes closed, still wearing the
purple Vera Wang gown she wore to the awards ceremony last night. Her two giant cats are curled up on the
bed next to her.

'Shouldn't we leave her alone if she's still asleep?' I
whisper, turning to leave. 'Surely this can wait, whatever
it is?'

She catches me by the wrist. 'Don't you see, Sophie?
Don't you remember anything? She's not asleep.'

'She looks asleep to me,' I whisper. 'Why do you want
to wake her up?'

'For God's sake, Sophie!' Angel hisses back at me. 'She's not asleep. I *can't* wake her up.' She pauses. 'Don't you understand what I'm saying? She's not asleep. She's dead.'

I actually laugh. Surely she's joking?

'Don't be ridiculous!' I exclaim. 'Of course she isn't!' I walk confidently over to the bed where Enola's glossy straight hair is fanned out over the pillow. I notice there's a short ladder in the toe of her sparkly black tights, totally normal after a riotous night out celebrating a win, surely? But as I get closer I can see that her skin has a weird kind of pallor. Almost blue. I reach out and touch her hand, snatching mine back as I feel that hers is ice cold.

Oh God. But no. She is fine, surely. It clearly turned into a big night last night and . . . she's sleeping it off. She's just a bit cold, it's still early and maybe the heating hasn't come on yet. I take her by the shoulder and shake her, gently at first but becoming more vigorous with each shake. 'Enola. Enola! Wake up! Wake up!' By now I am shouting. The two cats leap up, jump off the bed and dart from the room. I turn to Angel, tears coming now. 'What's wrong with her? Why won't she wake up? We need to call an ambulance!'

I pull out my phone and go to dial but Angel catches my hand with hers. 'Sophie. Wait. It's too late for that. We can't do anything to help her now. There's no point calling an ambulance. Surely you can see that?'

I look back over at Enola and, oh God, there's no

denying that now that I've shaken her and she's slumped into a different position, lying unnaturally and her skin that weird colour, she looks all wrong. I go back to the bed and gently touch her chest. It's not moving. I know that you're meant to feel the wrist for a pulse, but even when I learnt that as a Brownie I always struggled to put my fingers in the right place and could never feel anything. I feel nausea rising and dash into the en suite bathroom, throwing up pure liquid until there seems to be nothing left to come out. Did I not eat anything last night? No wonder I feel so awful.

I flush the loo and then go to the sink to splash my face with water and rinse my mouth. I dry my hands and face and it suddenly feels too intimate to be in Enola's bathroom touching her things, using her towels when she is out there lying dead on the bed. I retch again but there is nothing left.

I go back out into the bedroom and look directly at Angel, trying to avoid looking at Enola.

'But what happened to her?' I ask. 'How can she be dead?'

'I think it was most likely an overdose,' Angel says, grimly.

'An overdose?' I ask. 'But how? Enola never takes drugs.' We all have to be careful when we're out in public because Emery and Trixie like our image to remain squeaky clean, but when it's just us, or we're with people we trust, we all tend to dabble. Except Enola, who always has a total stick up her arse about that kind of thing. Had. Oh God. I can't think things like that about a dead girl. What the fuck happened here? Unless . . .

'You mean she killed herself?' I ask, incredulously. 'No. No she didn't. Why would she do that? She wasn't the type. And she and Max were going to get married! I heard him propose to her, when we were on tour. She had everything going for her. She wouldn't do this. Especially not now.'

Angel sighs. 'Do you really not remember?'

'Remember what?' I demand. 'There was the awards ceremony, and then we went out to a bar, and then . . . I don't know. I vaguely remember being here, and then someone said I was too wasted and Max took me home. But Enola was fine then. I'm sure she was.'

Angel nods. 'Yeah, she was. But we were celebrating. You were on a massive high, you'd scored some GHB at the club and wanted us all to take it. Enola said she didn't want to, you had a massive row about it, you were quite insistent. You said she was spoiling everyone's fun, accused her of thinking she was better than everyone else, which obviously she did, but she stuck to her guns. Then she told you you had to leave, you refused, Max managed to persuade you, but before you left you thought it'd be fun to spike her drink. Teach her a lesson about being so superior, you said to me.'

My hand flies to my mouth. A vague memory of arguing with Enola at some point of the evening springs into my head and admittedly I've never liked her all that much, neither of us did, but . . . 'Really?' I breathe. 'But then . . . then what happened?'

297

She shrugs. 'We all calmed down, pretty much everyone had left by then except for us and the boys, I ordered taxis and we started watching some MTV while we waited for them to arrive. You and Max took the first one, then Liam went, and I must have fallen asleep in front of the TV. And then when I woke up . . . she was here like this.' Angel gestures vaguely towards Enola. 'I guess at some point she felt she wanted to lie down and moved up here to the bedroom.'

I am staring at her still lying there on the bed. How can this have happened? It just doesn't seem . . . like a real thing.

'But, then . . . shouldn't we call someone?' I say, somewhat pathetically. 'I mean, we can't just leave her here!'

My head is buzzing. There's something niggling at the back of my head but I can't quite work out what it is.

Angel paces over to the window, seems to stare out at nothing, and then paces back again. 'We should, in theory, yes. But we need to think about this first. It's too late for Enola now. There's nothing we can do for her. In many ways, this was nothing more than a tragic accident.'

She pauses. The penthouse feels unnaturally silent for a few seconds and for some reason it makes me want to cry. I glance at Enola again and then look away. I can't bear it.

'However, it's entirely possible that not everyone might see it that way,' Angel continues. She sounded frantic when she called earlier, but now seems weirdly calm. 'You gave her a Class A drug against her will. It wouldn't be a huge stretch to imagine that some people, maybe her family, the police or even the courts, might argue that her death is your fault. That you killed her.'

68

Early hours 2 July 2024
Las Vegas
Charlie

Max goes through to the bathroom and I hear him switch on the taps, and then smell something sweet as I imagine he adds something like the bath oils they probably supply in these kind of places. I pour two glasses of champagne, dropping in some of the Fentanyl I brought with me – it's brilliant what you can get on the dark net these days. It won't kill him and it might not even send him to sleep if he's used to it, but it'll certainly make things easier later on.

Noticing the deep grey robes hanging in the open cupboards, their empty sleeves crossed in front of themselves in a kind of protective hug and with a pair of disposable slippers tucked jauntily in a pocket of each, I quietly ease off my dress and wrap myself in one of the dressing gowns. Partly because it will probably be

300

marginally less embarrassing than undressing in front of Max, pulling my dress off over my head in an ungainly and awkward way where he can see me, but also because I've never in my life been anywhere as luxurious as this and the robe looks so comfortable and inviting. I wrap it around myself and it is so soft that it almost feels like an embrace. It's massive – so enormous that it comes down almost to my ankles.

I push my feet into the slippers – also huge but so springy and soft it feels like I am walking on clouds – and walk through to the bathroom, picking up the two glasses I have already poured and the champagne bucket with its glistening bottle.

The bathroom is indeed like Angel's – there is a large round bath right in the middle of the room. Max is sitting on the edge with his feet on the floor, still in his pyjama trousers, pushing various buttons on a console. Different coloured lights are turning on and off in the tub, and the rhythm and shapes made by the roiling bubbles keep changing.

'Look at all these functions!' he says. 'Madness. I mean, how many different options do you need on a Jacuzzi?'

I smile and hand him the glass with the Fentanyl, putting the bucket down on the edge of the bath. 'Cheers,' I say, clinking mine against his. I take a large sip, hoping that he will do the same, and to my delight he does even better than that, he downs it in one. 'Mmm. Nice. I'll have another one of those, please,' he says.

I refill his glass, place mine down on the edge of the

tub and, as discreetly as I can, slip off my robe and slide under the water.

It's a long time since I've been fully naked in front of a man and, even though my feelings about him are mixed to put it mildly, this isn't just any man, it's Max Heaton. So I'm even more self-conscious than I normally would be in this situation, not that I would ever actually be in this situation or anything like it. I have never been in a Jacuzzi, and I've never even shared a bath with a man. I have no idea how to behave so I try to arrange myself so that the bubbly water covers as much of my modesty as possible and sip from my champagne, trying not to look embarrassed.

I avert my eyes as Max slips off his pyjama trousers and slides into the water next to me. He finishes his champagne again, pours himself another glass and tops mine up. 'Well, this is very rock star, isn't it?' he says.

I laugh. 'I bet you do things like this all the time.'

He sighs. 'Not really. I have all this kind of set-up at home, but it came with the house and it hardly ever gets used, if I'm honest. A hot tub and champagne isn't all that much fun on your own. Back in the day maybe it was, when Enola and I . . .'

'Is that your fiancée? The one you mentioned earlier?' I ask, seizing on his mention of her. 'Why don't you tell me about her?' I'd love to hear some stories about Enola. I feel like I know everything there is about her to know but there's always a chance he might tell me something new.

He looks me in the eye. 'She was a wonderful

woman. But she's gone now.' He moves closer to me. 'I can't change that. No one can, sadly.' I feel his hand on my thigh and then he slides it around to the inside and upwards.

'Can I kiss you? I know that some of you . . . ladies don't like to be kissed.'

'That's OK,' I say, somewhat breathlessly. 'You can kiss me.'

He moves his face towards mine and before I know it, we are kissing. I feel his hand move up the side of my body to caress one of my boobs. He starts to push me against the side of the bath and he gets up on his knees and then his hand is between my legs and I gasp and feel myself getting carried away by it all but then I remember why I am here and that I need to stay in control.

I push myself up and him down so that his head is resting on the ledge of the Jacuzzi and I am on top of him, kissing him deeply, grinding myself against him. His hands are on my waist pulling me towards him and I feel that he is hard and I push down onto him because I am never going to get this chance again and for a moment I want to feel what it might have felt like to be Enola. He lets out a deep groan and I move backwards in the tub so that he moves too, his head sliding into the water and he slides all the way down so that his back and head are on the bottom of the Jacuzzi under the water. I hold his wrists down against the base of the tub and I can tell that for a few seconds he thinks it is all part of the fun and then he realizes it isn't and starts to squirm but I continue to hold his arms down and move forward to sit on his chest to make extra sure he can't move and it doesn't take long until his movement stops but I stay where I am, still sitting on him to be doubly sure, letting go of his arms and touching myself until I come. Then I get out, dry myself off, get dressed and leave, the water in the Jacuzzi still bubbling and jumping. I put the robe and slippers I was wearing in a laundry bag to take with me, as well as the glass I drank from – mainly to remove any traces of me, but also because they all have the hotel's logo on and they will make nice souvenirs. I go back into the other room, take some cash from his wallet which I can hopefully use to buy a concert ticket from a tout, and then I'm ready to go.

69

'What? Of course I didn't kill Enola. Don't be stupid,' I say in response to Angel's frankly outrageous assertion. 'Don't be ridiculous. What's to say she didn't take the drugs of her own accord? No one can prove she didn't,' I add, uneasily. I am not a killer. 'We can tell them that.'

Whoever 'they' are. Enola's mum? The police? I feel my heartbeat quicken. Shit. This is really, really serious.

Angel nods. 'We could say that. But everyone knows Enola doesn't take drugs. It was her thing, wasn't it? She was always on about the evils of drugs in the press, giving us disapproving looks whenever we partook and, be honest, have you ever seen her take anything? Even once?'

I shake my head.

'Exactly,' she continues. 'I don't think an accidental

overdose would be accepted as the truth by anyone. A post-mortem would show exactly what she took – and it was GHB you gave her, hardly a drug for beginners.' She pauses. 'And don't forget about the big row you had with her. Loads of people heard that – not just me and the boys, but some of the other guests too. They might not have got the ins and outs of what it was about, but they'd have been aware of it. There were still a few others around then, though your row kind of killed the mood and they left not that long after. So that's not going to look good for you. They might even find the dealer you bought the drugs from at the club eventually, once they find the drugs in her system and go looking.' She pauses again. 'But if there's no body, no one knows that she's even dead, there's no autopsy, and most of that goes away.'

God. What a mess. No wonder I'm feeling so wrecked this morning. 'So what are you saying?' ask, uncertainly. 'Surely we need to call the police and ambulance and hope for the best? I don't see what else we can do?'

'No. It's too risky. They won't believe you. You spiked her, you killed her,' Angel says, matter-of-factly.

'But . . . what are you suggesting?' I haven't had much sleep, my head is pounding and I simply can't properly process what is happening here, let alone what Angel seems to think we should do about it.

'It's never been any secret that Enola isn't like the rest of us,' she continues, 'and that she's always found all the fame stuff harder than we all do. A lot harder. Plus she's had those letters arriving and the stories about her

306

leaked to the press. That's stressful for anyone. Things with Max are up and down to say the least. She's had a lot going on in her life lately, and not all of it good.'

I swallow down a wave of nausea. Those letters we sent seemed like a laugh at the time, a practical joke. We thought it was hilarious coming up with the wording, imagining her reading them, wondering if she'd take them seriously or dismiss them as trivial nonsense. But now they're starting to take on a whole different complexion.

'I think we should hide her body, and set things up to look like she's gone missing,' Angel states baldly. 'People can assume she's done a Walter Mitty or that she's killed herself, as they wish. It doesn't really matter either way, as long as it puts us in the clear, or rather, *you* in the clear.'

'But . . . it's too late for that, isn't it?' I counter. 'Enola's . . . still here.' I can't bring myself to refer to her body, to make it even more real. She is still Enola, even if she's dead, surely? 'Eventually someone will find her. We'll need to tell the police,' I say firmly. 'It's the best thing to do. Anything else . . . it's too risky. As well as simply being wrong.' I take my phone out again but I hesitate as a thought strikes me. 'Why did you call me about this anyway? Why didn't you call the police?'

She touches my arm gently. 'Because I care about you, Sophie,' she says, softly. 'And I know that even though you spiked her drink, you probably didn't intend to kill her.'

'Of course I didn't mean to kill her!' I snap. I'm starting to feel sick again as the implications of what has happened sink in. And what a load of bollocks. Angel doesn't give one shiny shit about me. There's something else going on here.

'OK, if I'm honest, this doesn't look good for me either,' she adds, obviously seeing that I'm not buying what she's saying. 'Even on the off chance the police did believe she took the drugs of her own accord, which is extremely unlikely, both of our careers would be over. A drugs death isn't good for our profile – suspicions would always remain. The fans would hate it, and Emery would no doubt cancel our contracts and make sure we were finished in the industry – he's a powerful man, as we all know. That would be it for us both, no question.'

My head is spinning. I can't process this. It's too much.

'It's too late for Enola. But it's not too late for you,' she simpers. 'If we get rid of her body, we can keep ourselves out of it.'

I can't believe she's really suggesting this.

'So . . . what are you thinking we should do? How would we even get her out of the building without people seeing? And where would we . . .' I want to ask where we'll put her, but it feels too macabre. God. What is wrong with me? Why am I even considering this?

'Getting her out – easy. She's so petite I reckon we can fit her into a big suitcase. I've had a look around the penthouse and there are several that might work. As for where to put her . . . I've had a few ideas. Obviously it's vital that once she's gone, she's gone. If her body is found, there'll be a full-on murder investigation and we're back to square one. Only worse.' She pauses. 'Square minus one? Is there such a thing?'

I'm appalled that I'm even listening to this. And horrified that Angel already seems to have thought this through in such detail. 'No,' I say. 'I know we weren't exactly mates with her, but Enola was a person. She deserves better than that, just being . . . dumped somewhere like rubbish.'

Angel shrugs. 'It's your call. But what you did amounts to manslaughter. And if it comes to it, I'm saving my skin. You poisoned her, not me. If you'd rather I tell the police that, then fine, I'll do that.'

I feel a flash of anger combined with fear as Angel finally shows her true colours.

'What I suggest will result in a better outcome for both of us,' she continues, 'but if you choose to tell the police what happened, it will certainly be you who will bear the brunt of it. The maximum sentence for manslaughter is life, I just looked it up.

'Granted, you may get less than that given the circumstances,' she adds, 'it's not as if you're a drunk driver or something. And you probably didn't mean to kill her.'

'Probably!' I shriek. 'Of course I didn't!'

Angel ignores me and carries on as if I haven't spoken. 'But I'd say that taking into account the involvement of Class A drugs, your profile, and Enola being who she was, they'd feel they need to make an example of you, and you'd almost certainly be spending a good few years inside. Do you really think you could cope with that? I know I couldn't.' She shudders. 'I'd rather be dead.'

I don't know much about prison beyond what I've seen on TV, but Angel is right – I wouldn't be able to cope. And, whatever happened last night, and however awful the consequences, nothing can be done to change it now.

'But why are you helping me?' I ask again. 'It's not . . . well, it's not like we're really *friends* is it?'

She gives me a dark smile. 'I'm not quite as heartless as you might think, Sophie. I thought I'd give you the chance to save yourself. And as I said, I don't think you killing Enola would be particularly great for my career, as things stand. But, cards on the table, there *is* something I want in return, and I think you'll find it's a small price to pay.'

70

2 July 2024
Las Vegas

Online news report:

Lead singer of boy band This Way Up Max Heaton was found dead in his suite at the Jupiter Hotel in Las Vegas this morning.

His room was opened by hotel staff when he failed to turn up for a concert rehearsal.

According to unconfirmed reports, the singer was found dead in the bath, and appears to have drowned. An empty bottle of champagne and a single glass were found on the edge of the bathtub.

A spokesperson for the Jupiter Hotel where Mr Heaton, the other members of This Way Up, Breathe and their entourages are staying said: 'We are deeply saddened by this tragic turn of events.

'While a full investigation will be carried out, Mr Heaton was alone in his room when he was found and there is no suggestion that this is anything other than an awful accident.'

There has been speculation that the comeback concerts are 'cursed' after Breathe lead singer Angel Williams experienced chemical burns and then electrocution, and both bands suffered from suspected food poisoning after eating in the hip celebrity hang-out Tazu Tazu, an accusation strongly denied by the restaurant.

A British Breathe fan who did not wish to be named said: 'It's awful about Max of course but what I really want to know is if the concert I booked tickets for is going to go ahead. I've spent a fortune on plane tickets and a hotel room, and now it might turn out it's all for nothing.'

It's not only in recent days that the bands have had a run of bad luck. Back in 2008, lead singer Enola Mazzeri went missing and no trace of her has been found since, dead or alive.

'Some people say this is Enola's doing,' says showbiz reporter, Trey Knightly. 'Some are claiming that all these unfortunate events are down to her, back from hiding, somehow entirely off grid for several years, and out for revenge. Others seem to think it's her ghost, seeking revenge from beyond the grave.

'But obviously that is nonsense. The incidents which have befallen the band members since they arrived in Las Vegas are no more than a series of unfortunate accidents, and perhaps, though we shouldn't speculate, sadly, a suicide. What we are all waiting to hear about now is if the final concert will go ahead.'

71

2 July 2024
Las Vegas
Sophie

'The final concert will have to go ahead,' Emery is saying.
'There is simply no question of cancelling it. It will cost
us an absolute fortune given that we are already going
to have to refund the people who came to the first one
as it was cut off so prematurely. I'm not going to be out
of pocket just because someone decided to get too pissed
and fall asleep in the bath. God knows if our insurance
would cover cancellation on those grounds and even if
it did, it will take months or even years to sort out. Not
to mention the loss of goodwill with the fans. And the
venue. I've got plenty of other bands I wanted to send
here, and if I find—'

'We can call it a tribute concert,' Trixie interrupts,

cutting off Emery's rant in full flow, thankfully. 'Get everyone lighting up their phones and waving them around while Liam sings "U and Me". We'll set up an online book of condolence and see if we can get the lights made into something which looks like a wreath spelling out Max's name for the back of the stage. I'll get on to that right now.' She goes back to her phone and starts frantically scrolling and tapping out messages.

I open my mouth to say that all sounds pretty taste-less but quickly close it again. I've got my own reasons for wanting the concert to go ahead so good taste will have to take a back seat for now.

'Those rumours have ramped up about all the stuff that's been happening being down to Enola again,' Trixie adds. 'Some people really do have nothing better to do than spend all day online coming up with conspir-acy theories,' she mutters, still scrolling and jabbing. 'It's totally beyond me how anyone finds the time.'

'Thankfully Angel has been cleared to perform with a few caveats from the doctors about what she can and can't do, otherwise the stage really would be half empty,' Emery says tactlessly. 'Liam, obviously you will take Max's part. I'll tee up one of the better backing singers to do yours – Kyle plays guitar, doesn't he?' He pauses. 'Actually, no, tell you what, let's have two of them acting as Max, one playing guitar, the other singing. Maybe Kyle and Ronan. Make the point that Max can't be replaced just like that.'

315

He looks at Trixie for approval and she looks up from her phone and nods. 'Like it,' she says. 'Like it a lot.'

'Though it could be argued,' Angel interjects, 'that as we are simply going ahead with the concert anyway, he *can* be replaced just like that?'

Emery shoots her a look. 'With that kind of attitude, perhaps we should be looking to replace you too,' he sneers. 'Especially now that you can't perform to the best of your abilities after your various unfortunate incidents?'

Unusually, Angel turns deep red. 'It's hardly my fault if you send us to a venue with dodgy electrics and put us up in a hotel where the chambermaids can't tell the difference between bleach and shower gel,' she spits back. 'I'm lucky to be alive. I'm still considering suing, you know. Perhaps I should include you in my lawsuit, as it's at your behest that I'm here at all.'

'Children, this is getting us absolutely nowhere,' Trixie interrupts.

'Absolutely agree,' Emery says. 'Let's get on with this so we can all do what we need to do and go home. Tomorrow, we rehearse, again. I'll get some suitable words written about Max from somewhere. Maybe we can do a song we don't usually do in his honour, I'll have a think about that. Bit like when Elton did that "Candle in the Wind" version at Diana's funeral, that kind of thing.'

Not sure comparing Max with Princess Diana is especially appropriate, but I don't say anything.

'Then the concert is going ahead, come hell or high-water. After that, we go home and I hope I never have to see any of you again. I don't think I can have been in my right mind when I agreed to this reunion – I must have simply been blinded by the amount of money I could make. But this is not an experience I want to repeat.'

72

Sunday 7 December 2008
London
Sophie

'You want me to quit the band?' I repeat. It seems like both the most and least obvious thing for Angel to ask of me. The success of Breathe and who is going to be lead singer is surely the least appropriate thing that could be on our minds, or that we should be discussing right now. But at the same time, Angel has always hated that she isn't lead singer, she's never made any secret of that, and with Enola gone, being the self-serving bitch that she is, it's bound to have been the first thing that came to her mind.

'Uh, but I don't think it works like that does it?' I say. 'As far as I remember, our contracts are water-tight. Emery made sure of that – I don't get to leave just because I feel like it.'

'I'm sure you can come to some arrangement,' Angel says briskly, 'plead special circumstances because of Enola's death, say you're too traumatized to go on or whatever. The worst that'll happen is that you'll get cut out of future royalties or something like that. Maybe have to pay back a few thousand or so, but you've got the money – you can afford it.'

'What? Why should I do that?' I splutter.

'But you're right about our contracts being very restrictive,' she continues, totally ignoring me, 'and it is because of our terms and conditions that I can't simply *choose* to go solo, Emery would make sure of that. But were you to *leave* that would be different – as obviously then there would only be me left. Then I'd get the solo career I'd wanted in the first place – I never wanted to be lumped in with the rest of you. Of the three of us, I was the only one that originally auditioned alone for *The Chosen*. Did you know that?'

What? Why is she going on about this now?

I open my mouth to say something – I'm not even sure what, but she interrupts.

'It's absolutely your decision, Sophie, I don't want to make you do anything you don't want to do,' she says. 'If you'd rather go to prison, then that's fine. Entirely up to you. Say the word and we'll call the police.' She says this as if she's offering me the choice of Wagamama or Pizza Express, something that doesn't matter and are both equally appealing in their own way.

'But we need to decide now, for obvious reasons,' she

adds, tilting her head towards Enola. 'We can't afford to hang around while you read the small print of your contract and negotiate with Emery.'

Oh God. Am I really going to do this?

I can't go to prison. I just can't.

'OK,' I agree. 'We'll do this. And then once the news is out about Enola going missing, I'll tell Emery that I'm leaving Breathe.'

73

3 July 2024
Las Vegas
Sophie

I still can't believe the size of this place – apparently it seats 20,000 people. We've played bigger concerts before at places like Wembley and Camp Nou, but somehow this feels massive, probably because of being indoors, or perhaps it's that infinity staging thing they've done with the magic lights.

Then again, maybe it's because we know it's our last concert ever. Perhaps because there are fewer of us onstage and it feels weird. Perhaps because I have finally found the strength to make an important decision and I know what I'm going to do. And because of that, nothing will ever be the same again after tonight.

I look at 'Enola's' empty microphone stand and for a second I feel like I might throw up. She is not going to reappear, I know that. But I feel her presence, all the time. Every day. I've tried to escape it, but I can't. She is always there. I need to finish this. Make things right. Do something I should have done many years ago. It's the only way I can find peace, I'm sure of it.

Max's death cemented it for me. Not because I had any particular affection or positive emotions towards Max – I don't – but it made me realize just how messed up this all is. People dying because of jealousy and greed. I can't let things drift on in the same way for ever and ever. It's karmically wrong. I need to take action.

The new 'Max' wreath in lights has already been lit at the back of the stage. Though it's not a physical wreath in any sense at all – it's a massive LED screen with the word picked out in what feels like 1,000 gaudy colours, with lilies and other flowers all around the edge. It's about the most tasteless thing I've ever seen.

One verse of 'Loud and Proud' has been rewritten as a tribute to Max, and it is terrible, with the worst kind of rhymes and references imaginable. I know they were short of time, but whoever did it included these lines:

> *We lost a beautiful spirit,*
> *But sometimes that's how it goes, innit?*

And:

> *So devastating to lose thee*
> *In the Jacuzzi.*

For fuck's sake.

Just awful. But really, none of it matters now. I have decided what I'm going to do, and after tomorrow, it will all be over.

74

Sunday 7 December 2008
London
Sophie

Getting Enola into the suitcase is horrific. Her limbs have already stiffened and even though she is tiny, it's a real struggle and there is a point at which I worry we're going to have to cut off a limb to make her fit. I vow to myself that if it comes to that, I'm going to change my mind, call the police and do the prison time.

Is this really the best way to get her out of the building? Couldn't we have rolled her up in a rug? I'm sure I saw a TV show where they did that. That would probably leave us more open to being spotted though.

Angel and I are both sweating by the time she is finally in and the case is closed, and I'm already starting to wonder if I am doing the right thing. But sadly, I guess there is no 'right thing' in this kind of situation. All the options are horrific, just in different ways.

'So what now?' I ask. 'What are we going to do with her?' I pause. At least putting Enola in the suitcase has taken away the problem of getting her out of here without being seen.

'Are we putting her in the river?' I continue, as, being so close to the water, this has been my assumption. 'Shouldn't we have weighted the suitcase?'

Angel shakes her head. 'No. We might be seen throwing her in. Plus there's too much risk of her floating, or eventually the case might disintegrate and then . . . anyway, no. That's a terrible idea.'

'I assume you've got a better one?' I snap. Fuck. What is happening here? How did I end up talking about how to dispose of a body in a dead woman's penthouse? Perhaps this is a nightmare. Perhaps I will wake up soon.

'As it happens, I do,' Angel says, smugly. 'They're pouring the concrete for the floor of the gym downstairs tomorrow. I live in the next block along which has the same road entry point and there's a sign telling residents that we won't have vehicle access during certain hours because of the lorries. If we can put her in there, once the concrete is in, we're home and dry.'

'But . . . won't the workmen see the suitcase?'

She shakes her head. 'I don't think so. They've already done something similar in my building – if it's anything like what they're doing there we can drop the case down quite deep and cover it with debris hopefully. Let's go and have a look, and if it doesn't look like it's going to be a goer, we'll think of something else.'

* * *

We go down in the private lift all the way to minus 1. When the door at the back of the lift opens – the opposite side to where we got in – and we look out into literally pitch black – there is nothing to be seen at all. I stifle the urge to scream – it feels like we are looking into an abyss, or into hell. *Stop being so melodramatic*, I tell myself. It's not hell or an abyss of any sort. It's an unfinished underground gym. That's all. The area above is going to be a garden, I remember Enola wanging on about that now – yet another plus of her amazing penthouse, so much better than anything else anyone was living in.

I am too old to be afraid of the dark. Even so, I keep my finger firmly on the 'open door' button while I gather my thoughts instead of simply stepping out. 'Have you got a torch?' I ask Angel. 'We need some light.'

She puts her hand in her pocket, fishes out her phone and switches the torch on.

It doesn't give out a lot of light but it's just about enough. Bloody hell. It's somehow even more frightening now we can see what is in front of us. It's still a black void, with no floor. Instead, there are kind of wire columns sticking up into what I can't help but think of as a dark chasm.

'They're pouring the concrete tomorrow,' Angel says. 'And as you see it's black as night down here. As far as I know, the cement comes in via a big pipe from outside from one of those lorries which go round and round – what are they called – cement mixers?' She pauses. 'I saw them doing that when they did ours. But even if it's not quite that, I don't think they're going to be in here peering down into the ground and looking too closely. Do you see how deep it is?'

Angel aims her torch downwards where at least six feet below us, quite possibly more, I can see a rough floor covered with what looks like loose stones. 'The case is black, isn't it?' she continues. 'I reckon if we put it down there and chuck a few stones over, the chances of it being spotted in low light are minimal, even if there is any need for anyone to come in and look in here tomorrow, which I doubt there is. And once the concrete has gone in . . . well. They're not going to dig it up without a very good reason, are they?'

We peer down into the darkness together. It's a horrific idea, unconscionable, but . . . I can't think of a better one. And the more I think about it, the more convinced I become that I can't go to prison.

I feel tears threaten again – why did I spike Enola's drink? What a stupid, ridiculous thing to do. I have taken her life and ruined mine probably, just because of some stupid, petty jealousy. What was our row even about? I don't remember. Whatever it was, it certainly wasn't worth this.

Right now, I'm not particularly bothered about Angel ejecting me from the band. I don't think I want anything to do with this kind of world any more. Living with the knowledge that I've taken someone's life? That's going to be hard.

But it's too late to do anything about that. And I imagine I can do more to repent and atone on the outside than I could rotting away in a prison cell. I can do something to help others, surely. I am going to make sure I do.

'OK,' I say. 'Let's do it.'

In life, Enola was petite, but in death, she seems to weigh an absolute ton. The suitcase has wheels but one seems to be stuck and manoeuvring it into the lift seems to take for ever. On our way back up to the penthouse earlier we stopped off and stole a ladder, there is plenty of this kind of stuff lying around as almost the entire place is still a building site.

'Right then,' Angel says as the lift door opens. 'We'll drop the case and then climb down to put some stones and stuff over it. That make sense?'

'I guess,' I agree. She pushes the case to the edge of the lift and it pitches forward, landing with a surprisingly loud thud. It feels entirely disrespectful and unceremonious, and even though I am not a religious person, I find myself mentally saying a little prayer. *Please, God, forgive me. Look after Enola. But let me be OK too. I will make it up to you. And her. I'm sorry. I really am.*

'Now we need to climb down and cover it up,' Angel says, brisk and businesslike. Part of me wishes she'd say 'her' rather than 'it' – Enola is still a person after all, isn't she? But perhaps that would make things worse. Perhaps Angel is referring to the suitcase rather than Enola herself, maybe trying to distance herself in the same way that I am. But even so, how can she be so calm?

She lowers the ladder and rests it against the wall

next to the lift. 'I'll stay here keeping the lift door open and shining the torch,' she says, taking her phone from her pocket and switching the torch on. 'Between the light from the lift and the phone torch there'll be enough for you to see what you're doing. You go down and cover the case in stones.'

I look at her in horror. 'Me? Why me? Why can't you climb down? This was your idea after all.'

Even in the dim light I can see her face harden. '*Might* I remind you that I am doing you a favour here Sophie?' she hisses. 'If you want to bin this off and call the police, that's fine. It's up to you.'

'OK, I'll go,' I snap. 'But promise you'll keep the light on me all the time?'

'Of course,' she says, 'but get on with it, will you? It's creeping me out being down here.'

I don't like ladders at the best of times and all of the current circumstances are obviously making my fears worse. I gingerly step onto the first rung and make my way slowly down. Angel is true to her word and keeps the light on me, but as I finally reach the bottom and step off a thought occurs to me – what if she pulls the ladder up and away? What if she leaves me here in the blackness with nothing but a dead body for company? Would I even be able to get out by myself? Could this whole thing be a complete set-up? Is she planning to leave me here with the body and call the police or, God, to be covered with concrete for ever?

I feel my heartbeat quicken and take a deep breath. No. Even if I couldn't climb up I could call out – I'm not

going to be buried alive. But being left with the body –
Enola – that remains a possibility, doesn't it? But I'm
here now. I'll need to trust. Get on with it, and get out as
quickly as possible.

'Now get some stones and cover up the case as best
you can,' Angel says. She casts the dim light of the torch
around. 'Look. There's some decent rubble over there,'
she adds, indicating a pile a couple of metres away from
me. 'But it's almost impossible to see the case even as it
is so we should be OK.'

'I'll cover it up though, better to be sure,' I say. As I
move to the left a little towards the pile of stones, suddenly the light goes out and I am plunged into darkness.

75

4 July 2024
Las Vegas
Sophie

I thought the atmosphere at the concert might be somehow more muted tonight after Max's death, but if anything, the crowd seems even more excited than on the first night. Admittedly last time we didn't get too far through the playlist before it all went entirely pear-shaped, so maybe things would have ramped up later, but tonight, I thought it would be kind of sombre. Funereal, even. But no.

The crowd is screaming – nothing particularly coherent – that seems to be the one thing that Trixie and Emery hadn't thought through when they came up with the idea of us having a reunion concert together. Back in the day, at the boys' concerts they'd chant 'This Way Up, This Way up,' while stamping their feet or clapping their hands, and at ours 'Breathe, Breathe,' or, if I'm honest, more often 'E-NO-LA, E-NO-LA', but now they don't know what to chant because we are two bands and some are their fans and some are ours. I imagine most are still Enola's, and she's not here. Emery should have thought of a name. Anyway, it is too late now and none of this matters. It will all be over very soon – that's the most important thing. I can't wait.

We are hanging above the stage in our pretend balloon baskets, me on one side, Angel on the other, Liam waiting in the wings to run on after we land. Fuck! How did it come to this?

The opening follows the same pattern as originally planned – the music building to a crescendo before we make our respective entrances. Angel walks gently rather than leaping and bounding down the steps, and looks like she's leaning harder than usual on the silver trouser-clad dancers. But once we meet Liam in the middle of the stage, the music suddenly dies and the lights go down on the stage. There is a gasp from the audience as the auditorium is left in total blackness, bar the hideous enormous 'Max' wreath at the back of the set still illuminating the stage and the first few rows.

'This one is for my friend and colleague Max,' Liam says into his mic in a sorrowful, gravelly voice. 'May he rest in peace. All of us up here, and I'm sure all of you down there . . .'

A whoop goes up from the crowd which he leaves to grow and continue along with shouts of 'We love you Max' and similar, before Liam concludes: '. . . are broken-hearted.' He pauses to allow more whoops and shouts before punching the air and shouting: 'Hope you and Enola are happy now together, mate, wherever you may be!'

He stares wistfully at 'Enola's' microphone stand as the crowd go absolutely mental. I feel a lurch of nausea – why has he so overtly referenced Enola being dead? We have always been under strict instructions never to respond directly to questions from the press about what we think happened to her if we can possibly avoid it. And Trixie has been very clear that whatever our own beliefs might be, and whatever the most obvious answer is as to whether Enola is alive or dead, in public we are to stick to the narrative that we hope she is happy living her secret life on a sunny beach drinking lots of cocktails or something similarly idyllic. That we would love nothing more than to have her return to us, if and when she is ready.

So Liam has gone way off script there, and will probably get a telling-off from Emery and Trixie later, but the crowd is loving it.

Angel clearly decides that the cheering has gone on long enough and strums the opening chords of 'Loud and Proud', which we are all performing together. The lights come back on brighter than before, the crowd goes wild and the concert is back on track.

I'm glad I'm only on backing vocals and that Angel was her usual pushy self, ensuring that she was in the prime spot. I'm so nervous about what I'm going to do, my voice is wavering all over the place. I'm pretty sure no one will notice though, as Angel is belting it out as if nothing has happened to her – she seems to have recovered really well from her various incidents – and Liam, though his voice was never as strong as Max's, has stepped up to the challenge admirably.

Liam shouts, 'Light up your phones for Max! Let's see them in the air!' as he waves his hand above his head. A few seconds later, the whole auditorium is alight with phones being waved aloft, side to side, in unison, as we sing the rewritten-in-honour-of-Max verse with its terrible lyrics, at about half the usual tempo and with a new, mournful tone for the occasion. My voice even cracks a little as I sing. I'm not particularly sorry that Max is dead, if I'm honest; underneath the cheeky chappie exterior he presented to the public he was a coercive bully, but the whole scene is moving even so. Like when a film makes you tear up even though you're not involved with the action, and the characters aren't even real.

I notice the cameraman zoom in on my face and see on one of the giant screens that I am crying. It probably doesn't matter and I can write it off as grief or shock, not that it will matter after tonight anyway. But more to the point, I need to hold it together. I can't lose my nerve. I need to do what I need to do. This has gone on long enough.

The song ends with an extra-long guitar solo from Liam, a final chord, and then the stage plunges into darkness again with only the gaudy 'Max' still lit up.

The audience continues to whoop, cheer and wail. But we have agreed (or rather, Trixie and Emery have told us) that only the beginning and the end of the

334

concert will be fully devoted to Max in this way, for the rest, it should be business as usual. Partly because there simply wouldn't have been enough rehearsal time to change the entire set, and also because in truth, an entire homage to Max and mournful versions of our songs all the way through would get tiresome for everyone. It's not what people bought into when they got their tickets, and it's not what they have come here for, many travelling halfway across the world.

I brace myself for what I am about to do – the end of 'Max's section' somehow feels like the right time and that is what I had planned, but before I know it, Angel is strumming the opening chords of 'We All Love You', our second relentlessly upbeat number one, and the lights ping back on at full beam. The dancers run onstage in their Moulin Rouge-style cancan costumes, and the crowd starts screaming.

I have missed my moment. I'm going to have to make it through the rest of the concert, and then do what I need to do.

76

Sunday 7 December 2008
London
Sophie

I scream into the darkness. Oh my God. I can't see a thing; this half-built gym or whatever it is going to be is completely pitch black. All my worst fears are coming true. Angel is abandoning me here, in the depths of hell with a corpse. I should never have trusted her – never have listened to her. 'Angel!' I yell. 'Put the light back on!'

'Calm down!' she says, quietly. 'And stop shouting for fuck's sake! Do you want someone to hear us? My battery died. You'll have to manage with the light of the lift. Just get on with moving the rubble over the case, and then we'll both get out of here.'

I have never felt so grubby in my life as we get back in the lift and go back up to Enola's penthouse. There's nothing I want to do more than dive into a really hot shower, so hot that it scalds, and scrub and scrub until I can no longer feel my skin. But there's no way I want to linger any longer than necessary in the home of the woman we just buried, let alone use her bathroom, and I also already know that however many showers I have and however hot the water, I will never be free of this feeling. Everything has changed forever.

'So, what now?' I ask. I look around the room. 'Is there anything else we need to, erm, do?' I've watched all the crime documentaries, all the effort murderers have to go to, to make sure that everything is clean, that no trace of them is left. The place is a mess, a riot of bottles, overflowing ashtrays, and worse.

'Well, the fact that there was a party here last night is in our favour as everyone knows we were here anyway and there will already be everyone's DNA all over the place, so we don't have to worry about things like wiping fingerprints or, I don't know, bodily fluids or whatever.' She pauses. 'For the sake of appearances though, it's better that we get rid of the obvious drugs stuff, as at some point, the police are bound to be called.'

'When do you think anyone's likely to notice that she's missing?' I ask.

Angel puts on some latex gloves which we picked up along with the ladder and takes what I recognize to be Enola's phone from its bespoke case and taps out a message. 'Well, I took the precaution of sending Max a text this morning from Enola's phone saying she was hungover and going to stay in bed and that she'd see him at rehearsal. I figured it was best if people thought she was alive for as long as possible. I'll send another now just for good measure . . .'

Worst hangover ever! Going to sleep now but thinking of u xx

'There,' she says. 'I'm pretty confident he won't turn up unannounced or anything, as I happen to know they had yet another row the other day about him being too clingy.'

She scrolls through the phone and taps out a few more messages before putting it down on the counter.

'Done,' she says. 'Messaged her mum and Emery too. If we're lucky, no one will notice she's gone until . . . Tuesday when she doesn't turn up for rehearsal.'

Oh God. This is all so confusing.

'And then what will happen?' I press. Angel seems remarkably calm about all of this. Eerily so.

'Well, I guess they'll try to call her and there'll be no answer – we shouldn't take the phone because I think they can track where it's been if they want to, can't they? Not sure, but better to leave it here to be on the safe side.' She pauses. 'Either that, or throw it in the river. Let's have a think about that one.' She pauses again. 'But when they find they can't get hold of her, eventually someone will no doubt realize that something odd is going on, come and see there's no sign and . . . well. I imagine they'll start an investigation, but given that her phone and bank accounts won't have been used, the

338

logical conclusion will surely be that she's offed herself.' She pauses. 'Or, if we take her passport, left of her own accord and doesn't want to be found.'

'But . . .' My head is spinning. How can she be so calm?

'All you have to do,' Angel continues patiently, as if talking to a toddler, 'is tell the truth. Up to the point you left the party. You were very drunk, obviously you don't mention any drugs. You went home in a taxi, with Max, because we were all worried that you wouldn't get back safely in the state you were in. That is easily corroborated, by Max, and by the taxi driver if it comes to that. I'm sure he can be traced if the police decide they want to do that.

'You stayed at home all day, except for a couple of walks to clear your head, to cover us in case anyone saw you leave your house,' she continues. 'You were as surprised as anyone else when Enola didn't turn up for rehearsal. You're horrified that she seems to have gone missing and are praying for her safe return.'

'And you . . .'

'I'll say I stayed over, because I did, crashing out after drinking too much and falling asleep in front of MTV, which is the truth. I can claim I assumed Enola was still asleep when I left, which I will be doing shortly. As she appears to have been messaging her boyfriend and mum this morning, this will stand up her still being alive nicely.

'Then later the police or whoever can surmise that Enola went missing at some point between me leaving and her sending her messages this morning, and her not arriving at Tuesday's rehearsal, or whenever it is when someone comes to check on her. By then she'll be under the concrete, and I can't imagine the developers would let them dig it up on a whim unless they had very good reason to think she was under there, but it would be even better if . . . ooh I know!'

She opens up Enola's laptop which is on the kitchen worktop and powers it up. 'I learnt how to pre-schedule emails the other day,' Angel says. 'So let's do one of those too. Here we go . . . I am taking some time away,' she says out loud as she taps. 'It has all become too much. I hope you will forgive me.'

She clicks, scrolls and presses, peering at the screen. 'Schedule to send for the day after the rehearsal and . . . done!' She looks up and beams, delighted with her cleverness. 'And I'm going to see if I can find her passport and get rid of that too. If that's not here, it'll add another layer of mystery and options. The assumption will naturally be that she's either done a runner or killed herself. Help me look. Where do you keep yours?'

'Um . . .' I don't want to tell her where I keep my passport now that I've seen exactly what she's capable of and nor do I want to help her look for Enola's, both because it feels so intrusive but also because I can't wait to get out of here. But equally I can see that what she's saying makes sense. 'Does she have anything like a study?' I say, without answering the question. 'Or even just a desk? Somewhere like that would probably be the best place to start.'

Angel points upwards to a mezzanine which I can now see has a large wooden desk by a window looking out over the river, with bookshelves on an adjacent wall. 'She does. So pretentious – what does someone like her need a desk for of all things? We have "people" for all that sort of boring admin stuff. But good thought – I'll go and have a look up there now. As soon as I've got the passport, we should get out of here. One at a time, obviously.'

'What about the cats?' I ask. They are winding around my legs, purring and looking up at me hopefully. 'She wouldn't leave without making sure they're OK. We need to make it look like she's thought about that.'

'Yeah, good point,' she says, banging around in the cupboards to find the cat food and filling the bowls to the brim. The cats start chowing greedily as soon as the bowls hit the floor. Angel tops up the water bowl, then roots around in the cupboards to find more bowls which she fills with more food and water.

'There. They'll be fine for a few days. Have you seen the size of the catio thing out there? They'll probably barely notice she's gone.' She goes back to the computer. 'But I'll add a line to the email asking that someone makes sure her cats are looked after because she's not mentally in the right place to do it at the moment. That seems like the kind of thing she'd say.' She taps away for a few seconds. 'There. All done.'

Once Angel has found the passport (top drawer of the desk, unlocked, so not hard) she sends a few more texts from Enola's phone (still wearing latex gloves, so it takes a while) to improve the timeline, as she says.

'Now, I'm going to go. You hang out here a few minutes longer to be absolutely sure we're not seen together. Put your hood up and make sure no one sees you leave – there are no cameras around here yet as there's still so much building work going on – I checked. After today, we never speak of this again, ever, by phone, by text, or anything. It simply never happened.'

She drops Enola's passport and keys into her bag and disappears into the lift.

77

3 July 2024
Las Vegas
Charlie

Redlight: I saw what happened to Max! Well done! So proud of you! I know Enola would be too.

Enolasbestfriend: Thank you. It felt good.

Redlight: I knew you were the right person for the job. You aren't like the others. You saw through what they were doing. Pushing her away like that. No one can replace someone like Enola.

Enolasbestfriend: Do you think she'll come back now? Now that Max is out of the way? Maybe she'll even appear at the concert tonight? There's still time.

Redlight: Let's hope so. Fingers crossed.

78

4 July 2024
Las Vegas
Sophie

I get through the next ninety minutes or so on auto-pilot, going through the motions as I focus on what I am planning to do as the concert comes to an end. The crowd doesn't seem to notice or care, and appears utterly delighted with our performance – Angel and Liam are both revelling in their new positions in the limelight, and that really comes through. The musicians and dancers are wholly professional and completely on their game, and really, there is no reason for them not to be I guess – they are lucky enough to be one step removed from all this.

Angel is clearly loving her new guitar – a gift from the hotel, no doubt in the hope that she won't sue. According to them, nothing untoward was found in the shower gel. She doesn't believe them – I'm not sure I do either.

But none of that matters any more. Nothing matters any more.

As we reach the point in the concert before the final song, the lights dim again and a hush falls over the stadium. 'Before we sing "Big You Up", one last time for Max,' Liam says, 'we're each going to say a few words about what he meant to us.'

Emery was already talking about re-releasing the song that we're about to sing in its new melancholy, cello-accompanied version. There really is no marketing opportunity he won't leap at.

The LED walls of the venue are suddenly covered in scrolling words along the lines of 'Max, you are our hero', 'Rest in peace Max, hope you're with Enola now', 'There's another angel in heaven tonight and he plays a Gibson', all messages from the online book of condolences, apparently. Overlaid are pictures of Max smiling, singing, all at his best, obviously. None of him snarling at Enola because he thinks she's looked at someone the wrong way, or passed out after yet another massive bender.

'But we're going to keep it short,' Liam continues, 'because if Max was here, he'd say that no one wants to hear any of that maudlin shite, they're here for the music.' Whooping, cheering. *Come on, come on. Let's get this over with*.

'But he's wrong,' Liam adds. 'We know you all loved him. We want to share our love for him with you.'

More whooping and cheering.

'Max was my best friend, would do anything for

anyone, and we'll miss him like crazy,' Liam shouts. 'Goodnight Max, wherever you are. Rest easy now.'

All lies. Liam and Max have barely spoken for years before we all ended up here, as far as I know, and Max was about as selfish as they come. Wouldn't do anything for anyone unless he thought there was something in it for him. But people always say nice things about the dead, don't they? And it's not like any of it matters now.

'Max was the glue that held us all together,' Angel cries, a clearly contrived sob in her throat. 'We, I mean Breathe and This Way Up, we loved each other like family. Always in our hearts, Max, always.'

Ugh. Pointless platitudes from both of them which anyone could say about anyone, pretty much. And not true, none of us loved each other, ever. Max might think he loved Enola, but he didn't. Not really. He wanted to possess her. These days I think we have all been so damaged by the whole experience I wonder if any of us is capable of loving anyone – most certainly not each other.

But the crowd are all screaming and crying and yelling, and now it's my turn and there's no putting it off any longer. I am going to do it. I am. No going back.

'Max . . .' I start hesitantly. There's no point in me repeating the kind of nonsense they've been spouting given what I'm going to do next. It'll all be over then, no going back. Might as well go out with a bang. 'Max . . . was like all of us. There was probably some good in him. But there was also bad. Enola . . . was scared of him. He was controlling. A bully, even. I'm not going to stand here and tell even more lies like Angel and Liam. There have already been far too many lies, stretching back for very many years. It's time that people know the truth.'

I stare fixedly at my microphone, which I'm amazed hasn't had its sound cut yet – either Emery and Trixie aren't paying attention, or they think it'll look worse if they cut me off. Trixie is no doubt thinking that she'll put out a statement about me being tired and emotional, or the grief getting to me or something. She's probably mentally drafting a press release already. Or maybe she doesn't care what I say about Max now, given that he's dead and that me coming out with this kind of stuff is bound to get us more press coverage. That's more likely. But she doesn't know what I'm going to do next – and that what I'm saying now will become as good as irrelevant.

'Max and Enola were not the perfect couple they presented themselves to be,' I continue. The crowd has become quieter than I'd have ever imagined a group of this size could be. What are they thinking? Do they assume this is all part of the show? 'And when she disappeared, there were some in the know who thought Max had driven her away.' I pause. The vast venue is still almost silent, bar a slight resonant echo from my words. 'Others thought she'd killed herself because she found the pressures of fame too hard to cope with, or that she couldn't bear to be under Max's control any longer and couldn't think of any other way to escape. There was even that theory doing the rounds that she was simply phased out in a planned operation by her management.'

347

The crowd starts to murmur and there is an occasional shout of something or other, I can't make out exactly what, but I get the impression they're not exactly pleased with what I'm saying. I glance to my left where I see Angel staring at me in horror.

I look out towards the crowd again. 'But none of those theories is right. Enola did not disappear of her own accord, and Max did not kill her. She is never going to turn up and use that stupid microphone that we have left on the stage for her. Not tonight, not ever.'

The crowd goes silent again. I clear my throat.

'And the reason I know this, is because Enola is dead. Because of me. I killed her.'

79

4 July 2024
Las Vegas
Charlie

I had no idea a stadium of that size could turn so silent. There is almost no sound, and then a murmuring starts up again in the crowd as they seem to be asking themselves whether this is a joke? Part of the act? Or something else?

My heart starts beating faster in my chest because what if what she says is true? Could I have got it so wrong after all these years? Why would Sophie kill Enola?

Can it be true that she's never coming back? Can Enola really be dead? I can't cope with that. I can't. I need Enola in the world. I need to know that one day, she will be here again. That she's OK.

I push my way through the crowd, I need to get away, to think. All these years I've been convinced Enola was still alive, out there somewhere, hiding from Max, not wanting anything more to do with Breathe. I thought that if I could get rid of him, and punish Angel, then maybe she would come back. And one day I could tell her what I'd done for her and I could finally be the friend to her that I've always wanted to be.

I wasn't the only one – Redlight knew it too. They helped me plan this. We knew it was the right thing to do. The only thing which might bring Enola back to us.

Did I kill Max for nothing? Perhaps it doesn't matter, as he made her life a misery but Sophie . . . how could I get it so wrong?

I don't know what to do with myself. All this planning, everything I did, all for nothing.

80

5 July 2024
Las Vegas

Online news report:

Breathe singer Sophie Moffat was led away in handcuffs last night after a shocking claim made onstage that she killed fellow band member Enola Mazzeri more than fifteen years ago.

Miss Moffat is currently being held in Las Vegas police station where it is likely she will be questioned by police before being repatriated to the UK, where the alleged crime was committed.

A spokesperson for Breathe said: 'Sophie was clearly very upset following Max's death and not thinking straight. She didn't fully realize what she was saying, or its implications. It has been a very difficult few days.

'We hope this misunderstanding will be quickly ironed out and she can be released.'

Meantime, a new version of 'Loud and Proud' recorded as a tribute to This Way Up band member Max Heaton has shot to the number one download slot on Spotify.

81

5 July 2024
London
Roxie

Of course I knew that Enola wasn't coming back. Until Sophie's confession, which I have to admit I was *not* expecting, I was ninety-nine per cent sure that my sister had taken her own life. I didn't know how or where, or why her body hadn't been found, but I knew how unhappy she had been all the time she was with Breathe. In spite of all her wealth and the trappings of fame, her environment was toxic.

But her issues went back much further than that. She and I both grew up messed up, just in different ways. Mum focused too much attention on her and too little on me, and we both suffered for it. Had Enola had a better childhood, felt like she was unconditionally loved by Mum, she might have been better able to deal with what came later. Sophie and Angel ignoring her. Liam as good as raping her. And not having the nerve to leave her dysfunctional relationship with Max because she didn't have the confidence that anyone else would love her.

But Mum was little more than a child when we were born, and I don't blame her for falling short as a mother – in her own way, she did what she could. And I have found contentment of a sort. My life might not look like much to most, but I have everything I want and enjoy my online life. I don't need real people.

Except Enola. I miss her terribly. She understood me, she didn't judge me. She and I, we might have been very different, but we were a unit even before we were born. Not everyone has that. It's something very special. I will never have that again with anyone. It's a big part of the reason why I don't even bother trying when it comes to friendships or relationships. No one is like Enola, so I am better off on my own.

I blamed the others in both of the bands for her death, of course. While I was convinced she had killed herself, I felt sure she was very much driven to it by the others. Most of all by Max, by being coercive and controlling and generally a shit boyfriend, but also by Angel and Sophie being downright nasty to her. As well as always making sure she felt like an outsider, Enola was pretty sure they were leaking stories to the press about her, and I suspect they were behind some of those nasty letters too. And Liam . . . Enola always tried to play down what happened between them at *The Chosen*, but I know it affected her more than she let on to me.

I didn't have it in me to physically do anything to take revenge on any of them, I knew that. I can barely leave my flat these days, and it's been like that for years. Taking on something like this would be too much for me. Impossible.

What I am good at though, is being online, and doing my research. And I realized that with a little bit of effort, I could get someone to do what needed to be done for me.

I'd kept an eye on the Breathe forums over the years, which later morphed into Facebook fan groups. I knew who the avid posters were, which ones seemed the most unhinged or obsessed, and which ones still kept Enola as their favourite. They tended to keep the same pseudonyms even as they moved between forums. I had noticed Enolasbestfriend as being pretty obsessive about my sister, though she was far from the only one. But it was when she was arrested at the party at the aquarium in Barcelona that she really grabbed my attention.

From her posts online and the press reports of her court case, it was easy to put the two – Charlie and Enolasbestfriend – together. And it became clear that this woman genuinely believed that Enola had been replaced by a doppelgänger because Enola wanted to escape from Max. That she had decided she no longer wanted to be in the band, and management didn't want the world to know that she had left Breathe. Charlie's conspiracy theory had a kind of elegant if totally deluded quality to it as so often conspiracy theories do, and initially I followed the case, and her online posts about how unfair it all was, simply out of fascination.

And then Enola went missing. Enolasbestfriend, or Charlie Dixon as I by then knew her to be, was beside herself and was on the forums day and night. Initially guarded about her theories, by the time she'd been through the court case and her story was in the press, I guess she felt there was no longer any point in holding back. She was convinced that the stand-in had been introduced to allow Enola to escape from Max and the band, at the same time as the tanker crash happened, which some days she also seemed to believe had been set up as some kind of distraction.

And while she was clearly utterly deluded, I realized that she was also my ideal right-hand woman.

A little bit more research once I knew her real name threw up that Charlie already had form – she ended up with just a suspended sentence and a restraining order for the Barcelona incident, but it didn't take much digging to find out that she had previously been obsessed with a young actress, and this had led to a charge for GBH against someone that she had felt was causing her idol harm.

Online, I started to agree with her ludicrous theories and sympathize with her. Amazingly I wasn't the only one and, incredibly, these theories about Enola are still out there. Enola is still 'sighted' fairly regularly, everywhere from Bolton to the Bahamas. Some, like Charlie, still believe Enola had a double. A few believe it was me.

I only stood in for Enola a couple of times in the very early days of Breathe, for a laugh, but as I started to find the company of other people more and more difficult, it stopped being fun. Enola sometimes tried to persuade me to do it again in the last few years before she disappeared, but I always said 'no'.

After a while, I started to slide into Charlie's DMs. She didn't mind, I was an ally, as far as she was concerned. I never told her that I was Enola's sister. We mainly talked about Enola, but as time went on, we talked about anything and everything and she seems to believe we became friends. We never met, but as neither of us leave the house more than necessary (especially me) there was never any reason to contrive an excuse. We understood each other's social anxieties, but more importantly, I knew she'd do anything for Enola.

Initially we mainly talked by DM on the forums, then on Facebook Messenger, and more recently on WhatsApp, on a burner phone of course. She never knew my real name, I told her it was better that way for security, so we continued as Enolasbestfriend for her and Redlight for me, a nod to the prostitute in the Police song I was named after. Like so many things when it came to me and Enola, I'm not sure Mum had thought that name through, nor, indeed, naming Enola after a plane that dropped an atomic bomb. She just liked the songs.

It didn't take much to push Charlie into doing what I wanted her to do. Right from the start she had violent feelings towards all of the band members. But she isn't the sharpest tool in the box, and not that great at planning, so I simply helped her achieve her aims.

Some might call it grooming. I call it revenge.

She did well. She has one more task, and we've already discussed it. She won't be hearing from me again.

82

2 a.m. Sunday 7 December 2008
London
Angel

'You stupid bitch, Enola!' Sophie is shouting. 'It wasn't only because of you we won the award tonight! We're part of this band too, you know!'

Enola is standing by the window in her stunning purple Vera Wang dress, the lights of London twinkling through the plate-glass wall behind her. It's late and she is looking a little dishevelled by now, but still, though I hate to admit it, beautiful.

I loathe her.

She looks at Sophie in confusion.

'Why are you shouting at me?' she asks, almost timidly. 'I never said anything like that.'

'Oh yeah, sure you didn't,' Sophie sneers.

I have set this up. A few minutes ago I told Sophie that I heard Enola say to a journalist that she is the only true talent in Breathe and that Sophie and I are just passengers in the band. I didn't hear her say anything of the sort – I invented it completely.

But I knew it would set Sophie off. She's always a big drinker on nights out and the fun thing about Sophie is she often loses her memory. In the past I've had a brilliant time teasing her about what she got up to, imaginary awful men she got off with or indiscreetly gave blow jobs to under the table or in the back of taxis.

But tonight I need to make absolutely sure that she doesn't remember a thing when she wakes up so I've popped a roofie into the last drink I served her just to be sure. Should also help ensure that she's sufficiently wasted for me to send her home when I'm ready to get rid of her too.

We've already decided what is going to happen.

'Sophie, come on,' Max says. 'You've had enough. Let's get you home.'

'I don't need an escort!' Sophie snaps. 'And I'm not ready to go.'

'I'd like you to go,' Enola says, slow and measured. 'And that goes for all of you,' she adds. 'It's been a long night, I'm tired, it's my place, and I don't want any of you here any more.' She glances at Max. 'I just want to be on my own,' she adds, almost hoarsely, as if she might cry. Enola hates a row – Sophie shouting at her like that will have upset her, as I knew it would.

'Babe,' I say, touching Sophie lightly on the arm, 'come on. We're winding things up now. It's time to go. I'm going to call some taxis. Max can drop you off,

360

make sure you get home safely. That OK for you Enola?'
I ask.

She nods and gives me a grateful half-smile.

'I read a story in the paper the other day about a serial rapist who they think might be a taxi driver,' I add. Another lie. Sophie is both thick and a total catastrophizer, so it's easy to manipulate her with stories like these. It suits me best if Max goes with her for several reasons. I need him out of the way, but I also like the neatness of it. Get him involved in what's going to happen, even if unwittingly.

Everyone except me is absolutely wasted, as I very much hoped and assumed they would be. I've been deliberately taking it easy all night – not so much that anyone would notice, but enough that I can keep a clear head.

I call a couple of taxis from a nice company, the one the record company uses when we're not in limos. The kind that send a driver who wears a shirt and tie and won't sell pictures of us to the press if they want to keep their contract.

'Thirty minutes,' I say. 'Liam, I called you a taxi too. I'll walk, as my building is right next door. How about everyone calms down and we watch some MTV until they arrive? I'm going to make everyone some herbal tea.'

I can see that the fight has already gone out of Sophie – that'll be the roofie I slipped into her last drink – as she slumps down onto the sofa and stares disinterestedly at the TV. Her head lolls onto Liam's shoulder and he puts his arm around her. It's actually quite sweet. Enola is in an armchair with a face like a slapped arse, but I know what I can do to sort that out. Not sure where Max is now – guess he's gone to the loo. Hopefully he's not taking another line or anything. I need everyone to leave on cue.

Once the kettle has boiled, I make the teas and drop a roofie into Enola's drink, along with some sugar to make sure she doesn't taste it. I put the Emma Bridgewater mugs on a Conran tray and take them over, making sure Enola gets the one with the big E on it.

Enola gets up and stumbles blearily up to her bedroom when the first taxi arrives, mumbling something at me about letting myself out, then Max and Sophie leave together. I watch MTV for about ten more minutes and then follow Enola into her bedroom with Liam. She is fast asleep, as I knew she would be. He holds her arms and I smother her with a pillow, as planned. I wasn't sure I'd be able to hold her still and press the pillow down at the same time, but as it turns out, she barely moves. Enola always made sure she stayed in the forefront of the band by sucking up to Emery, and with her still in the picture, I'd never stand a chance of getting what I deserve.

Half an hour later, Liam leaves. And a few hours later, I call Sophie.

83

2025
London

Online news report:

The trial of Angel Williams, former member of top girl band Breathe, began at the Old Bailey today.

Miss Williams has pleaded not guilty to preventing a lawful burial and perverting the course of justice.

Former bandmate Sophie Moffat is meanwhile awaiting sentence after pleading guilty to the manslaughter of Enola Mazzeri in 2008.

Following Ms Moffat's shock confession to the murder during a Breathe and This Way Up concert in Las Vegas on 4 July 2024, ground penetrating radar revealed what is believed to be the star's body encased in concrete in the basement of the building where she once lived.

Miss Moffat claims that Miss Williams helped her dispose of the body in 2008, a claim contested by the defendant.

Discussions are ongoing with the building freeholder as to whether the remains can be safely disinterred. Meantime Kimberley Mazzeri, the mother of the pop star, currently living in the penthouse where her daughter is now believed to have been murdered, has put the property up for sale for an asking price of £10 million pounds.

The hearing continues.

84

2025
London
Liam

Bloody hell.

I thought I had missed being a pop star, but those two concerts in Vegas were enough to last me a lifetime. And now having to go and give evidence about something that happened so long ago on a night when I probably could barely have even remembered what happened the next day.

I had the shock of my life when Angel took that overdose in Las Vegas. I thought she'd finally found a conscience after all these years, felt remorse for what she did. And that scared me, because if she had, and was going to confess to what we did, I needed to make sure she didn't take me down with her.

I mean, Angel's always acted like she didn't care about what we did to Enola, but you can't kill someone and not have it come back to haunt you. I know it does me. I told myself that we did what needed doing at the time, but the enforced therapy I've had in my various rehab stints has made me see that the drinking and gambling is a way to escape from myself, which I can't shake however much rehab I do. The therapists don't know exactly *what* I'm escaping from, obviously, but I can see they probably have a point. I guess however much Angel tried to do the same, she could never quite manage it. Hence the overdose when we were in Vegas. I assumed both the bands being back together after all those years had brought it all back to her, as it clearly had to Sophie.

Angel claimed it was an accident but, well. I wasn't so sure. I thought she was becoming a liability. Only she and I know the truth about what happened that night. Max unwittingly played his part by getting Sophie out of the way for us, as we'd planned, but he never knew the truth of what happened once he left.

I had thought for years that Angel basically felt the same as me, that what we did needed doing, that it was justified, but the suicide attempt, well. She had become a loose cannon as far as I was concerned.

I'm not a roadie, but I know my way around an electrical circuit after retraining when things went pear-shaped after This Way Up. Angel always insisted on using a vintage electric guitar that once belonged to some rock icon, so it only took a bit of fiddling with it to make it dangerous.

It wasn't foolproof, I knew that, but I was happy to wait and see what happened. I couldn't risk doing anything that could be traced back to me. It had felt like a close enough shave last time, with Enola. We'd all been questioned as the last people to see her, but as no one knew whether she was actually dead or had simply left, it all tailed off pretty quickly, at least as far as our involvement was concerned.

As it was, the electric shock didn't kill Angel, but that turned out OK, because Sophie headed it off by claiming she killed Enola, as we took the precaution of leading her to believe she did all those years ago.

It had started out as a joke, of course, me and Angel larking around about how much easier our lives would be without Enola. Angel, so that she could be the star of the show. Me, so that I didn't have the crushing and constant worry that Emery, Max or the papers might find out that I'd basically raped Enola all those years ago. I didn't see it like that at the time, of course, but times have changed since then and after what she said at the party in Barcelona, I could see she kind of had a point.

Plus, in spite of my huge earnings when we were in This Way Up, it was never enough, and I figured that a bigger slice of the royalties for 'All The Way' wouldn't go amiss either. Who could have predicted when Enola and I wrote it together to perform on *The Chosen* it would go on to be one of Breathe's biggest hits and make a shit load of money because it would be used in a car advert?

Angel and my plan snowballed and snowballed, and before I knew it we were doing it. It was Angel's idea to set up Sophie so that Angel could get her way and be the star of the show, and also as insurance for the future – if Enola's body was ever found, we could point the finger at Sophie. We knew that Sophie would go along with what we wanted if we told her she was going to go to prison otherwise – she had always been weak and suggestible in just about every way possible.

Angel also nicked Sophie's watch to drop in the case with Enola as an extra precaution in case the suitcase was ever found – though it seems like that won't be necessary now that Sophie has confessed. She also had the foresight to take Enola's keys, which she disposed of along with the passport. We got what we wanted, and felt like we had all bases covered.

And with this coming to court now, nearly twenty years on, it's simply Sophie's word against Angel's – there's no concrete evidence against her. Angel is claiming she has no knowledge of what happened to Enola, with her defence team suggesting Sophie must have returned to the penthouse using Enola's keys, which were never found, and acted alone. The jury may or not believe Angel, but without any relevant forensics and with it all having happened so long ago, her lawyer says it's unlikely they'll convict because there will always be reasonable doubt. Then again, I guess he has to say stuff like that to charge the eye-watering fees he does.

I had to go to court today to give evidence. I stuck to what I'd said in my statement all those years ago – that I didn't remember much except that Sophie and Enola had had a big row. Everyone knows I've been in and out of rehab all of my life, so it's not much of a stretch for the jury to believe I don't remember much about a night many years ago.

When I wasn't speaking, I was pretty much holding my breath in case Angel decided to squeal on me. But deep down, I knew she wouldn't. Not because she gives a shit about me, or indeed anyone other than herself, but because it would make things worse for herself. As things stand, she's only up for concealing a crime and preventing a lawful burial or something like that, and the likelihood is she won't be convicted, apparently. It's Sophie who is up for the actual killing. If she squeals on me, Angel not only reveals that she's been lying all these years, she implicates herself for murder too. So I'm pretty confident she won't do that. She held the pillow over Enola's face, after all.

I'm looking forward to getting home, putting all this behind me. The journey has been a few hours, I've listened to some music and am starting to feel a little more relaxed. My junction is approaching, and I put my foot on the brakes. But something is wrong. The car isn't slowing down. What the fuck? I push my foot further to the floor, but nothing happens. There's a loud bang. And then nothing. Nothing.

85

Enolasbestfriend: I did what we talked about. I saw him leave court so it should be happening about now.

    I stare at the phone, but the single tick remains resolutely grey.

Enolasbestfriend: Redlight? Where are you?

Enolasbestfriend: Redlight?

Acknowledgements

They say it takes a village to write a book (or something like that), and that was definitely the case with this one.

First thanks go to the team at HarperCollins, especially editor Kate Bradley who put up with quite a lot of toys out of the pram with this book with grace and patience. Also to Morgan Springett for always being happy to answer seemingly any question from me, however annoying, as well as lots of general help. Thanks to my brilliant agent Gaia Banks for her help with absolutely everything book-related and always being willing to listen, as well as her colleagues at Sheil Land, especially Lauren Coleman for the lovely foreign editions.

Thank you to Charlotte Webb for the copyedit and Simon Fox for proofread, and to beta readers Fran Bevan, Sarah Clarke and Lucy Dixon for such useful and thoughtful input. Thanks to Claire Ward for yet another brilliant cover and apologies for all the tweaking – absolutely love the finished version.

Thanks for Facebook friends for input on just about everything from 2008 fashion, whether readers will understand what 'dressing to the left' means (sadly apparently not, because I thought it was funny) and questions about dog care (which was just too complicated in the end so Enola ended up with cats instead). Special thanks this time to Leah Hardy and Sally Nicholls for their suggestions for brilliantly terrible lyrics. Obviously all these questions were important research and not just faffing about online. An extra mention also to the Witches for always being hilarious.

Thanks as usual to Alex who originally came up with the seed of the idea for *The Penthouse*, as well as the ongoing support with everything, and for coming with me to Las Vegas on my research trip, even though it wouldn't be your first (or even 100th probably) choice.

And thanks to all the readers for picking this up of course! I'm grateful to every one of you.

If you enjoyed *The Penthouse*, don't miss out on
Catherine Cooper's other gripping thrillers . . .

Four friends. One luxury getaway. The perfect murder.

French Alps, 1998

Two young men ski into a blizzard . . . but only
one returns.

20 years later

Four people connected to the missing man find
themselves in that same resort. Each has a secret. Two
may have blood on their hands. One is a
killer-in-waiting.

Someone knows what really happened that day.

And somebody will pay.

They thought it was perfect. They were wrong . . .

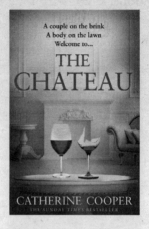

A luxurious chateau

Aura and Nick don't talk about what happened in
England. They've bought a chateau in France to
make a fresh start, and their kids need them to stay
together – whatever it costs.

A couple on the brink

The expat community is welcoming, but when a
neighbour is murdered at a lavish party, Aura and
Nick don't know who to trust.

A secret that is bound to come out . . .

Someone knows exactly why they really came
to the chateau. And someone is going to give
them what they deserve.

A glamorous ship. A missing woman.
A holiday to DIE for . . .

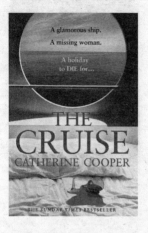

A glamorous ship

During a New Year's Eve party on a large,
luxurious cruise ship in the Caribbean, the ship's
dancer, Lola, goes missing.

Everyone on board has something to hide

Two weeks later, the ship is out of service, laid
up far from land with no more than a skeleton
crew on board. And then more people start
disappearing . . .

No one is safe

Why are the crew being harmed?
Who is responsible? And who will be next?

The perfect escape, or the perfect trap?

When a select group of influencers and journalists receive an exclusive invitation to a luxury resort in the Maldives, it seems like the ultimate press trip.

But when the island is cut off during a storm and people start dying, it looks like someone has murder in mind.

Are the guests really who they seem to be, or does each one of them have a secret to hide?

Something they would kill for?